PETER
PO

C000052630

REGINALD Evelyn Peter Southouse Cheyney (1896-1951) was
born in Whitechapel in the East End of London. After serving
as a lieutenant during the First World War, he worked as
a police reporter and freelance investigator until he found
success with his first Lemmy Caution novel. In his lifetime
Cheyney was a prolific and wildly successful author, selling, in
1946 alone, over 1.5 million copies of his books. His work was
also enormously popular in France, and inspired Jean-Luc
Godard's character of the same name in his dystopian sci-fi
film *Alphaville*. The master of British noir, in Lemmy Caution
Peter Cheyney created the blueprint for the tough-talking,
hard-drinking pulp fiction detective.

PETER CHEYNEY

POISON IVY

DEAN STREET PRESS

Published by Dean Street Press 2022

All Rights Reserved

First published in 1937

Cover by DSP

ISBN 978 1 914150 87 6

www.deanstreetpress.co.uk

CHAPTER ONE
RUB OUT FOR ONE

WAS I pleased or was I? I'm tellin' you that kickin' around Alliance Nebraska never pleased me any; more especially when I say that I have been rusticatin' in this dump so that I am already beginnin' to think I am growing hay in my hair. But I reckon that the ways of the main "G" office is nobody's business, an' I have also got an idea at the back of my head that they have kept me kickin' around this spot all this time so that the bezuzus I started over the Miranda van Zelden case could die down.

It looks to me like they have got something pretty good boilin' up for me because I reckon if they are pulling Myras Duncan down from Chicago and plantin' him to contact me in New York, the job is not goin' to be one for sissies, because I'm tellin' you that this Duncan is a tough ace "G" man, and that guy has got more medals for cleaning up mobs than you ever heard tell.

I reckon a train is a great spot for thinkin' things out. All the while I have been in this train I have been sittin' back letting my mind play around. There is a lot of guys think that being a "G" man is a mug's business and that's as maybe; but I'm tellin' you that if you are a guy like me who likes to see things happen sometimes an' who falls for contrast, it's a great business, that is if they don't get you first, an' all the time I am wonderin' just what the lay-out is going to be on this job an' just what is going to happen to Lemmy Caution before I hand my ticket in and sign off the charge account.

It is eight o'clock when I arrive. I check out of the depot and get along to some hotel near West 23rd Street where they don't know me, and I register myself as Perry C. Rice, an' I do a little talking in the reception that would show anybody that I was an egg and butter man who thought New York was a nice place for strangers only a bit big.

After this I give myself a bath an' I dig myself out a tuxedo, the sorta cut that a guy like this fellow Rice would wear. After which I get around the town a bit, absorb a little bourbon, an' about ten o'clock at night I jump myself a taxicab and I scram down to Moksie's on Waterfront.

This Moksie's is the usual sorta dump. It's a place I don't know because I ain't acquainted with New York any too good, my not havin' operated around there very much, which looks to me like the reason I have been picked for this job. But it is the usual sorta waterfront dive where you can win yourself any amount of bad hooch an' anything else you're looking for including a split skull an' a free dive in the East River with a flat-iron around your neck.

When I go down the steps a lotta tough guys give me the once over, but they don't look very surprised so I imagine they have seen guys in tuxedos before. In one corner is a bar an' behind this bar is a big guy—I hear 'em call him Moksie—an' I tell him that I am drinking rye straight an' that he looks as if he would like one too. I am right about this. I then start givin' him a lotta dope about good times in Mason City where they make bricks an' beet sugar, an' by the time that I am finished talking these guys have got a definite idea in their heads that I am such a hick that ferns will start growing outa my ears any moment.

I stick around this dump for about twenty minutes and then some guy comes down. He is middle-sized guy an' he is round and plump an' smilin'. He is wearing a good grey suit an' he has got a big pin in his scarf. His right hand is stuck in the armhole of his waistcoat an' I see that the top joint is missing from the little finger, so I do some mathematics an' conclude that this is Myras Duncan, my contact, otherwise Harvest V. Mellander.

He's got a coupla dames with him an' it looks to me like he is making a play that they have been showin' him around the town. They go over to a table an' they sit down an' presently some thin feller comes in an' takes the two janes away.

I just don't do anything at all. I just stick around.

Pretty soon this Harvest V. Mellander comes prancing up to the bar, an' believe me he is puttin' on a very good act that he is good an' high. He buys himself a four-finger shot of bourbon an' whilst he is drinkin' it he looks at me an' sorta grins.

"Listen, kid," he says, "I wouldn't try anything on with you, but ain't your name Rice an' ain't you from Mason City?"

I look at him an' I tell him yes, an' say how would he know a thing like that. He tells me that he knows it because he once had a car smash on Main, an' don't I remember taking him in for the night.

I then do a big recognition act an' we start buying drinks for all an' sundry, and in about an hour's time we have got this place jazzed up good, an' plenty so that nobody takes any notice when this guy Myras and myself scram off to some table at the end of the room with a bottle of bourbon an' start tellin' stories about the old days.

I turn my hand over so that he can see the razor cut which I got off some mobster four years before. He pours me out a drink.

"O.K. buddy," he says. "Now get a load of this. You an' I are chasing daydreams because believe me the job we're on is so slim that nobody knows anythin' about it including me. I suppose you don't know nothin'."

"You're dead right," I tell him with a big hiccough. "I don't know a thing, Harvest. What's it all about? Is somebody goin' to shoot the President or what?"

He lights himself a cigar. All around the other guys in this place are making plenty noise an' we can talk easy.

"It ain't quite so bad as that," he says, "but it's this way. The Bureau's got this tip-off that somebody is goin' to try something funny with a gold shipment that's goin' to Southampton England in a week's time. Well, how anybody in the Bureau reckons that any palooka can get at that gold I don't know, but that's the idea that's flying about, an' you gotta handle the works. I'm here to give you the low-down as far as it goes an' I'm scrammin' out in a coupla days leaving you to carry the baby.

"The Bureau reckons that they've forgotten you down in this part of the world an' anyway you're elected."

I light myself a cigarette and have a little more bourbon. I reckon this sounds good to me.

"Listen, Harvest," I say, "where do they get all this fancy stuff from. It sounds to me like a pipe-dream from a police nose. Maybe the cops around here have been goin' to the movies or somethin'."

He grins.

"That's what I figured in the first place," he says, "only it ain't like that. It's this way. One night there is a schlmozzle in some swell joint, an' some tough egg gets smacked over the front-piece with a bottle of White Rock, an' it don't do him no good neither, see? This guy just goes out like he had listened to two lullabies at once an' he never comes round again.

"Any how they run this guy down to Bellevue in a patrol wagon, an' he gets delirious an' starts shootin' off his mouth about this and that. Finally this guy starts talkin' about the gold shipment an' does he know all about it or does he? He knows the amount to be sent over, the boat it's goin' on, the U.S. Treasury order for movin' it an' what will you. He knows the whole piece an' where he got it from is nobody's business.

"Carson, a New York 'G' man, was takin' it all down in short-hand, after which this palooka passes out and hands in his dinner pail before he comes round again, an' so that is that, an' where do you go from there?"

"You certainly ain't got a lot to work on," I tell him. "Ain't there anything else on the job?"

"That's just it," he says. "I can't tell you a thing. All I've been doin' is to go around here an' try an' get contacts with the outside of the mobs so as we can try and get wise to any one who is plannin' to pull something funny over that shipment, but up to the moment I have drawn a blank.

"Now you know as well as I do that there are only about five bad men around this City who are big enough to try and get away with a pinch of a shipment of bar gold worth about eight million dollars, so I reckon all you can do is to contact those five guys here, get in somehow, let 'em play you for a sucker, lose your money, but try an' get next to 'em."

He pulls a toothpick out of his vest pocket, an' he starts gettin' to work on his back teeth. All of a sudden he gets a big idea an' I see his eyes change. He looks across at me an' he grins again.

"Say listen," he says. "I'll tell you something else that might amuse the children. Directly Carson shoots in a report to the Bureau they put me on this job an' I pick three good boys from police headquarters an' start to do a little investigatin'. I put these guys on doin' a quiet muscle-in act on any mob or really tough egg they can contact, an' the joke is that the whole lot of 'em has had the works one way or another. McNeil—a nice kid from Queens— got himself shot near Brooklyn Bridge, nobody knows how. The second guy—Franton, a wise dick—was found in East River with a card in his pocket inside a waterproof tobacco pouch he used to carry with 'Come around again some time' written on it, and the third feller, a tough copper with brains, was taken off the dope squad to do this one, an' he got smacked down with a blackjack so hard that he never even knew they'd hit him. So what do you know about that?"

He stops talking because a lotta new guys have come down into this dive, an' a bunch of 'em come around our table.

"O.K.," he says, lettin' out a phoney hiccough that could be heard a mile away, "now get a load of this. I've got one or two people workin' for me, people I've picked up, people who get around places and hear things. I don't mean 'G' men, I mean just ordinary pikers. I gotta scram outa here now. You meet me at Joe Madrigaul's place at one o'clock this morning. Maybe I can show you somethin'."

With this he shakes me warmly by the hand, an' waltzes out of this dump.

I sit there an' I do a bit of quiet thinkin' because this job does not look so easy to me. It looks like chasing a needle in a whole lotta haystacks. At the same time what Mellander has said is true. There are only about five mobsters left the in City of New York who would have the nerve or the organisation to try and pull a break like this and even then they'd be bughouse, but I reckon his system of musclin' in on this case from the outside on the chance of picking something up is good, an' that looks like the only way this job can be pulled.

In any event I have always found it a very good thing not to start any trouble until it comes up an' hits you. Too many guys have had to use hair restorer over goin' out an' meeting a whole lot of grief before it got there, an' I have been too long in this thug chasing game to get excited about anything very much.

The only thing that is worryin' me at the moment is that my good friend Mr. Mellander has left me to pay the bill which when you come to weigh it up is not so hot, an' while I am waitin' for the guy who is lookin' after our table to bring me my change I am doin' some quiet thinkin'.

I am thinkin' that this is a break for me anyhow. It looks like a job for the brain trust all right, and I start to hand myself a bouquet for getting it.

Then I come back to earth. I remember also that I have not got through with this yet, an' that I am just as likely to win myself a royal smack in the puss an' a nice bronze casket, as a citation from the Director, an' it looks to me as if I had better look out for myself plenty.

Still, after I have finished the bourbon, and got my change it looks to me like this New York can be a very interestin' place.

Also, they tell me, they have some very swell dames around here which is a thing that I am very interested in at any time providin' that it does not interfere with the business in hand.

And after these ruminations I scram.

I go back to my hotel dump, an' I lay on the bed an' I begin to do some heavy thinkin' about this gold bullion bezuzus. Because it looks to me like there is a leak somewhere if all these police dicks have got themselves bumped off just hangin' around and tryin' to make some sense out of what is goin' on. Mark you I ain't surprised that these coppers have got themselves in bad because I have often noticed that a police dick will go out for too many contacts in order to keep himself wised up as to what is goin' on, an' some of these contacts are not so good an' go shootin' their mouths off all over the place, after which some mobster gets wise to the game an' starts a little target practice on the bull.

That's why they started this "G" man business. They reckon that we have got to work on our own an' not get tied up with the coppers unless we have to, which believe me is a thing we don't do unless the have is spelt with one helluva big "H." Another thing is that we are a mixed lot of guys an' you can pick practically any sort of class of guy from a "G" division any place. There is guys who meant to be lawyers an' guys who meant to go on the stage an' guys who have taken a run out powder on some dame—in fact there is every sorta guy you can think of an' a lot you'd never dream of.

I am also feelin' a bit pleased that they have put me on to this job because it is a big sorta job, an' if they are takin' Myras Duncan off it an' leavin' it to me then I reckon that they think I am the cat's lingerie, an' I don't mean maybe, an' I am also thinkin' that they musta been sorts pleased with the way I handled that Miranda van Zelden case in England with the English cops.

From here I start rememberin' Miranda an' what a swell piece she was. Believe me that dame had got a figure that woulda meant a lot to a blind man. I also start wonderin' just what sorta dames I am goin' to run across in this case that I am on, an' whether I am goin' to contact any swell lookers whilst I am tryin' to rub in on the mob that is plannin' this gold snatch.

Because I am a guy who is very interested in women, an' I am tellin' you that women are very interestin' things an' that if a woman ain't interestin' then she oughta go an' see somebody about it, because even if you are as ugly as a bunch of stale frank-furters you can still have that sorts something that makes guys go goofy an' start writin' in an' orderin' correspondence courses on "How to acquire a mysterious personality" an' all that sorta punk.

I'm tellin' you women are the berries an' I mean just that, because I have noticed things about women in cases I have been in on an' in nine cases outa ten if you handle a dame the right way she will spill the beans an' wise you up to something you are after even before she knows that she has got her little mouth open. In fact I will go so far as to say that some swell mobster's pet in Missouri once gave me the low-down on a hot ice prop-osition just because she liked the way I showed my teeth while I was yawnin' my head off when she was tellin' me how much she would like to tear her best friend's ears off.

By now it is half after midnight, an' I reckon that it is time that I got a move on an' met up with Harvest V. Mellander at Joe Madrigaul's place, which is only a ten minute run in a cab from where I am. So I doll up a bit, an' just before I go I have a meetin' with myself as to whether I should pack the old shooting iron because Lemmy Caution without a Luger under his arm is about as much use as a lump of pickled pork to a rabbi, especially when I come to consider that these palookas have been givin' the heat to these previous guys, but after doin' a bit more thinkin' I conclude that this guy Perry Charles Rice would not pack a rod, so I leave it behind an' believe me havin' regard to what happened this was a durn good thing for Perry Rice *an'* Lemmy Caution as I hope to tell you.

You oughta know that it was a swell night when I got outside an' what with the shot of bourbon an' me gettin' this bullion case I am feelin' like the guy who four-flushed the pot in a poker game when the other guys forgot to ask him to show his openers.

Pretty soon I get around to this Joe Madrigaul's place which is called Madrigaul's Club Select, which looks to me like a good crack because this Joe Madrigaul, who is a Greek, was one of the original forty thieves if some of the stories I have heard about him are O.K.

It is a swell dump—like the night club you always see on the movies, only with real liquor. There is a gold sorta entrance an' then you go along a wide passage an' up a few stairs an' through some doors an' you check your hat at a place on the right. In front of you is a few more wide stairs an' then a dance floor with tables all around it an' a curtained-off stage on the floor level right at the end. Away on the left, half-way to the stage, is a little passage with a blind end an' some telephone booths in it. Right dead on the right-hand side down near the doors is a bar with a couple of bar tenders in fancy white coats shakin' 'em up. The band platform is on the right of the stage with a little door beside it, and there is a band playin' some hot tune with a swing that would make Caruso wish he had been a song an' dance guy.

I check in my hat an' cross over to the bar, an' as I open my mouth to say "rye" I catch a look at a guy who is on the other side of the room. Now there is something familiar about this guy because he is pretty high an' is yet steady on his feet an' when I have another look I see that this guy is Jerry Tiernan, a reporter on the *Chicago Evenin' Sun an' Gazette,* an' I get the jitters because this palooka knows me for Lemmy Caution an' I reckon that I have gotta tell him to keep his trap shut about my being a "G" man otherwise there is likely to be some sweet complications.

Now you oughta know that this Jerry Tiernan is a right sorta guy an' that I have made use of him once or twice before now, an' that he is very hot at findin' out things that you do not want checked up through the office. He is also a guy with a lot of sense an' knows how to keep his trap shut, so I ease over across the floor and grab him just as he is about to stagger off some place.

"Listen, Hangover," I say, "just take a pull at yourself an' meet your old friend Perry Charles Rice who is down from the old bond-sellin' racket in Iowa, an' I hope you ain't too drunk to get that, big boy, an' like it!"

Mind you this Hangover is well gone—he was one of them guys who is always half cut anyhow an' I don't suppose he'd ever been any other way for years—but his brain is workin' all right because he looks at me an' grins an' says:

"Well . . . if it ain't the old Perry. . . . What are you doin' down here you ol' son of a hoodlum. An' how's the big bond salesman? Let me promote you to a big drink, Perry. . . ."

An' with this he grabs me by the arm an' takes me back to the bar where I tip him off that I am down here on a little business an' that he is not to forget that I am Mr. Rice—the stuff you use at weddings—an' that if he does I am liable to go haywire an' cane the pants off him with stingin' nettles.

After which I turn around and start to give the once over to this Joe Madrigaul's place. This is a swell place I'm tellin' you an' cost some sweet dough to sling together. There are plenty people there eatin' and drinkin' and they look like heavy spenders to me.

I was wonderin' just why my friend Harvest V. Mellander had got me to go along to meet up with him there, an' just how this place broke in the little bit of business we had on, an' I am not surprised anyhow because I reckon that more thuggery starts in night clubs the world over than in any other sorta place.

Just then I see something that makes me catch my breath an' gasp. I see a dame!

This dame is comin' out of the little door by the side of the band platform at the end of the dance floor on the right. An' although I have seen plenty swell dames in my life I have never looked at one in this class.

I reckon that some of you educated guys have heard of that Greek dame Helen whose face launched a thousand ships. Well I'm tellin' you that this honey's face would have launched the United States Navy an' a couple submarines. She was tall an' she moved like a queen. She had a figure that would have kept Rip Van Winkle awake just so's he could wonder whether he wasn't dreamin' it. She had an oval face that was as white an' as perfect as marble, an' there was two lovely eyes lookin' out of it that sorta looked right into you an' then out the other side.

Was she swell? . . . I'm tellin' you that this dame had a mouth that was so perfect that you had to look again so that you knew you wasn't takin' yourself for a ride.

An' she had a guy with her. This guy was so ugly he could have got himself a free scholarship into a college for gargoyles. I'm tellin' you that it hurt you to look at him. He was short an' plump an' white faced. An' he was frightened sick. I've seen some scared guys in my time, but none of 'em had anything on this baby. When it came to bein' frightened he was ace high.

They stand there for a minute in front of the door as if they was undecided about somethin'. Then, just as it looks as if they was goin' to sit down at one of the tables near the band platform another guy comes out of the door an' joins in.

This last guy is a slim, wiry, good-lookin' feller. He has gotta clean cut sorta face but he looks so tough that he would like to pull cats' legs off. You know, one of them cruel mugs. He is certainly dressed up an' looks swell, an' he has gotta coupla diamonds twinklin' in his shirt front that never come out of no five and ten.

He smiles at the lovely dame an' says somethin' an' then she turns around to the gargoyle an' says somethin' to him. After this they turn around an' go back through the little door.

I am sorta interested in this set-up, an' I turn around to the bar lookin' for Hangover so's I can ask him one or two questions about these people, because I reckon that Hangover is the night club king, there ain't any place in Chicago or New York that he ain't next to. I don't know whether I told you before, but Jerry

Tiernan is one swell crime reporter an' his paper just lets him do what he likes an' he gets around plenty I'm tellin' you, an' has been of use to me more than once in jobs I was on.

I look around this place some more. It is certainly a swell joint. It has filled up considerable an' they have a good trade. There is lots of champagne corks poppin' and some of the women are pretty lookers an' can swing a mean hip.

Hangover is standin' by the end of the bar drinkin' rye and talkin' to some red neck who is payin' for it, so I ease over an' I get the news-hound on one side an' I ask him if he knows who the dame was that just went through the little door. I tell him that she was a very swell dame an' a heavy looker an' does that help him in the identification parade.

He looks at me an' he grins. This guy Hangover has got a sickly sorta musical comedy grin; maybe because he's met so many murderers. He says:

"That's Carlotta, Perry. Don't you know Carlotta? Well . . . you'll have to meet the lady, only mind your eye Perry, because you might get yourself burned. Didn't you ever hear that dope about the moth an' the flame?"

He takes another gulp at the rye.

"She's a honey," he says, "but oh boy, is she bad? An' Perry, can she sing?"

He then goes on to tell me that this Carlotta is a dame who sings in the cabaret at this club, that she is a hot momma an' that plenty guys have handed themselves a smack by getting next to her. This dame, according to Hangover—an' I'm tellin' you that he knows his stuff—has gotta sorta Cleopatra complex an' she believes that every guy with a wad that looks like bein' worth takin' is good to play Marc Antony opposite her. Hangover also tells me strictly confidentially that the gargoyle-faced palooka is a fellow called Willie the Goop by the boys around the night clubs.

This Willie the Goop has got a real name—Charles Frene—but nobody ever thinks of using it, an' apparently he has got one big crush on Carlotta an' is hangin' around tryin' to make her good an' hard.

By what Hangover tells me this Carlotta is plenty tough, an' she is aimin' to cash in on the Gargoyle proposition, this guy having more money than he rightly knows what to do with.

Well, I was gettin' so interested in pickin' up this local colour that I very nearly forgot my date with Myras Duncan—or rather Mr. Harvest V. Mellander—an' when I look at my watch I see that it is twenty minutes past one and that he is good an' late, which surprises me because I have always heard that this guy is a dead shot for bein' any place at the time nominated.

I stick around for a few more minutes and then I have an idea that I will get through to this Moksie's dive on Waterfront where I contacted Duncan, an' find out if he has left any message or tried to contact me—that bein' the only place where he would know he could get me—an' so I feel in my pocket for a nickel an' I walk around behind the tables on the left-hand side of the Club up to the little passage where I'd seen a telephone booth.

When I got to this place I see that it is a little passage about fifteen feet long an' there are three telephone booths in it, all painted cream an' gold to match the decorations and with little pleated curtains over the windows. The passage is lit with three little electric bulbs like lilies, one over each booth.

I go down to the end booth an' I open the door. I oughta tell you that I went to the end booth because you can see the other two—they bein' opposite each other—from the club floor an' I am not particularly keen on drawin' attention to myself.

I take a look at the directory an' I find the number of this Moksie's dive an' I get my nickel ready an' I open the door, an' I get a considerable shock.

Because propped up against the wall with the telephone receiver in his hand an' his hat slipped over one eye an' a little trickle of blood runnin' down on the floor is nobody but Myras Duncan, otherwise Mr. Harvest Mellander, an' somebody has given him the heat good an' plenty, having shot him three times at close range, there bein' obvious powder marks on his light grey suit.

Now this business does not please me at all because it stands to reason that I cannot find out very much about this business now, Duncan being very dead, an' it also looks like there was some folks around here who are not very well disposed to "G" guys like myself, an' that they are probably plannin' to make things a bit difficult for me now that they have disposed of Mr. Mellander.

So I close the door an' I go back to the bar an' I have a shot of rye all by myself an' I do a little quiet thinkin'. After which I go outside to the place where I checked my hat an' I ask the jane behind the counter if she has gotta bit of cardboard about twelve inches by twelve inches.

This baby is a nice jane an' she falls for the come on look I give her, so she cuts out the bottom of a white cardboard box she has got an' she gives me this an' also a bit of string that I asked for. I then slip her a buck an' go off to the wash-room.

Up in the wash-room, which is up a little flight of stairs, I take out my fountain pen an' I start doin' a big printin' act on this bit of cardboard, an' when I have done it I run the string through two little holes I have punched in the corners, an' I put it under my coat an' I go back into the club.

I have another rye at the bar an' then I ease round to the little telephone passage on the left an' I take a quick look in the end booth an' I see that Mr. Mellander is quite undisturbed and is still very dead.

I then shut the door, an' havin' done this I hang the notice that I have printed up in the wash-room, which says "OUT OF ORDER," on the door handle of the death booth, and I ease out again an' go over to the bar an' buy myself a big one.

Because it looks to me that this case is goin' to be a very interestin' case.

CHAPTER TWO
ONE FOR WILLIE

BY THIS time I have come to the conclusion that there is some guy around this place of Joe Madrigaul's who knows a coupla things. It is also a cinch that whoever it was bumped Myras Duncan is pretty well on to the fact that he was operating on this bullion case an' it looks like that the same thing is goin' to go for me.

So it looks that someone in this bezuzus is a fellow who has got some sorta access to things pretty high up which must be a fact when you remember that Duncan told me that the original thug in this case who was slogged over the head talked a lot of stuff when he was bughouse as to what was an' what was not goin' to be done about this bullion.

All of which does not help me any an' it looks to me that the only thing that I can do is to stick around this dump an' just wait for something else to pop, although I have got a sneakin' conviction that the next thing that is goin' to happen is that somebody is going to pull one on me.

The thing that concerns me right now is just how long Myras Duncan has been stuck in that call booth. I am also interested to know as to whether he got himself shot before he had made the call or afterwards, because I am thinkin' that maybe he was calling me an' that if he got the heat after he rung up there might still be some message for me at Moksie's; so it looks like it is goin' to be a good thing for me to do to get through to Moksie's an' ask whether anybody rang up with a message for Mr. Rice, but on second thoughts I reckon I will ask Hangover to put this call through because just at this minute I feel I would like to stick around by the bar an' not go any place where somebody could iron me out.

So I ease over to him an' wise him up to the fact that I would like him to go over to the phone box an' ring through to Moksie's an' ask if anybody put through a call for Mr. Rice, to which he says O.K. an' I watch him as he goes round the left of the dance floor stoppin' here an' there to wisecrack with guys he knows. I see him turn into the little telephone passage an' I see too that he does not go into one of the boxes that I can see from the bar, but is evidently goin' to walk down to the box at the end. After a bit I see him come back an' go into one of the other boxes, an' I breathe a sigh of relief because it is a stone certainty to me that he has seen the "Out of Order" notice on the end box an' given it the go-by.

Anyhow he does this phoning an' comes back an' tells me that nobody has called up Moksie's an' asked for me, after which he says he has got a date some place and asks me where I am stayin' in New York an' fixes to come round an' have a drink with me. He then has some more rye an' scrams.

Two three minutes afterwards the band put up a big roll on the drums an' the lights in the club begin to fade out. Right then the whole place is in darkness except for just an occasional wall light here an' there throwing a dim light round the tables at the sides. Then a spot light is put on the curtains at the end of the floor. They part an' standing' there in a black dress that looks as if she was poured into it is Carlotta. Say, what have I been doin' all that dame's life!

I guess that Hangover was right when he said that dame could sing. I'm telling you that most of them mugs in that place of Madrigaul's had sampled mostly everything goin'. I reckon they'd heard plenty singers before, but when this dame starts handin' them out a slow swing about how she was always lookin' for love an' never gettin' any, well I reckon you could have heard your-self wishin'.

By the time she has come to the end of the chorus an' has started on the second verse, I am thinkin' that maybe I could go for this dame plenty—that is providin' I could look after myself in the process, an' not get my fingers all burned up like Hangover said.

It also looks to me that when she has finished her song she will probably go over an' join Willie the Goop, the gargoyle-faced guy, who is parked by himself at a table on the right—the table nearest Carlotta, an' I have got an idea that I would like to get better acquainted with these two guys. It looks to me that I owe this Joe Madrigaul's place one for Duncan. Besides which I am a naturally curious cuss.

So I leave the bar an', takin' it quiet, I start edgin' my way round the backs of the tables on the right of the club up towards Willie's table. I am careful not to make any noise or draw atten-tion to myself.

When Carlotta is about half-way through the second chorus, I reckon I am about ten feet from Willie the Goop's table, but I cannot see him because the electric wall bracket that is behind his table is not switched on owin' to it bein' too near the stage. I am just goin' to light myself a cigarette when I hear a sorta plop. It is a sound that I have heard before. It might be a champagne cork bein' pulled only it is too soft. There is a funny metallic tinge in it. I know what this noise is. It is the sound that an automatic makes when its fired with a silencer fitted over the barrel.

Right now Carlotta has finished the chorus. She makes a bow an' the lights go up, an' there is a roar of applause, but believe me it stopped good an' quick when everybody in that place saw that somebody has blasted Willie the Goop good an' proper. He was slumped forward on the table in front of him, an' his head had knocked over the vase of flowers that was standin' in the middle of the table. The white tablecloth an' the napkins were stained red and the stain was gettin' bigger.

I just stopped where I was. I was watchin' Carlotta. She never bat an eyelid. She just took a sorta quiet look at what was once Willie the Goop an' then turned an' walked up-stage, an' the curtains came down behind her.

I reckoned she had gone off to her dressin' room.

The next thing I know is that Joe Madrigaul is standin' on the steps at the entrance to the dance floor. This guy looks good an' scared I'm tellin' you.

"Latees an' gentlemens," he bleats. "I wanta you to keep mos' quiet an notta move or anything until the cops come, because it looks like to me thata they may wanta ask plenty say-so because somebody has shoot dees guy!"

An' with this he shuts the double doors behind him an' locks 'em. There is one helluva hubbub goin' on in this club. Everybody is talkin' at the top of their voices an' crowdin' round the table havin' a look at what was Willie. A lot of the women are pretendin' to be very shocked, but I notice that they only get shocked after they have had a good look.

I take advantage of this spot of hey-hey to ease up past the back of the table an' to walk through the little door on the right of the band platform which is now empty, the bandmen having joined the rest of the mob on the floor. I find myself in a little passage runnin' down by the side of the stage an' I walk down this, cut across backstage an' go through another passage. This

looks to me like dressin' rooms an' at the end I can see one door a
little bit open an' a light inside. I reckon that this will be Carlotta's
room an' I also reckon that I can hear voices inside an' I make
two guesses that Carlotta is havin' a conversation with the well-
dressed hard-puss guy who was talking to her an' Willie the Goop
just after I came into the Club.

I walk along an' I push open the door, an' I go in. I find that
I am right in my guess because Carlotta is sittin' down in front
of her dressin' table with her chair screwed round talking to the
guy who is sittin' in the corner of the room smokin' a cigarette.
He looks up.

"And what do you want, feller?" he says.

I grin.

"Sorry to butt in like this people," I say, "but I was just lookin'
around and it seemed funny that you guys should decide to hold
a meetin' out here just when somebody's got themselves shot on
the dance floor. Say," I say, lookin' at 'em both, "wasn't this guy
a pal of yours?"

She didn't say anything an' he throws his cigarette stub away
an' gets another one out. He is lookin' at me most of the time with
his eyelids drooped over his eyes.

"Why the hell don't you mind your own business, pal?" he
says. "I reckon this is a free country, ain't it, an' I'd like to know
who asked you to go gumshoein' around the place askin' questions. Who are you anyway?"

I grin some more.

"My name's Rice, from Mason City, Iowa, an' I'm around here
because a pal of mine, Jerry Tiernan, a reporting guy, promised
to introduce me to this dame. He was just goin' to do it, but he
had to go, so I thought I'd come around an' do it myself."

I look at the dame.

"How're you makin' out, kid?" I crack.

She looks up and she speaks. Its a funny thing but I've never
known a swell looker whose voice matched her face and figure, but
this Carlotta dame was the exception that didn't prove anythin'.
She'd got a voice that was as good-lookin' as her face. It was maple
syrup, I'm tellin' you, but it didn't go with the expression in her

eyes while she was lookin' at me. I told you they was lovely, didn't I, but you shoulda seen 'em now. They was lookin' at me like a pair of hard green cats' eyes. They was just tough.

"I'd be glad to know you, Mr. Rice," she said, "but it looks to me as if this ain't the time for introductions, an' it looks to me as if you might be answering a few questions yourself instead of asking them."

She turned to the fellow in the corner.

"I saw this guy, Rudy," she said. "I watched him while I was singing my number. I saw him coming up behind Willie's table, and I reckon that he might know something about that shooting himself."

Rudy looks at me an' he grins.

"Maybe you might at that," he says. "It looks like the cops might like to talk to you, Mr. Rice."

I grin some more.

"O.K.," I say, "but you know it ain't as easy as that. If you shoot a guy you have to have a gun, an' a gun is a thing that I never carry. They go off an' hurt people sometimes.

"Listen, baby," I say, "talkin' about who killed this guy outside. It looks to me like somebody could have ironed this guy out through that little door on the right, the door that leads back-stage." I grin some more. "I wonder if you got a gun," I ask him.

He gets up.

"Listen," he says. "You scram outa here. Nobody asked you to come around in this dressin' room, an' you're not wanted. Scram, otherwise it might not be so good for you. If anybody wants to ask questions around here, its all right if they're a copper, otherwise they might get a smack in the puss."

I tip my hat to the dame.

"O.K., children," I say. "Mr. Rice is never a guy for sticking his nose in where it ain't wanted. I'll be seein' you. So long. An' don't do anything I wouldn't do myself!"

With this crack I turn around and walk back through the little door on to the Club floor, where there was a lotta excitement breakin'. Some police lieutenant an' four guys from the Homicide Squad are kickin' around there askin' questions, an' no sooner do I appear than this lieutenant guy, whose name apparently is Reissler, gets his hooks on to me an' starts givin' me the works, because it looks like Joe Madrigaul an' one or two other palookas have seen me easin' round the side of the Club gettin' up towards Willie the Goop's table, an' it looks as if they are spottin' me for being the killer.

The lieutenant gets very tough with me, but I tell him to ease off an' that if he is accusin' me of murder I would very much like to see the gun that I did this job with, but that if he wants to ask me straight questions nice and quiet maybe I'll do business.

He then asks me where I have been, an' I tell him that I have eased off in in order to have a few words with Miss Carlotta who is a very swell dame, an' the sorta proposition that we do not meet very often in Mason City. I also point out to him the little door at the back an' that somebody could have croaked this guy Willie the Goop by comin' through the little door which was in darkness whilst Carlotta was singin' her number, giving him the heat an' then scrammin' outa the dance floor.

The lieutenant tells me that when he wants my advice he will ask for it, to which I crack back that that is O.K. by me an' that I have read detective books myself.

Just at this moment Carlotta an' the guy she calls Rudy come through the door an' the lieutenant lines them up too. To cut a long story short this cop, who is pretty good an' intelligent, pulls it down to the fact that it was somebody within about ten fifteen feet radius of Willie that gave him the heat, an' he reckons that he is taking everybody who was within that radius at the time, includin' me, down to headquarters for a little pow-wow.

He also lines up Carlotta an' her boy friend Rudy an' takes 'em down too, because he says he reckons it was a bit screwy them being out the back instead of bein' on the dance floor after this guy was shot.

Whilst all this palooka is goin' on I do not say anything at all. I have lit myself a cigarette an' I am wonderin' just how long it is going to be before some smart guy discovers that there is another perfectly good stiff in the shape of Myras Duncan *alias* Mr.

Harvest V. Mellander who is still stuck in the telephone box with the receiver to his ear.

I am also wondering very quietly to myself whether the exchange will be able to tell me at what time that phone box was disconnected, that is if somebody has been tryin' to get through on it, after Myras Duncan was shot, because if this is so it will give me a very good idea as to the approximate time that somebody erased Myras out.

I am disturbed in these ruminations by the arrival of the patrol wagons, and we are all shepherded down to headquarters, where they proceed to do a big questionin' act. By keepin' my ears open I get myself some information and discover that Carlotta's name is Carlotta de la Rue which sounds good an' phoney to me an' makes me imagine that her real monniker is maybe Lottie Higgins.

The guy with her is a guy called Rudy Saltierra, an' I must say that this guy seems pretty calm an' collected an' don't seem to be worryin' about anything at all.

When they start to give me the works I tell 'em that I am Perry Rice from Mason City, Iowa, an' let it go at that. But I am not mug enough to show 'em my Federal badge or do any big acts as to who I really am, otherwise I reckon I may spoil the whole bag of tricks, an' I am only hopin' that by some means or other I will get through this check-up without the works being blown.

It looks like Carlotta an' this guy Saltierra are all right because everybody could see where Carlotta was an' she tells 'em she walked back stage because when the lights went up an' she saw this guy Willie was ironed out she thought that she was goin' to faint. This guy Saltierra had got a cast-iron alibi because some guy back-stage who works the lights says that from where he was he could see the door of Carlotta's dressin' room which was open, an' that Saltierra was sitting there at the time the shootin' was done.

Just when I am beginning to be good an' bored with all this, a diversion arrives in the shape of Hangover, who has absorbed a whole lot more rye an' is standin' up only by force of will an' a copper's arm.

It looks like he has heard about this shooting business an' scrammed back to Joe Madrigaul's place right away where he has discovered that I have been taken down to headquarters, an' he has blown in to tell this Reissler that I am a perfectly good an' innocent citizen an' I have just come down to New York; that I have never been in Joe Madrigaul's place before an' that I am the sorta guy who would not know what to do with a gun even if I won one at a church raffle.

All this stuff, combined with my general attitude which has been just like how I think Perry Rice would behave, gets me outa this jam, an' the lieutenant comes over to me an' tells me I can scram out of it, but that I had better not be quite so fresh when cops are askin' me questions, to which I ask him how would he like me to be because I am that way, an' also that I am not very used to talking to smart city coppers, after which he tells me a few things about myself an' I scram.

When I get outside I wait for Hangover an' when this guy comes out I say thank you very much, an' he says he thinks that we should go an' drink some bourbon some place because it is obvious to him that without him lookin' after me I am liable to get myself into trouble around New York.

I say that this is O.K. but that I have got one or two private things to do, an' that he will be doin' me a big favour if he comes round an' sees me tomorrow mornin' at my hotel as there are one or two things he can do for me. He then falls into a cab an' goes off some place.

I hang around for a minute or two, an' I start walkin'. When I have walked half a block I see this guy Rudy Saltierra lightin' himself a cigarette, an' he sees me. He grins, an' I see that when this guy grins he looks more like a coupla tigers than ever.

"Well, Mr. Rice," he says, "I reckon you had a swell experience your first night in New York. You'll be able to tell 'em all about it when you get back home."

"You're tellin' me," I say. "I reckon that's a swell first night for anybody to have in New York. They always told me this was a tough place."

He grins.

"Well, that's the way it goes," he says. "Say, what about comin' along an' having a little drink some place with me? I reckon I could show you a thing or two that wouldn't hurt your eyesight."

I say thanks but I have got something to do. Another thing to go on all I want is some coffee, I am off liquor at the moment. I say this because I can see way down the block an all night coffee bar an' I think maybe he will fall for the idea. He does.

"O.K., buddy," he says, "you can get some coffee along here. I'd like to buy you a cup—New York hospitality."

He grins some more.

We go along to this coffee bar an' he orders two cups of coffee, then he puts his hand in his pocket to pay for it an' the light from behind the bar falls on him an' I see somethin' that is very interesting to me.

I have told you that this guy Rudy Saltierra is a very snappy dresser, an' I am wonderin' just why it is that his tuxedo does not match up with his pants, because I can see that his evening pants are made of a sorta barathea cloth but that his jacket is a black herringbone, an' I think that this is a very interesting thing for reasons which I will wise you up about in a minute.

Whilst we are drinkin' this coffee, this guy asks me a lotta questions about Mason City, but he don't win anything here because I know all about this place an' could answer up like I was really born there.

After a bit I say that it is about time I was goin' an' I say thanks a lot, an' I tell him that I hope I will see him again round Joe Madrigaul's place. He says that I surely will but that it would be a good thing if I did not go walkin' around back-stage unless somebody asks me to, an' he sorta suggests by his attitude that this dame Carlotta is his own personal property and that anybody else who plays around is liable to get a poke in the snoot.

Just at this time a yellow cab is passin' which I stop an' I tell the driver to drive me back to the Hotel Court where I am stayin', an' I do this good an' loud so that Rudy can hear me. When we have driven a coupla blocks I tell the driver to change direction an' drop me somewhere around the back of Joe Madrigaul's Club, because I have got a whole lot of ideas floatin' about in my brain box that I would like to check up on.

When I get outa the cab I go round to the back of this club an' I see that it abuts on a sorta alleyway. There are some windows on the street level which are all barred up an' I reckon that about eight feet below them will be the club floor. I walk along a bit an' I see a little window just above my head, an' I work out that this will be the window that looks into the dressing room passage.

There is nobody around in this alley an' after I investigate a bit I find a garbage can. I take this garbage can back an' I stand on it, an' I do a little heavy work on the window with a little cold steel tool I always carry, an' within about five minutes I have got this window good an' open. I get down an' take the garbage can back to the place I got it from. Then I go back to the window, take a jump, pull myself up, get through it an' shut it after me.

It is pretty good an' dark inside an' the only light I have got is a little tiny flash that I have got in the cap of my fountain-pen, but I do my best with this an' I find that I am right about being in the dressing room passage.

I walk along this an' over the stage part of the floor an' through the curtains an' into the middle of the club floor. I have seen some depressing sights but I do not think there is anything so depressin' as a night club when it is closed. The cleaners have not been at work owin' to this killin' I suppose, an' away on the left in the dim light that is coming through some glass windows at the top I can still see the red stain on the table cloth where Willie the Goop handed in his dinner pail.

I walk across the floor an' I go into the little telephone passage. I see that my "Out of Order" notice is still on the door an' I look inside an' I see that Myras Duncan is still there. It looks to me like nobody has been around here an' discovered him yet. I then go back an' sit down at a table. The guys who was at this table must have been a bit upset at the shootin' because I see that they have left a bottle with some bourbon in it there, so I help myself to a drink an' I proceed to do a little quiet thinkin'.

Sittin' at this table in the sorta dim light with this dead guy Duncan standin' in the telephone booth not thirty yards away, tryin' to get a hunch on just how all this business around here broke, may seem funny to you, but then maybe I am a funny sorta guy. I do not mind dead men one little bit; it's the live ones I'm afraid of.

Out in the middle of the dance floor is a long white streamer—you know one of them things that you throw at other guys; that sorta unwinds itself, an' it seemed to me just at that moment that life was like one of them streamers, only in the case of Mr. Harvest V. Mellander someone had broke it off with a snap. I am also thinkin' that although I do not know this guy Duncan very well, yet he seemed a good guy an' had got himself a good rating as a "G" man, an' it looked that I would have to do something about him bein' bumped off like that.

An' then—I don't know why it was—I got an idea. It was so funny an' screwy that just for a moment I thought I had gone a bit nuts myself, but after thinkin' around things it did not seem so strange. Maybe, if you've been listenin' to what I've been sayin' you mighta got the same sorta idea yourself.

But I soon bring myself back to earth because it don't do anybody any good to indulge in pipe dreams in the middle of deserted dance clubs at four o'clock in the mornin' an' the thing that I had got to do was to find where Rudy had thrown his other dinner coat.

Just at this moment I wasn't worryin' too much about the Myras Duncan bump off. That could look after itself for a bit. The thing that was engrossin' my attention was Willie the Goop bezuzus, an' this was the way I reckoned that it was done.

I told you that this Rudy Saltierra was a snappy dresser an' that I noticed at the coffee stall that he was wearin' an odd dinner coat. Well it looks to me like Rudy had slipped through the little door by the side of the band platform while this Carlotta was doin' her number an' had sorta walked quietly in the darkness up to Willie the Goop's table. When he got there he had shot this mug Willie through the pocket of his jacket after which he had scrammed good an' quick an' changed it. If this is right then he had that jacket parked some place an' it looks to me like the place was Carlotta's dressin' room.

I get up an' I walk quietly through the stage curtain an' through to the dressin' room passage. Carlotta's room is locked but I have got prizes for doin' little jobs on locked doors an' it takes me about two minutes to fix the lock an' open the door.

I go in an' I lamp around. The air is sorta sweet an' heavy—you know how a room gets when the window ain't open an' the dame who has the room uses a lotta powder and perfume there—an' I stand there sniffin' an' it is almost as if this dame Carlotta is in the place because I reckon this honey uses a swell sorta perfume that I wouldn't even forget if I was dead.

I start gumshoein' around this place openin' drawers an' lookin' into closets but I don't discover nothin' very much only that this dame Carlotta has one helluva nice taste in lingerie—an' that she wears stockin's so sheer that it was almost a sin to turn 'em over in the drawers.

After a bit I give up lookin' around here an' I go out in the passage and start lookin' for a likely place for a gent to temporarily park a tuxedo that he don't want to be found wearin', an' whilst I am workin' around this passage with my fountain-pen flash I am thinkin' that Rudy Saltierra is sure comin' back for this jacket some time an' it might not be so good for Lemmy if he decided to come back right now, especially having regard to the fact that I am not heeled having left the old Luger at home because I am playin' at being Perry Rice.

Right down at the end of the passage, near where the window is that I came in through, is a wash-basin—the sorta thing that it put there for stage hands to use, an' up on the wall, well above this basin is a cistern. I look around until I find a step-ladder which I see at the other end of the passage an' I put it up against the wall an' I feel along the top of this cistern, an' oh boy am I right? I get one helluva kick out of this because parked on top of the cistern is a tuxedo an' when I look at it close I see that it is made of barathea an' also that there is a flower in the buttonhole just as it was when I saw Rudy wearin' it earlier in the evenin'.

I get down the step ladder an' turn the coat over an' sure as shootin' there is the bullet hole through the right hand pocket an' it looks as if my idea about the way that Willie the Goop got his is dead right. I then slip my hand into the breast pocket of this tuxedo an' I fish out a letter an' I get kick number two because I can see that this letter is addressed to Miss Carlotta De La Rue at Joe Madrigaul's Club Select, an' I begin to wonder just what this letter is doin' in Rudy's pocket.

I then read the letter which is written in a pretty lousy sorta handwritin', just as if the guy who wrote it had been comin' out of a jag at the time, an' it says:

"Carlotta, I have not the time to write much to you just now, but I must see you and talk to you tonight. I am both worried and frightened at my discoveries of today, and I am even more worried and frightened for you.

Why it was necessary for you to string me along when you are already tied up to Saltierra I don't know. Maybe it was for money, but even if this is so and even if you are as heartless, as cruel, as mercenary and as scheming as I have been told, I must still see you for a few moments this evening.

I cannot possible telephone my news. It is too important and much too secret. I shall see you at the Club tonight and speak to you after your number.

"Willie."

I put this letter back in the envelope just like it was, an' the envelope back in the tuxedo an' then I walk up the ladder an' I put the tuxedo back where I found it an' I leave it for Saltierra to find when he comes for it.

When I get down the ladder I sit down on one of the rungs an' do some more thinkin'. It is a stone ginger that this letter is in Saltierra's coat because Carlotta had given it to him to read after she has got it. It stands to reason that this Willie the Goop had come along to Joe Madrigaul's place to shoot his mouth about somethin' or other, an' Rudy just wasn't goin' to have it; an' it looks to me like this dame Carlotta has probably given Rudy the tip off that it is about time that somebody gave this Willie the Goop an earful of hot lead an' Rudy has listened and said yes.

I reckon that I am not too displeased with things just at this minute because they are beginnin' to shape up a bit, an' maybe if I wait a bit I shall have somethin' I can get my teeth into.

I listen a bit but everything is quiet, so I take a chance and light myself a cigarette, an' then I gumshoe back across the dance floor an' I go over to the telephone passage feelin' my way along in the darkness an' I go into one of the booths at the entrance of the passage an' after puttin' my handkerchief over the transmitter so that some wise guy will not recognise my voice I ask for Police Headquarters.

When I get it I ask for Lieutenant Riessler. Presently this guy comes to the telephone. I ask him if he is him an' he says yes an' who am I.

"Listen, honeybunch," I tell him. "I know that you are just a big flatfoot with leaves growin' around your knees through standin' in one place too long, but there are a couple things I think you oughta know.

"First of all let me tell you that if you will send a patrol wagon around to Joe Madrigaul's place you will find a stiff in the telephone box. This stiff is a guy called Harvest V. Mellander an' somebody shot him tonight three times, so it looks as if they meant it. Secondly this guy has still got the receiver in his hand so that this telephone box will have been disconnected since the time he was shot.

"Now maybe I can tell you some more, so if you are a good guy and will check up with the telephone company what time this phone box got disconnected through the receiver bein' picked up, an' will put an ad. in the personal column of the New York Evenin' Mirror tomorrow tellin' me what the time was, then maybe I will telephone you again some time.

"The second thing is that you oughta believe in Santa Claus, because I'm him, an' what would you do without me, sweetheart?"

I then hang up an' I scram outa this Joe Madrigaul's place good an' quick, because I reckon that the lieutenant will be down pronto. I get through the little window an' I walk around a block or two an' I get myself a cab an' I go back to my hotel an' I proceed to get myself to bed, because believe it or not, I am very tired an' my old mother usta tell me that a man needs three things. Lots of good nourishin' food, lots of sound sleep an' the love of a good woman. Well anyhow I have got the food an' the sleep part an' I am still gumshoein' around lookin' for part three.

Somehow I wish this dame Carlotta was good, but my unfailing instinct—as the lady writers call it—tells me that she is just another of them dames who would prise the gold stoppin' out of a sleepin' guy's tooth.

CHAPTER THREE
A SPOT OF HOOEY

NEXT mornin' I get up good an' early an' whilst I am shavin' I take a long look at myself in the mirror an' wonder just how long I am goin' to be all in one piece, because you have gotta realise that this business of mine can be a not very healthy profession. I have known lots of guys in the service who have been just as big as I am—an' I am tellin' you that I weigh two hundred pounds an' have a face that is so ugly in a nice sorta way that dames are always inclined to lean on me in moments of trouble—an' who have got all sorts of things that I have not got such as education, but even this has not prevented them from gettin' themselves ironed out by some thug.

Which just goes to show that education ain't everything.

At the same time I have got something that the Director calls a "nose" for satisfyin' my natural curiosity in ways not always adopted by other guys, an' they tell me that this is what makes me a good dick. But just at this moment I have come to a conclusion about a coupla things, one is that I am very interested in this guy Willie the Goop, whose real name is supposed to be Charles Frene, an' point number two is that I have got to remember that I am investigatin' this bullion snatch an' I reckon I must not worry myself about these murders except when an' where they touch this gold business.

But it looks to me like it will be a very good thing if these New York coppers, who will be hot to find out who has bumped Myras

Duncan an' Willie, do not get ahead too fast, otherwise all my ideas are goin' to be all balled up.

When I read the newspapers I see that the killings of Charles Frene an' Harvest V. Mellander, whose body was discovered by this cop Riessler about thirteen minutes after I telephoned him, have been put down to some mobsters who was operatin' in the Club. It also says that the cops think they will be pinchin' somebody within two three days.

This is a thing that any cop, in any country, thinks, an' it don't mean a thing.

Well it is a cinch that they have not got anything on Rudy Saltierra because he is alibied by this electrician guy who works the lights at the club an' who said that Saltierra was sittin' in Carlotta's dressing room the whole time. But as I happen to think, personally speakin', that it was Saltierra who bumped off Willie the Goop, than I reckon this electrician guy is in on the game, an' I reckon that I am goin' to have two three words with this palooka an' maybe will try a little rough stuff with him.

So having thought all this out, I take myself down to the telegraph office an' I send off a wire to the Director's Office in code:

Special Agent Lemuel H. Caution to Director, Federal Bureau of Investigation Washington (Decoding Room). Report Myras Duncan shot last night Joe Madrigaul's Club Select New York identified by me to New York police as Harvest V. Mellander stop Report man about thirty blonde brown eyes oversized nose and mouth very ugly weight approximately 185 pounds height approximately five feet eight inches known as Willie the Goop otherwise Charles Frene shot same venue within say two hours of Duncan killing. Please arrange delay investigations of local police in order that situation may develop stop Please arrange give me full information of Charles Frene Hotel Court under cover of bond advertisement circular addressed Perry C. Rice stop Please enclose full details next gold movement United States to England and advise whether bullion will be moved to ship from United States Assay Office or Federal Reserve Bank of New York stop Am temporarily cleared of suspicion on part of local police in Charles Frene killing, but am probably still under observation suggest my real identity not disclosed anywhere stop

Having got this off my chest, I then go back to the hotel an' give myself a shot of rye because I think that very soon a lot of interestin' things are going to happen around here shortly—anyway I hope so.

At half-past ten Hangover arrives an' he is full of news an' bourbon. He asks me whether I know that there has been another killing at Joe Madrigaul's place an' that some guy Mellander has got himself bumped off in the phone box, an' I says yes I have seen this in the papers. He says that it looks to him as if this stuff is goin' to make a pretty good story an' he is goin' to get around and get himself a coupla lines on it. I reckon he is very pleased with all this bein' a reporter.

He also says he does not know what I am doin' around Joe Madrigaul's place last night but that he guesses that I am on a job of some sort, an' that if he can be of any use to me I have only got to say the word.

Now I have been thinkin' about Hangover an' I have come to the conclusion that it is much the best thing for me to do to tell this guy what I am really doin' in New York. Maybe you will think that this was not such a hot thing to do, but it looked to be right just at this time, an' I feel that I am goin' to follow my nose for a bit, so I tell him about the stuff that I got from Mellander last night.

I tell him who Mellander was an' I also tell him that it looks to me like these two killings was tied up with this suggested attempt that is goin' to be made on the bullion. That this is a cinch as regards Duncan an' probably it goes for Willie too. I also tell him that he will be doin' a very good job of work for me if he will give me the low down on this guy Rudy Saltierra an' that I would like to have this pronto.

He is very pleased with all this an' says that I am a great guy to wise him up about this story, an' he will keep it under his hat until I give him the say-so to break with it an' that when I say go he reckons that this is goin' to be one of the biggest crime stories that he has ever pulled in a long career of liquor, dames an' what have you got. After which we drink a little bourbon an' he goes off to see what he can find out.

By this time it is twelve o'clock an' I put on my fedora an' I go round to Joe Madrigaul's place an' I ask to see this guy, an' I see him in his office. This Madrigaul is not at all unpleased to see me, because he is a bit excited about havin' all these murders around his club, an' I don't think that he minds the idea very much because it looks to him like a lotta guys will come around just to see the place where these fellows got bumped, which just goes to show that most guys is only interested in some other guy after he is dead.

I put on a very good act about last night, an' bein' taken down to headquarters an' grilled, an' I tell him that when I get back to Mason City I bet I will make the folks' hair stand up when they hear about the sorta stuff that goes on around here in New York an' that I have been pulled in as a suspect. I then tell him that I have always been interested in detective stories, that I practically read one every week an' that I reckon if I had been a dick I would have made very good. I also say I have got a lotta theories myself about these murders; that it looks to me like this guy Willie the Goop was shot by somebody who came through the pass door on the right of the band platform.

He falls for this an' says that this is not so because just on the other side of the door, fixed up on a platform on the wall, is the electrician who works the lights an' this guy can see all round back-stage, an' that the only fellow who could have come through an' shot Willie was Rudy Saltierra, an' this electrician guy says he was in Carlotta's dressing room all the time.

I say that this is very interestin' an' has this guy got any theories about what happened. He falls for this too an' takes me across the club floor to where this electrician is at work looking after the lights, an' I have a talk with this guy whose name is Skendall, an' this guy tells me how nobody back-stage could have done any shootin' or gone through the pass door unless he had seen 'em.

This Skendall is a big sorta guy an' looks tough. By this time I have come to the conclusion that he is a first-class liar an' that he is fixin' an alibi for Rudy Saltierra very nicely. I also reckon that I will have a few quiet words some time with this Skendall an' will probably argue with him with a sledge hammer.

Anyway it looks like I am doin' a good mornin's work an' so I suggest to Joe Madrigaul that we should sample a little rye at my expense an' this idea goin' with him we go back to his office an' we proceed to do a little quiet drinkin'.

This Joe Madrigaul is the usual sort who runs joints like this, an' he is not a bad guy in his way, an' after I have talked for a bit to this cuss I come to the conclusion that it is more than likely that he don't know what is going on around this dump an' is probably bein' played for a sucker by the Carlotta-Saltierra mob who are certainly givin' themselves a pretty good break some way or another.

So I tell him that this Carlotta is a nice piece of work an' that I could go for her in a very big way myself an' he says that is all very well, but that this Carlotta is Rudy Saltierra's girl, and that I had just as soon start playin' baseball with a coupla Bengal tigers as try an' muscle in on the same. I also get it out of him that it is Rudy Saltierra who got this dame the job singin' at the Club which is why he is always hangin' around.

Madrigaul wises me up that Saltierra is a tough baby an' that he is a racketeer in a big way. Nice an' quiet mind you, but still big, an' that he is a very nasty tempered fellow an' can always get somebody to do a big rubbin' out act with any guys who start gettin' fresh. The guy goes on that it looks like Rudy is real stuck on the bundle of frills an' that Madrigaul wouldn't be surprised if Rudy didn't do somethin' silly like marryin' her or somethin' equally screwy because it looks like Rudy has said to Madrigaul that this time it is different an' that he is goin' for this dame in a different sorta way to all the others, which is all very well but still sounds like a lot of hokum to me because I know these racketeers an' their little way of takin' a run out powder on a dame after they have told her a lotta bedtime stories about what they will do for her if she is nice an' says yes papa all the time.

After this pow-wow with the Greek I scram outa this place and get myself some eats at a quick lunch an' do some more quiet thinkin'. It looks to me like I have gotta force the pace a bit if I am goin' to get next to what these guys are at; that the best thing I can do is to get around an' have a little talk with this Carlotta dame an' try an' see just how she is shapin' in this business.

Maybe you will think that this was not a clever thing to do, but I have always found that takin' the bull by the horns is some-thin' which gets results—even if it is the bull who gets the results.

I then go into a drug store an' look up the name of a florists near Joe Madrigaul's place, an' when I have got this I ring the Club an' say to the girl that I am the florists an' that Miss de la Rue has ordered some flowers from us but that we have lost the address an' can they oblige. She falls for this an' gives me Carlotta's address on Riverside Drive at West 113th Street an' I jump a cab an' go around there pronto.

When I get there I see that this is a pretty swell sorta apart-ment house an' that by the looks of the place this Carlotta must be makin' some sweet dough doin' this torch singin' act around night clubs. I get her name off the indicator on the ground floor an' I go up in the lift an' walk straight along the corridor until I come to the door of the apartment an' then I rap on the door an' stick around until it is opened by some coloured maid who is all dolled up like you see 'em in French farces.

As this girl opens the door I look over her shoulder an' I see another door—on the opposite side of the hall behind her—close, an' I reckon that Carlotta is in alright, but when I tell this maid that I want to see Miss de la Rue she says she reckons that Miss de la Rue is out an' that I had better get in touch with her at the Club Select where she will be that evenin', because Miss de la Rue don't receive at her apartment.

I tell her that for what Miss de la Rue don't receive I hope she will be truly thankful, an' as she steps back to shut the door I put my foot inside an' just push. She then begins to do a big squawk, so I tell her to behave herself an' not get excited, an' I walk across the little hall an' I rap on the door opposite an' I open it an' go in.

It is a swell sorta drawin' room an' looks very pretty. It is full of women's fall-di-lala, an' Carlotta wearin' a very attractive loungin' gown is sittin' at a table writin' a letter. When she heard me she spins around an' looks at me like I was somethin' that crawled out from under a rock.

"An' what do you want," she says. "Didn't somebody tell you that I wasn't at home?"

I put my hat down an' I sit down an' I light a cigarette. She is tappin' on the floor with her foot because I'm tellin' you that she was properly het-up, an' I might also tell you that this dame has got the swellest feet an' ankles that I have ever seen an' I have seen considerable.

"Now listen, Miss Carlotta," I say, nice an' gentle like. "Don't get me wrong, because I wouldn't like you to come to any wrong sorta conclusions about me because I am a guy that has gotta terrific respect for women because believe it or not my mother was a woman an' my father always taught me that it was wrong to hit a woman while there was a good train service runnin'."

This Carlotta then gets up an' does a big high hat act. She says that she is really not interested in what my father said to me, an' that will I please state what I want otherwise she is goin' to ring for the lift guy an' have me thrown out on my ear. I then look very sorrowful an' say that I have always known that my lack of education an' book learnin' would get me in a jam some time, an' that if I had known I was goin' to meet up with her I would have spent my whole life takin' correspondence courses so I would talk like a radio announcer.

She then starts tappin' with her foot some more, an' I tell her that when I saw her the night before she just hit me for the boundary an' that I have never seen anything like her before, an' that I am just plain nuts about her, an' that my pal Jerry Tiernan had promised to introduce me to her only that was all messed up by this shootin' business, an' that I have taken a great liberty in bustin' in like this but that I am due to leave New York almost any time now an' that I just couldn't go without seein' her.

All the while I am doin' this this dame is lookin' at me in a very suspicious sorta manner, but at last I see that I am beginnin' to get away with it, an' I see her eyes sorta soften, an' I reckon that she has fallen for this spiel that I have put up.

Because it is a funny thing but it don't matter who or what a dame is or how tough she is you have only gotta pull a lotta stuff about bein' nuts about her an' in nine cases outa ten she will fall for it just because women—ever since the world began—have wanted guys to fall for 'em. An' you can take it from me that if the serpent in the Garden of Eden hadn't been wise to this fact then we none of us would even be here, an' Adam would still be wearin' smoked glasses an' not noticin' anything about Eve at all—at least not so it mattered.

She then says that maybe that is O.K. but that I should not go around bustin' into people's apartments an' anyhow what do I want.

I say that I am very worried because I reckon that the police are very suspicious about me an' this killin' last night, an' that although they have let me go I was very upset because there seemed to be some sorta idea flyin' about that I had shot this guy Willie the Goop which was a thing which was quite impossible for me to do anyhow because I would not hurt a fly.

When I have finished this business she gets up an' she gets herself a cigarette out of a box an' lights a swell silver ornamental lighter on a little table an' she brings the cigarette box an' the lighter over to me an' she gives me a cigarette an' lights it for me.

She stands in front of me while she is doin' this an' I tell you that this dame was certainly a honey. She has got a figure that is nobody's business an' she walks like a queen oughta walk if she knew her stuff. She is wearin' the same perfume that I remember from the time when I turned her dressing room over while I was lookin' for Rudy's other tuxedo, an' was that stuff perfume or was it? I'm tellin' you that it certainly was. It just did somethin' to me an' what with her standin' there lookin' down on me with those big lovely eyes sorta soft an' droopin' I had to remember that I was doin' a job otherwise I might have qualified myself for a big sentimental act an' messed up the whole bag of tricks.

Which is the way it always goes. Because I have found out that if ever you are on a case an' you meet a good woman—you know the sort that your mother wants you to get acquainted with—then she is always one of them with squat heels an' a square fringe an' she talks high hat an' makes you feel that you oughta take a course in table manners an' how to eat asparagus without havin' to wear a slicker; but if she is a bad one like this Carlotta then you can bet your last dime that she has got all the makin's an' that she wears the right sorta scent an' french heels an' that she looks like she was poured into her clothes an' she talks in that sorta voice that makes you think of raisin' a family quick, so as to get some new voters functionin' for Mr. Roosevelt's new deal before it starts gettin' any older.

After she has lit this cigarette for me she sits down beside me on the couch an' she waits for a minute an' then she says.

"Listen Perry, I reckon that you are the sorta man that I have always felt attracted to an' I reckon that it was something more than mere chance that sent you to Joe Madrigaul's place last night."

She gives a little sigh an' then she goes on.

"Yes . . . I think it was Fate that sent you there because I needed help so badly."

Then she goes on to say that she is sorry that she sorta suggested that I had anything to do with the Willie the Goop bump-off the night before, but that when I came around to her dressin' room she was very very upset, but that anyhow they knew that I couldn't have done it because I hadn't gotta gun. Then when she has said all this she looks at me sorta sad an' says what do I think about it because she can see that I am a man with a whole lotta brains an' that she is gettin' some ideas into her head about these killin's which are distressin' her a whole lot.

I then say what I said the night before, an' while I am talkin' I am watchin' her quietly in a mirror that is on the wall on the other side of the room, an' I can see that she is lookin' at me with those hard cats' eyes of hers an' I reckon that she is weighin' up just how much I am guessin' an' just how much I have guessed right.

I say that it is a cinch that nobody on the Club floor could have shot Willie the Goop because I am standin' just near his table, an' that although his table was in darkness because the wall bracket was not switched on, yet nobody could have got past me, and so

I reckoned that somebody musta come through the pass door on the right of the stage curtain and shot Willie.

I then ask her if that wall bracket by his table was always put out when she sang her numbers an' she says no but she reckons that something had gone wrong with it, an' I think she is right too because I bet this guy Skendall the electrician was in on this bump-off an' fixed it so that that particular light wasn't workin' so that the gunman could get away with the job. All of which makes me very determined to do a little talkin' some time with this Skendall.

After a bit she gives another sigh an' she says that it looks to her that I think that it was Rudy Saltierra that did the shootin', an' I say well I don't see how anybody else coulda done it, an' she reminds me that the electrician who works the lights back-stage had alibied Rudy Saltierra by sayin' that he never left her dressin' room, an' that besides this Rudy hadn't got a gun.

Now this is a new one on me because it is a fact that Rudy hadn't got a gun when we went down to headquarters, an' if he had used one on Willie he would have to have dumped it some place in the Club an' if this was a fact then I'd have thought that he would have left it along with his other tuxedo. But this don't mean anything really because I reckon that Rudy had a lotta time to slip the gun to somebody else, an' anyhow I am certain that there are more thugs in this game than I have counted on up to the minute.

But I play along with my little Carlotta an' I say that if she says that, well then I reckon it wasn't Rudy because this is the thing she wants me to say.

Then she gives another sigh an' she gets up an' she says that she reckons that I must run along now, but that if I stick around in New York she will always be glad to see me, an' then suddenly she sorta breaks down an' she sticks her arms around my neck an' before I know what I am doin' I am kissin' this dame like nothin' on earth just because it seems the right thing to do, an' believe me I didn't find it no hardship neither, an' you do not have to get excited about this anyway because I have always been partial to kissin' pretty women, that is providin' that it does not interfere with the business in hand.

Anyway this Carlotta hangs on to me like a clam on a lighthouse. She tells me that she is very unhappy an' that she is in a very bad jam, an' she sorta suggests that she is not really very stuck on this guy Rudy Saltierra, an' that she is beginnin' to go all goofy where I am concerned.

Now I take all this with a very large helpin' of salt because I reckon that this dame is playin' me along for a sucker.

After a bit I tell her that she should take a pull at herself an' that if she gets into any sort of tough spot she can always rely on Perry C. Rice, after which I say that if I do not have to leave New York too quick I will be around at Joe Madrigaul's place tonight so as to hear her sing some more, and she says that I must excuse her for breakin' down but that she ain't met a lot of men like me in her life, an' that I remind her of the countryside an' the wide open spaces, but I do not tell her what she reminds me of because I have got to keep this party nice.

I then take a fond farewell an' I leave, but when I get outside I walk round the block an' I come back the other way an' I stick around an' keep my eye on the apartment and sure as smoke about ten minutes afterwards a roadster pulls up an' out gets Rudy Saltierra lookin' like all the flowers in May an' he goes in.

I light myself a cigarette an' I scram out of it. I am very pleased with the afternoon's work because it is a cup of coffee to all the tea in China that this dame is spilling the works about me to Rudy an' that the pair of 'em have got the jitters about me an' that they will probably try something on which is just what I want 'em to do, because if you can get guys a bit rattled then they always do something they never meant to do an' give themselves away some place.

So I buy myself a cab an' I get back to the hotel an' I have a shot of bourbon an' lay down on the bed to do a little quiet thinkin'. After a bit I get up an' I take a look through the window an' down on the other side of the street opposite the hotel entrance I can see some guy standin' up against a cigarette stand an' just doin' nothin' at all. The guy is wearin' a light grey fedora well over one eye an' he is just smokin' an' ruminatin' an' keepin' an eye on the hotel.

Which pleases me very much because it looks to me like Rudy has got some mobster to keep an eye on me, an' this is one of them times that I like bein' kept an eye on.

But I reckon that from now on I am goin' to pack my shootin' iron because it looks to me that maybe these guys have got me marked for the spot an' I am tellin' you that I do not intend to go gettin' myself killed with my boots on, not unless I fall in the river after too much bourbon or some nice an' innocent reason like that which is a thing that can happen to anybody.

CHAPTER FOUR
ROUGH STUFF

AT SEVEN o'clock I gave myself a shower an' changed my clothes, after which I packed my grip an' I rang down to the desk to send me up my bill because I have got an idea in my head that when I have scrammed outa this Hotel Court I am not comin' back to it any more but will go live in some place where Rudy does not know where I am, because you have got to realise that I have got an instinct for trouble an' I have got a very large idea in my head that somebody is goin' to start somethin' with me pretty soon.

Because the way I figure it out at the moment is this: I reckon that this big act that Carlotta has put on with me this afternoon is for the purpose of getting next to me by puttin' the idea in my head that she is the little forlorn dame who has by some means or other got herself into the power of the wicked mobster Rudy, instead of which, as I have told you, Joe Madrigaul has told me that it was Rudy who got this dame the job at the Club, an' I reckon that the pair of 'em think that they are playin' me for a sucker.

I also think a lot of other things but as these are more or less theories at the moment I am not goin' to worry you with 'em, but I reckon that I will see how they turn out.

I then have my dinner an' at nine o'clock Hangover comes through on the telephone. He tells me that he has been hangin' around in the reporters' room at police headquarters an' that he has got a line on this guy Saltierra. Hangover reckons that Saltierra made plenty dough outa the liquor racket while repeal was on, an' since then he has been runnin' protection rackets around town.

I do not have to tell you what a protection racket is. You go along to some guy an' you tell the guy that he needs protection an' you say that you are goin' to do the protectin'. If he pays up, O.K., if not then you fix it so that he really *does* need protection, after which the guy either pays or else he usually wins himself a good-lookin' funeral.

Now accordin' to Hangover this Saltierra has got a whole lotta brains, that is he don't drink too much, nor talk too heavy, an' the guys who work for him are a very select bunch of thugs. They know their stuff an' they do not suffer from the usual mobster's habit of shootin' their mouths when they have been samplin' the rye well an' truly.

Hangover then asks me when is he goin' to see me, an' I tell him that I reckon that I will be around Joe Madrigaul's place soon after midnight an' if he wants to do me a big favour he will find out where this electrician guy Skendall lives because I wanta talk to this guy. He says this will be easy an' that he will meet me at the Club half after twelve.

I then go downstairs an' pay the bill an' I tell the clerk that I have gotta scram but that I will be around some time next day an' that I am expectin' some advertisin' matter that he might keep for me until I call in for it.

I then walk outside an' get a cab an' I can see that the guy in the grey fedora gets in one an' comes after me. I tell the guy who is drivin' my cab to run around a bit an' pull up in some quiet place an' he does this. When we pull up I see outa the back window that the other cab has pulled up about thirty yards behind us an' I get outa the cab an' I walk back along the sidewalk until I come to this cab an' I swing in suddenly an' pull the door open an' inside sittin' there smokin' is the guy in the grey fedora.

"Listen wise guy," I tell him, "I have been followed around before. I am now givin' you official notice that I do not like your face an' unless you scram outa here good an' quick I am goin' to bust you in the puss, an' how do you like that?"

He is about to say somethin' an' leans forward an' as he does this I catch hold of him by his scarf an' pull him towards me, an' I let him have a haymaker on the nose. This guy subsides in the corner nice an' quiet an' I then tell the driver that he had better stick around until his fare comes up for air.

Maybe this will seem to you to be forcin' the pace a bit but I know that a war is about to start at any minute now an' I reckon that I might as well be the guy who starts it, because strange as it may seem, I do not like these mobsters one little bit, first of all because they are mean cusses an' secondly because they have ironed out one two pals of mine at different times.

I then go back to my cab, drive around for a few minutes an' then stop at some little hotel where I check myself in as Perry Rice an' give myself a large shot of bourbon just to square things off.

I unpack my grip an' stick around for a bit, after which I go an' see a newsreel an' then I go back to this hotel which is called the Delamere an' I put on my shoulder holster with my Luger in it, an' I get myself a cab an' go around to Joe Madrigaul's place.

I reckon this guy Madrigaul was right about being pleased with the killin's because there is a lot of people around this place lampin' all over it an' gettin' a kick outa being in some place where some guys got themselves bumped off, which will go to show you the sorta thing that amuses people in these days.

Joe Madrigaul is standin' about the place dressed up an' with a red carnation in his buttonhole, lookin' very pleased with life an' we have one or two drinks together, an' tell each other stories. He also tells me that the police have been around to see him an' that they have got an idea that it was somebody who got outa the Club who shot Harvest V. Mellander an' that they probably left some pal inside who was sittin' at one of the tables behind me, an' that this was the guy who shot Willie the Goop, an' they reckon that this guy must have got up behind me an' shot round behind my back an' then scrammed out of it an' got through the doors before Joe closed them.

Madrigaul cannot understand this theory because the girl in the cloakroom which any guy would have to pass in order to get outa the Club says that nobody went by her, but still I reckon the police are doin' their stuff an' just layin' things off for a bit, an' that Washington has probably given them an instruction as per my telegram.

Pretty soon Hangover comes in. As usual he is half cut but fulla brains, an' he comes over to me an' says that he reckons things are goin' O.K. and that he hopes the information he gave me about Saltierra was of some use, an' that he reckons he can find out some more in a day or so. He also tells me that he has got another line but that he will not blow any thin' until he has checked up on it. He says that he has got an idea in his head that this guy Willie the Goop whose name was supposed to be Charles Frene, is not Charles Frene at all but somebody else, and that he thinks he can find out who this guy really was an' will let me know.

He also tells me that he has got the address of this Skendall; that this Skendall seems a right sorta guy an' has not got any sorta record with the cops in New York an' that he lives over some down-town garage. He then gives me this address an' I say that maybe I will have a talk some time with this Skendall.

Pretty soon Rudy Saltierra comes in an I see that he has got himself a new dinner suit, because his tuxedo an' pants are matchin'. He is also very nicely dressed with a white carnation an' pearl an' diamond studs an' buttons. He is very affable to me an' buys me some rye an' sorta suggests that when I have got tired of stickin' around this place he will take me some other places an' I think it is a good thing to tell him that I will probably like to get around with him a bit that night, although believe me I have not got any such intention.

He then gets very friendly an' I say that I reckon he is a very lucky guy to be tied up with this dame Carlotta because I reckon that this dame is the swellest femme I have ever seen in a long career, an' the guy who is next to a dame like that must be a swell guy. He says he reckons that is how it is an' that maybe after she has done her number we might drink a little glass of champagne together just to show we are all friends an' that there is no ill-feelin' about the tough cracks we had the night before.

He also sorta suggests to me that these killin's are nothin' to get very excited about, that they very often happen around a place like New York an' that nobody is goin' to get particularly het-up about them because these guys who get themselves bumped off are always tied up some way or other with mobsters, who are very bad people to get tied up with.

After a bit there is a roll on the drums an' Joe Madrigaul goes into the middle of the floor an' he says that how last night he is very sorry to tell everybody whilst Miss de la Rue was singin' her number with a spot light on her, that a guy was bumped off. He also says that some other guy was found ironed out in the telephone box an' he winds up by sayin' that he hopes nobody will mind this very much because they can always be sure of havin' a good time at Joe Madrigaul's an' that he will now present the famous Carlotta.

He then scrams out of it an' the lights go out an' a spot light goes on the curtains an' there is Carlotta. I have told you that this dame was a honey before, but if you could have seen that dame standin' there dressed in some flame coloured gown that sorta caught the spot light an' held it, I tell you it would have made your heart stop beatin'.

She sings the same number that she sang the night before, an' when it is over she goes back through the curtains an' the lights go up an' Rudy Saltierra gives me the wink an' we go up an' we sit down at the table that Willie the Goop was sittin' at, only this time I notice that the wall bracket behind him has been mended, so I reckon that this guy Skendall has been puttin' in a little heavy work on it.

After a bit Carlotta comes out an' sits down. She smiles at me an' I say how do you do, an' Rudy orders a bottle of champagne.

In a minute the band starts again an' everybody begins to dance. I am wonderin' why Saltierra does not dance with this dame Carlotta but he don't make any move an' I think that maybe the reason is that if he dances with this dame then he thinks that I might ask for one an' he is not so hot on the idea.

After a coupla minutes Carlotta says I have got a pencil because she wants to show us somethin' funny. So I give her the little silver pencil that I have got an' she shows us a little puzzle which she draws on the table cloth, which is very good if you like that sorta thing, but she does not return the pencil to me an' after a bit whilst Rudy is watchin' somebody on the dance floor I see her writin' something on the table cloth under her bread plate. She has a quick look at me an' then looks down at the plate, an' I get the idea that this dame has written some message down for me to read, an' I grin to myself because I think that these guys are goin' to start somethin' with me good an' quick.

I stick around for about another ten minutes an' then I say I must get along because I have got to see somebody an' as I get up, Saltierra asks this Carlotta if she would like to dance. I say goodnight an' they start dancin' an' I lean over the table an' move her plate, an' I see that she has written "apartment 3 o'clock," an' I reckon this is the tip-off that I should go round an' see her at three o'clock that night. Having absorbed this information which I do not think is so hot I scram back to the bar an' look for Hangover, but this guy has gone. I then check out my hat, grab a cab an' go back to my hotel.

When I get there I do a little thinkin' an' I come to the conclusion that I had better get this Skendall business over, because I reckon that this is important, an' that if I can pull an act with Skendall then maybe I can get confirmation about my ideas regardin' Saltierra.

I am realisin' all the time that I am walkin' down a blind alley, but at the same time you gotta understand that I had got a definite hunch that somehow I am slowly gettin' near to somethin' on this gold snatch which is the main business that is worryin' me right now.

This guy Skendall lives in a garage down town near Spruce Street. Hangover tells me that this place is a two floor place an' that Skendall lives over the garage. I have also discovered from Madrigaul that Skendall is goin' off early tonight havin' been kept late at the Club the night before over the shootin', so I reckon that I am goin' to talk to this palooka before he turns in an' gets too sleepy to think.

I change out of my tuxedo into a day suit an' I stick the Luger in my trousers waistband, an' then I go out an' jump a yellow cab an' tell him to drop me on the corner of Spruce.

While we are goin' downtown I wonder just how tough this Skendall is an' whether I am goin' to have trouble with him, but after a minute I think that anyway I will soon know so I might as well think about somethin' else. This is what they call logic.

After a bit we arrive on Spruce an' I pay off the cab an' stick around for a bit. Pretty soon I see the garage on the corner, two-three blocks down Spruce, an' I walk down the street an' light myself a cigarette standing on the opposite side of the roadway an' havin' a good look at the dump.

It is not much of a place. There is room for three or four cars, an' there is an old gas pump. There is a side door on the right of the garage that I reckon is a sorta private entrance to Skendall's place upstairs an' also, at the back of the garage, there is another door that might also lead up to the apartment above.

I pulla newspaper outa my pocket an' push my finger through so as to make a hole to see through an' then I stand, underneath a lamp an' pretend to read the paper, but all the time I am keepin' my eye on the fellow who is workin' about the garage, and who, right now, is fixing a flat tyre on one of the cars.

Just at this minute the door at the back opens an' a guy puts his head around the corner an' speaks to the guy in the garage. I see that the guy in the doorway is Skendall an' also that he is sending the other guy out lor somethin' because the other guy scrams an' I can see him hurryin' to a cigarette stand down the street, so I reckon that Skendall has sent him out to buy some.

Skendall stands for a minute in the back doorway an' then he goes, so I reckon that he has gone upstairs again. I look down the street an' I can see the garage guy still standin' at the cigarette stand an' so I ease across the road pretty quick an' go into the garage an' stand in a dark corner which is full of shadows.

A couple minutes afterwards the guy comes back with the cigarettes an' I watch him as he goes over to the door an' upstairs. A minute afterwards he comes down again and begins to play around with the flat tyre which is on a car in the front of the garage an' it is quite easy for me to slip across to the door an' open it and walk through, pullin' it shut behind me.

I find myself at the bottom of a flight of wooden stairs an' at the top I can see a slit of light comin' from a door. I go up the stairs, an' look around the edge of the door an' I look into a bedroom an' in the corner is Skendall in his shirtsleeves fiddlin' with a radio.

I pull out the Luger.

"Well, Skendall, how're you makin' out?" I ask him.

He spins around. He looks as surprised as if he'd trod on a snake, an' then he recognises me.

He grins.

"Why, if it ain't Mr. Rice," he says, just standin' there with his big hands hangin' down by his sides, "an' why the rod, Mr. Rice, an' what can I do for you?"

"You sit down there an' shut your head," I tell him, "an' take a tip from me an' get some quick thinkin' an do what you're told otherwise this gun's liable to go off an' you're liable to get yourself a coupla slugs in the guts."

He sits down, but he is still lookin' pretty cool, an' the idea crosses my mind that this is not the first time this guy has had a gun held on him.

"Say, Rice," he cracks. "Just what is this, a hold-up, an' what are you after anyway?"

I think I will try something on this guy, because I have figured out that if he was in on the shootin' of Willie the Goop then he must know the reason for it, an' it looks to me as if Willie knew somethin' that he wasn't supposed to know an' that's why they ironed him out.

"Listen, punk," I say. "You know this ain't a hold-up, an' you know what I'm doin' here. You guys gave it to Willie the Goop, who was a friend of mine just because he knew somethin' too much for you. Well let me tell you that you're going to tell me all about it an' like it, an' if you don't then I'm going to take you for a ride that you'll remember when you've got white whiskers an' double lumbago."

He gets up. This guy has got nerve alright.

"Yeah, bozo," he says. "Well now I'll tell you a few. If you fire that gun off up here there'll be half a dozen of my buddies around here inside ten seconds an' what they wouldn't do to you is nobody's business. You take a tip from me an' put it ..."

He breaks off an' takes a sudden dive at me across the room. I drop the gun an' my head an' connect with his jaw with my left elbow. He goes down, but he is up almost before he has hit the floor an' aims a nasty one at my head. I block it an' swing a right which misses, an' then we get into a wrestlin' act with nothin' barred.

I'm telling you that this guy Skendall was strong, but I'm also tellin' you that I am a little bit stronger, an' when I have thrown him an' fell on top of him an' banged his head on the floor half a dozen times he starts to go a bit funny an' weaken.

I get my fingers round his throat an' press my two thumbs on his windpipe. His eyes start poppin'.

"Now listen, sweetheart," I tell him. "Are you goin' to play ball or are you? If so indicate in the usual way. If not I'm just goin' to go on squeezin' until you are duly elected for the local morgue."

He is almost black in the face when he nods his head, an' I ease up the pressure.

"Now get this, Skendall," I say. "I reckon I'm on to you. First of all I want you to tell me about that little business last night at Joe Madrigaul's place. How did Saltierra kill Willie the Goop an' why? That's question number one, an' question number two is, who killed Harvest V. Mellander an' why? Now think quick and splutter before I start puttin' your eyes out."

I get up an' he gets up too. He is movin' pretty slow because he has got his hand to his throat an' I reckon that he is hurt some. The pressure I put on his throat would have strangled a coupla ordinary guys. He makes as though he is goin' to sit down on a chair that is standin' by the wall when suddenly he makes a dive for the door.

I have been expectin' somethin' like this, an' I get there first. I slam him one into under the heart with my right an' I follow with a left hook to the jaw. He tries to shape up an' so I give him a smasher on the mouth, an' what his teeth don't do to my knuckles is nobody's business. He goes down with a wallop an' I pick him up with my left hand an' smack him down with my right again just for luck because these mobsters like Skendall are just a pain in the neck to me anyway.

I sit down an' watch him. He is pretty well finished. He crawls up to his feet an' flops down in the chair by the wall with his head lollin' an' his tongue hangin' out. I reckon this guy is about all out for none.

"O.K. little precious," I tell him. "Maybe you won't start gettin' funny around here any more, because if you do I'm goin' to give you some treatment that I learned off the Phillipinos on the Islands, an' very likely you will be nutty when I have done with you. Now are you goin' to talk turkey or do I really get to work on you?"

He nods his head weakly. The last bust in the puss I have given him has hurt him an' there is a tear stealin' down one of his cheeks.

"Just too bad, ain't it?" I tell him. "It's O.K. for you guys when you are shootin' people in the dark at restaurant tables or givin' guys like Mellander the heat in call boxes, but when you get a smack in the puss yourself it don't feel so good, does it?"

"O.K." he mutters. "I'm talkin'. . . . Ouch. . . ." He lets go a groan, an' is swayin' so that it looks as if he is goin' to fall off his chair. I fall for this an' seein' that this guy is pretty badly knocked about I get up an' go over to him; but as I am gettin' near him I see his eyes move to the door an' I spin around.

In the doorway is the guy from the garage an' he has got a rod in his hand an' as I jump he squeezes it.

I feel the bullet cut through the sleeve of my coat just above the elbow, an' before he can fire again I am on him.

I'm tellin' you that I am annoyed. I reckon that there is plenty trouble in this world without any more from these lousy bums who are always durn brave when the other guy ain't got a gun. I fix this guy.

I punch seventeen different kinds of hell out of him. I paste him until he don't know which way he's pointin' or what his name is, an' by the time I have finished bustin' these two guys around the place I am really beginnin' to take an interest in the job. I just put my heart right into my work.

I lay off 'em when the garage guy is layin' on his face in the corner cryin' like he was needin' his mammy, an' Skendall has only got two teeth left, then I pick up my gun an' put it in my pocket. I take the shells out of the garage guy's gun an' throw it in the corner, an' then I run downstairs an' pull the garage shutters down. I close the place up, lock the doors, turn off the lights, an' then I go back again to my little playmates upstairs.

They are still lyin' where I left 'em, an' they are not takin' any interest in anything at all.

I walk along the passage an' I find a bathroom. I full a jug with water an' I bring it back an' throw it over these two heroes. Then I give 'em a drink out of the rye flask I have got in my hip pocket an' sit 'em both up on the bed like nice children.

Skendall does a bit of weavin' about an' then he opens his eyes an' sits up an' takes notice. His face looks like a map of China an' the garage guy's would have won prizes in the blancmange business.

I sit there lookin' at them. I wait two three minutes till they have got their wits about them an' then I dive into my secret pocket an' I bring out my Federal badge. I flash it at 'em.

"My name's Caution," I tell 'em. "Lemmy Caution. The guy who bust the Siegella outfit. The guy who brought in Mirandaz and Yellt. I wiped out the Green gang in Arkansas an' I pulled in Willie Jerelderez who used to like to see guys die slow.

"Now listen. You guys are either goin' to spill the beans or you're goin' to Headquarters booked on a charge of first degree murder of Willie the Goop and Harvest V. Mellander, an' an attempted murder charge of me—a Federal Agent. I know you never killed either of those guys but I'll pin it on you an' you'll fry for it.

"Now are you talkin' or are you talkin'?"

Skendall's eyes are poppin'.

"Jeez," he mutters. . . . "Lemmy Caution. . . . We give up. We're talkin'."

OVER in the corner I see a box of cigars, so I help myself to one, an' I make myself comfortable in a big chair that I pull outa the corner of the room. I have got the Luger lyin' on my knee just in case these guys should think they've got a chance to try somethin', although from the looks of it I do not think they will ever try a muscle act with anybody any more.

"Now listen," I tell 'em, "if you guys wanta make it easy for yourselves you're goin to be wise palookas an' come clean. You're in one big spot an' you know it. The only chance you've got is to shoot the works, an' what you've got to do right now is to answer the questions I'm goin' to ask you an' no holdin' out.

"Now first of all I wanta know what you know about the Mellander bump-off last night."

Skendall licks his lips.

"Honest, Mr. Caution," he says, "we don't know a thing. How that guy got his I don't know an' who stuck him up in that callbox is nobody's business. But I do know one thing, it wasn't Rudy Saltierra who done it, an' I'll tell you for why. I was workin' backstage the whole evenin' an' the first time Rudy went on the club floor was when he went through the pass door with this de la Rue dame—the one they call Poison Ivy—an' this guy Willie the Goop just before she sang her number."

"How did that dame get the monniker?" I ask him, "An what do you know about her anyway?"

He grins.

"She's a hot mamma alright," he says. "An' has she got what it takes or has she? I'd take a chance an' leave home myself if I could get my hooks on a honey like that—Poison Ivy or no Poison Ivy."

He takes a pull at himself an' I can see that his mind has been strayin' from business—if you know what I mean—an' I don't exactly blame him because this dame has certainly got the works. When they was handin' out the sex appeal they gave her an extra wallop for luck.

Skendall sorta sighs an' then he goes on.

"Rudy picked her up some place. She was singin' in some little dump; had got herself a trial night an' some playboy that Rudy was acquainted with an' who was tryin' to make this dame takes Rudy along just so's to stop any opposition from one or two other tough guys who was also tryin' to get a drag on Carlotta. Well, Rudy goes along an' this dame takes a peek at him an' lamps his diamond waistcoat buttons an' then she gives him one of them look-me-over-kid-I'm-hard-to-get sorta looks, an' Rudy falls like the guy who fell off the Empire State Roof. He goes bats about this dame an' in about two days she's got him right where she wants him, an' he ain't been the same guy ever since. All he thinks of now is just bustin' things wide open so's he can make a lotta jack an' get spliced up with this baby. But I reckon she's playin' him for a sucker because I usta see a lotta things at that place of Joe's an' I reckon that she was out for Willie the Goop who was more her style an' who they say would be durn rich one day."

I nod.

"How did Saltierra get into the club from back-stage?" I ask.

"He came in the back way," says Skendall. "There's a little door at the back that the staff uses. He always used to come in that way an' he used to leave his hat in her dressin' room."

"O.K." I say. "Now what about Willie? It was Saltierra fixed him, wasn't it?"

Skendall nodded.

"It was him all right," he said. "While the dame was singin' her number I saw him easin' across the stage at the back. He'd got his hand in his tuxedo pocket an' I knew he was goin' to bump somebody. Just when he gets underneath my perch he looks at me an' winks. Then he pulls the gun outa his pocket, an' I can see him lookin' at the silencer on the barrel. Then he puts his hand—the one with the gun in it—behind his back an' he opens the pass door an' goes through.

"He comes back right after an' he looks up at me an' says. 'Don't forget that I ain't been outa that dressing room over there. Remember you can see the door from that perch. Got that?'"

He shrugs his shoulders.

"An' what was I to do?" he says. "I ain't takin' no chances with Rudy Saltierra."

I grin.

"So he's tough, is he?" I said. "Now what did he want to shoot Willie the Goop for?"

He shrugs his shoulders some more.

"Search me," he says. "I don't know, but I reckon he's gotta way of fixing anybody that he don't want kickin' around. I wouldn't mind seein' him fried," says this Skendall, "so long as he didn't get me first, because I wouldn't be the first guy in my family that he's fixed."

I look at him.

"Yeah," I say, "who else has he been executin'?"

"He creased my brother," said Skendall, "an' I ain't forgot that yet. He bust him over the head with a bottle just because he'd had one or two too many an' gotta bit fresh."

I do a big memory act an' I remember the original guy that Duncan told me about—the fellow who talked about this gold snatch in his delirium—was hit over the head with a bottle. I nod my head.

"This was the guy who died down in Bellevue without comin' round, wasn't it?" I say. "What was he doin' with Saltierra anyhow?"

He grins.

"He was a big guy with Saltierra," says Skendall, "he knew all his business, but he was a close cuss an' he never talked to me. He got me that job around Joe Madrigaul's place, an' Saltierra used to look after me. He'd slip me fifty or a hundred dollars every week just for doin' my job there an' for doin' any odd thing he wanted done."

I turn to the other guy.

"An' what about you," I say.

He looks up.

"I don't know a thing," he says. "All I know is I run the garage here. It belongs to Saltierra. I look after the cars an' I keep 'em fit to go out on the road. This guy got me my job."

"That's right," says Skendall. "He didn't know a thing. He knows this place is screwy an' he knows it is a hang-out of Saltierra's. Say, can I have a smoke?"

I threw him across a cigarette an' he feels in his jeans for some matches an' lights it.

"We ain't big timers with Saltierra," he goes on, "I reckon he don't tell anybody much his business except maybe that dame Carlotta."

"Oh yeah," I say, "the dame. Tell me about her."

Skendall laughs, at least he tries to an' he stops when his face hurts him.

"He's nuts about her. Just plain nuts. Everybody knows he's bats about her an' I reckon she'll give him the works."

The cigar is not so hot so I throw it away an' light myself a cigarette.

"So she's a hot momma," I say.

He grins.

"An' how," he says. "I reckon that she an' Saltierra was takin' this guy Willie the Goop for plenty."

"Where did this Willie the Goop get his dough from?" I ask.

He shakes his head.

"I wouldn't know that," he says, "but I know he had plenty, an' I know that this dame Carlotta was playin' him along, an' I know that Saltierra knew it. I've seen 'em winkin' at each other behind his back."

"O.K." I say, "an' that's all you guys know?"

Both these guys hold their heads an' the way they do it makes me grin because they have got a swell pair of stiff necks between them through trying to get rough with me.

"Listen Skendall," I say, "there's just one more little thing. Where is Rudy Saltierra hangin' out? Has he got one dump or more? Where does he live an' has he got an office?"

Skendall hesitates for a bit an' I think that maybe he will hold out on me, but he does a bit more thinkin' an' then comes across.

"He's got a place on Ninth Avenue," he says—he gives me the number—"You go up the stairs," he goes on, "an' when you get to the top there's the front door of an apartment right in front of you. That's where he hangs out. But this apartment is a sorta office dump, although its furnished to look like an apartment. Rudy lives in the flat next door, the one on the left as you stand facing the door of the screwy one. All he did was to knock a door through the wall and stick a bookcase arrangement in front of it. He's at this dump pretty well every night. That's where the guys come to see him. When he wants to be out he just goes into the dump next door an' there you are. After that I don't know a thing."

I look at him.

"You wouldn't make a mistake about not knowin' any more, would you?" I say. "Otherwise I'm goin' to get plenty tough with you guys."

"That's the works," he says, "the whole works, an' I wouldn't hold out on you because I know we're in bad."

I believe him. I reckon anyway that these two guys are only small timers just kickin' around on the edge of the mob lookin' after the cars, runnin' the garage an' doin' the odd bits of dirty work that every mobster has to have done. The thing is that I have got to fix these two guys some way so they keep their traps shut, an' don't go spillin' the works about who I am.

It looks to me there is only one way I can fix this job. I've got to get these guys pinched an' although I don't want to contact anybody around here, this is the one time I have to do it. I speak to the garage guy.

"Listen you," I say. "You got any rope around here?"

He says yes, there is a coil down in the bathroom. I send him along to get this an' when he comes back, I stick him an' Skendall back to back on the bed, an' I tie 'em up so they'll stay that way.

When I've finished with 'em they've got about as much chance of getting loose as a pat of butter has of jumpin' outa hell. Then I get my hat.

"Now listen, you guys," I say. "I'm goin' to tell you something. I'm goin' to have you pinched, an' when the cops come for you you're goin' to keep your traps shut, you ain't goin' to say anythin' about what's happened here tonight, an' you ain't goin' to say anythin' at all about me. You'll be smacked in a cell an' you'll be kept there for two weeks. You won't ask to see anybody an' you won't talk to anybody. If you do your stuff like I tell you you can go at the end of that time, but if either of you guys so much as opens the corner of his trap about whom I am or what I've been askin' you I will frame you each for a coupla years if not more. Have you got that?"

They say they have got it all right. I say:

"Well, now stick around an' tell each other fairy stories, and when you gets outa this jam take a tip from me, go get yourself some job where you don't get mixed up with guys like Saltierra an' you won't get pushed around so much.

"So long, maybe I'll be seein' you."

They don't say a word. Both these guys have had quite enough to go on with. I switch off the light, I close the door behind me, an' I go downstairs through the garage, open the shutter, get underneath an' pull it down behind me. I have a look up an' down the street an' way down just past the cigarette stand where the garage guy got the cigarettes I see a call box.

I start walkin' towards this call box, an' when I have walked half-way I stop to light a cigarette. I look over my shoulder, an' behind me comin' round the corner of the street is a maroon coloured V.8. There is a guy drivin' it an' one by his side. This car squeals round the corner with its brakes on, an' then it shoots down the street in my direction like a streak of lightning.

There are some times when you do not even think, you just do somethin'. I did. I dropped flat on my face an' as I did so some guy in the back of this car starts playin' tunes on a tommy gun that is stuck outa the window. He sprays the wall behind where I was standin' an' I can hear the click as the bullets bite into the brickwork. Before I can look up the car is gone.

I get up, finish lighting my cigarette, then I scram across the road through a passage I see there, an' start doin' a double cut all over the place. Behind me as I go I can hear windows go up as the folks around stick their heads out to see what the shootin' is about.

I do five minutes quick walking turnin' this way an' that, after which time I come to the conclusion that I must have shaken off any guys who are still lookin' for me. Then I find a call box an' I go in.

I dial for operator, tell him it is a government call an' ask to be plugged through to the New York "G" Office. In two minutes I get 'em. I give 'em my code number an' tell 'em I'm workin' direct with Washington an' that I'm sorry to trouble them, but there is two guys tied up in a garage two blocks down Spruce. I tell the agent at the other end I've bust 'em about good an' plenty.

"I want these two guys pinched," I say, "frame 'em on some charge, anythin' you like, but keep 'em inside for a fortnight an' don't let 'em see anybody, an' they ain't to talk to anybody. I've made that plain to 'em, you might do it too."

"O.K." he says, and I hang up.

When I get outa this call box I light myself another cigarette an' I think about what I am goin' to do next.

Now I have always had an old-fashioned idea that if you are tryin' to find somethin' out a great thing to do is to start as much trouble as you can, because when trouble starts people begin to do a lotta things that they wouldn't do normally, especially if they are hidin' something up their sleeve an' I reckon by startin' trouble wherever I can an' makin' myself as unpleasant as possible that maybe I will get a line on this gold snatch.

You have gotta realise that up to the present in this business you know as much as I do, which you will agree is not a lot, except that there are one or two things stickin' out a foot which I am wise to an' which tell me I have got to be very careful about what I do unless I want to win for myself a nice casket in some cemetery which is a thing I am not particularly partial to.

I look at my watch an' I see that it is half past three an' I reckon that there is still time for me to have a little interview with Rudy Saltierra because there are one or two things I want to say to this guy, because I naturally do not like fellows shootin' at me with tommy guns, an' I think that anyhow it is time that somebody told this Saltierra mug just where he gets off.

Well, I think that first of all I will go back to my dump an' I will have a look an' see if Washington has sent down the information that I have asked for, so I jump a cab which I find crawlin' along, an' I go back to my original hotel an' I ask the night clerk if he has got this advertisement folder for me. He says yes an' hands it over.

I then get back into the cab which I have kept waitin' outside an' go round to my new hotel an' go up to my room an' I tear open the folder which is nothin' but a lot of bond selling copy an' right at the bottom I find the code sheet in answer to my wire. I decode this an' it says:

Your report received stop New York police will block investigation of Mellander-Frene killings pending further instructions this office stop Reference Charles Frene this mans name is Charles Velas Chayse stop He is adopted son of Harberry Velas Chayse well-known New York Wall Street operator and socialite stop Murdered man was of no occupation and has reputation of being heavy spender playboy most of his money going in night haunts and on dubious women stop Has had source of finance cut down severely of late by father who was unable to control his nocturnal activities as murdered man took the name Charles Frene in order to disguise identity stop Details next gold movement United States to Great Britain as follows additional movement of two million will go from Federal Reserve Bank New York today and will go to Southampton England on Atlantic cargo and passenger liner "Maybury" shipment originally intended to go on s.s. "Queen Mary" but altered at last moment in order to mislead any criminal attempt stop "Maybury" will leave New York within short period of delivery of bullion stop Take it that you have made necessary contacts in this matter via Duncan. Your identity not disclosed stop Good luck stop.

Now I reckon that this wire does not tell me anything very much except it is interestin' about this guy Willie the Goop, who looks to me to have been the usual rich man's son playin' around an' spendin' all the dough that he could get outa the old man who has got tired of the business and closed down on it.

With reference to the bullion shipment I cannot understand this at all because it looks as if by now this gold must already have been removed from the Federal Bank to this boat *Maybury* which will be clearin' out pretty soon if she has not already done so.

I reckon it was clever of the Federal authorities to take this bullion off a big boat an' slip it on to a small cargo an' passenger boat, that is unless whoever is after this stuff has been wised up to this move by somebody inside.

But anyhow if this gold has been got away it looks as if all this business is just a lotta hot air, an' that this brother of Skendall's who was the guy who did all the talkin' whilst he was unconscious at Bellevue must have been dreamin' it. Yet it looks durn strange to me that he shoulda known all the details an' I reckon that maybe there is somethin' to it after all.

Because right at the back of my head is the idea that Willie the Goop was ironed out because of somethin' to do with this gold snatch. It is stickin' out a couple miles that somebody gave Myras Duncan the heat because they knew he was workin' on this job.

I am in a bit of a spot because I don't really know anything very much yet. I know that it was Rudy that bumped Willie an' I have also got another very big idea as to how Duncan got his too, but I am still not gettin' any nearer to this gold bezezus which, when you come to think of it, is what I am drawin' my pay for.

Anyway, I burn this wire an' give myself a shot of rye, after which I go downstairs, an' I go into a call box in the reception an' I get the telephone number of this address that Skendall has given me on Ninth Avenue where Rudy Saltierra is hanging out, after which I do a little business with the reception clerk.

I slip him ten dollars an' I tell him that I am about to play a joke on some friends of mine an' I give him Rudy's telephone number which I have just got an' tell him that he is to ring this number in twenty minutes' time an' ask for Perry C. Rice which is me. He says O.K. he will do this an' I then get a cab an' drive round to this place.

It is not a bad sorta dump an' there is some night guy downstairs an' when I ask for Mr. Saltierra he says O.K. he is on the third floor. I go up in the lift which is one of those things you work yourself, and when I get out I see the little flight of stairs like Skendall told me leadin' up to this doorway, an' there are other apartments on either side of the door an' I reckon that the right hand one is Saltierra's second apartment just like Skendall said, an' that it is a pretty good idea for him to have an arrangement like this because it means that he can get outa his own flat through this door on the right if he wants to.

I slip my hand into my arm-pit just to see if the Luger is working easy in its holster, an' I ring the doorbell. About two minutes later some guy opens the door. This palooka looks just about as tough as they make 'em, an' although he is dressed up to look like a butler he looks to me as if he should be usin' a blackjack instead of announcin' guys. He also looks at me with his mouth open, because I reckon that he is a little bit surprised to see me. I step into the apartment.

"Listen sour-puss," I tell him, "you just run along and tell Mr. Saltierra that Mr. Perry C. Rice would like to have a couple words with him an' tell him not to pull any fancy business about not being at home or something like that otherwise I am liable to burn the place down, an' look snappy because I don't like your face and I have a private graveyard way back home for guys whose faces I don't like. Scram."

This guy looks even more surprised an' I reckon that he is doing all he can to stop himself from crownin' me, but he slides off an' he comes back in a minute and says will I come this way. I walk across the hallway an' he opened the door on the other side.

I step into a room that is big an' very well furnished. There is a fire burning in the wall facin' me, an' standin' in front of it is Rudy smiling like a rattlesnake, and sittin' on the right hand side of the fireplace is Carlotta. She is also doin' a big grinnin' act. Sprinkled around the room are two or three guys who might be anything at all, but I reckon they are all mobsters.

"Well, Mr. Rice," says Saltierra, "this is an unexpected pleasure, because to tell you the truth I ain't used to receiving visitors at four-thirty o'clock in the mornin'."

"Just fancy that now," I say. "Anyhow," I go on, chuckin' my hat in the corner, "if you ain't very careful Rudy, you're goin' to be some place where you'll only get visitors on the day before they fry you."

I go over to him.

"Listen, you cheap punk," I tell him. "Will you tell me why I shouldn't smack you down an' then kick you into little bits?"

He looks surprised.

"Say what's eatin' you?" he says. "What's this all about, an' what do you think you're doin' bustin' in here an' trying to do a short-arm act?"

I grin.

"Listen Saltierra," I tell him. "I'm getting wise to you. Maybe you think that I ain't guessed that it was your mob who tried to give me the heat. What's the big idea? I didn't know I was so unpopular around here."

He shrugs his shoulders.

"I don't know what you're talkin' about," he says, "nobody around here has tried to give you the heat. We like you Perry, don't we boys?"

He turns to these thugs an' they are all grinnin' an' believe me if that mob liked me I would much rather be hated by a bunch of starvin' alligators.

He turns to Carlotta.

"Listen sweetheart," he says, "wasn't I saying just a few minutes ago that I reckoned that Perry Rice was a good guy?"

"Sure," she says, an' she looks at me an' then at him with that sorta insolent look in her eyes that makes me wanta take her hair down an' pull it.

He walks over to a little table an' he pours out a highball an' he hands it to me.

"Listen, big boy," he says. "Why don't you be your age, an' you can drink that drink because it ain't poisoned. Say—what do you expect—gumshoein' around the place sticking your nose into all sorts of things that don't concern you an' getting all worked up when the trouble starts?

"Don't you realise," he says, "that you can't do that sorta thing around here. Joe Madrigaul told me that you was easin' around his place doing a big private detective act. You take a tip from me. You stick to your bond selling an' give up this Pinkerton stuff, because it won't get you nowhere.

"An'," he goes on, "if somebody has tried to iron you out, well what did you expect? Ain't there enough trouble around here without you stickin' your nose in it an' tryin' to make some more.

An' what did you want to go round and see Skendall for? Maybe for all I know Skendall has got some tough fellows an' they just don't like guys from Mason City jumpin' around the place and asking a lot of fool questions, and maybe they thought that you was better outa the way, but it ain't got anything to do with me, an' I don't know anything about it, because I have been sitting here the whole evening since I left Madrigaul's place an' so have these boys."

"Oh yeah," I say, "an' how did you know I'd been down to Skendall's. It looks to me as if you knew what I was doing pretty well to-night."

He grins.

"Why shouldn't I know?" he says. "Skendall's a guy who works for me. He came through an' told me."

"You don't say, sweetheart," I tell him. "Well, let me tell you something. Skendall never came through to you on the telephone an' told you anything because I have bust him an' your other guy up in the garage so good that they ain't quite certain about what their name is, an' they ain't goin' to telephone you for quite some time. They're busy. I told 'em to beat it outa New York, an' they've taken my tip an' beat it."

The smile fades off his face an' I must say he looks surprised.

I turn to this dame.

"As for you, Poison Ivy," I tell her. "You're a swell lookin' piece of work, but to me you're just a big pain in the ear."

I finish my drink, an' I look round at the lot of 'em.

"I'm goin' to tell you guys something," I say, "an' that goes for you too you black snake," I say to Carlotta, "I got the low-down on you. I suppose you thought I was just the big rube up from the country who hadn't got enough sense to come in outa the rain.

"As for giving an imitation of being a private detective, why shouldn't I? It's a sorta hobby of mine an' way back in Mason City they think I'm pretty good at it too. I've had my ideas from the first that you was the guy who shot this mug Willie, an' I'm tellin' you Saltierra that before I'm through maybe I'll get you fried for it just because you tried to make me look a big punk an' just because you tried a big rub-out act on me tonight.

"It is also my opinion," I say, "that this dame Carlotta is playin' along with you. The guy who christened her Poison Ivy was dead right, only she's all poison and no ivy, an' I reckon she helped you along with the scheme, an' I reckon when you two guys found that Willie the Goop's dough was runnin' short an' he wasn't goin' to be much more use to you you gave him the heat. An' how do you like that?"

The situation is what they call tense. These four other thugs who are hangin' around the room sorta close in quietly. Carlotta is sittin' there still smilin' lookin' like all the devils in hell, an' Saltierra has sorta straightened up an' is lookin' at me out of a pair of eyes that are cold and hard like ice.

"Listen Rice," he says, "I reckon you're being rude, an' I reckon we're going to teach you a lesson, an' maybe when we're through with you you won't want to go stickin' your nose into nobody's business any more because it looks to me like I might as well be really tough with you, an' this is where you get yours."

Carlotta gets up.

When she got up there was a sorta pause. What the poet would call the lull before the waterworks bust. There is a pause because this dame just dominates everythin', an' I can quite get the idea about Rudy goin' haywire about her.

She has changed her gown an' she is wearin' black with a summer ermine cloak an' boy, is she good? She looks around the room like the Queen of Sheba after an extra good facial an' a water wave, an' then she looks at me.

Now maybe I have told you before that I have always gone well with dames. I have got that sorta something that they like an' even if I am as ugly as a couple bull-pups, still, it is that sorta ugliness that makes a dame go for you just because she likes to think that after people have looked at your mug an' gasped they will look at her an' breathe a sigh of relief.

An' when this Carlotta—this Poison Ivy—looks at me I get the idea that, tough as she is, I might still be able to pull the old Adam an' Eve on her.

"Listen Rudy," she says, "you don't want any trouble with this goop, not here anyway. This ain't the time to start something.

There's too much on,"—she looks at him sorta knowingly—"an' if you start something with this guy around here, what's the good?"

She turns round to me.

"Listen," she says, "you fool. You take a tip from me an' get outa New York good an' quick an' stay out. An' you can thank your lucky stars that I'm the sorta person that doesn't like to see anybody bumped off, otherwise it might not be so good for you."

"You don't say, Magnificent," I tell her. "Well listen, so far as I'm concerned you can save your good wishes, an' if any of these cheap yellow bellied thugs round here like to start something they can any time they like an' maybe it won't be so good for 'em.

"An' while we're on the job, honeybunch," I go on, thinkin' that I will start some trouble between this dame an' Rudy—"you don't have to try an' pull any of your hot pertater acts on me, because I have been vaccinated against dames like you, an' anyway you make me think of cold boiled beef.

"I suppose you think you was takin' me for a mug when you did that act in your apartment with me, cryin' all over the place an' tryin' to make out that Rudy here had corralled you against your will.

"You take a tip from me an' take a run out powder on yourself. Go some place—as far away as you can. Go to Hollywood an' get yourself some good monster parts an' you'll do fine."

Is she burned up or is she? She goes to pick up a decanter off the table an' take a swipe at me, but Rudy puts his hand out. I turn around an' talk to him.

"As for you doin' any big acts with me," I say, "you may like to know that a couple friends of mine know just where I am right now, an' if I don't get back home on time I reckon they're goin' to put a call through to police headquarters, an' maybe they'll be able to hang something on to you for once that you can't alibi out of."

He grins.

"Ain't you clever?" he says. "I reckon I've heard that sorta stuff before, an' I reckon we're going to give it to you."

He is just slippin' his hand round to his hip pocket when the phone bell rings an' I don't mind tellin' you that I breathe a sigh of relief that this reception clerk has done his stuff.

"There you are big boy," I tell him, "there it is."

One of these guys picks up the receiver an' speaks. Then he puts his hand over the mouth-piece an' looks at Saltierra.

"It's for him," he says.

"Excuse me," I say, an' I take the telephone outa his hand.

"O.K. brother," I say into the telephone. "Thank you for callin' an' if I am not back in fifteen minutes do what I told you to."

The guy at the other end is a bit mystified, but before he can do any more talkin' I hang up. I go over to the corner of the room an' I get my hat.

"Well, I reckon I'll be goin'," I say. "Take a tip from me Rudy, watch your step because I don't like your face, an' I'm going to stick around keepin' my eye on you, an' I'll take darned good care that I'm safe while I'm doin' it. In the meantime, so long, an' thanks for the drink. I'll be seein' you."

I turn around an' I open the door an' I cross the hallway. I get to the front door an' open it. I am just goin' to step out, when I hear a noise behind me an' I spin around an' there is Carlotta standin' in the doorway on the other side of the hall.

Is she marvellous or is she? Her eyes are blazin' an' she is standin' so tense an' icy that she looks like the Statue of Liberty in a snowstorm. Her breast is heavin' an' she is so het-up that she has to have a durn good gasp before she can get any words out.

"O.K. Mr. Wise Guy," she hisses. "I'm goin' to get you for this. You've got away with it this time, but before I'm through with you I'm goin' to watch you wriggle like a worm on a spike. No man is goin' to insult me an' live, an' when the time is ripe you're goin' to get yours an' you're goin' to get it slow so's I can watch you squirm—you cheap, wise-crackin' mug."

I have put on my hat but I take it off an' I make a low bow.

"That's O.K. by me, Gorgeous," I crack, "but take it easy or you'll bust your brassiere. Relax honeybunch just like Dr. Hay tells you. If you ask me," I go on, "I think you've been takin' too much red meat lately, an' maybe you need a little treatment."

I walk over to her.

"Listen Pet," I say. "There's only one thing I'd like to tell you an' that is that although you're all the world to Rudy you're just sour drippin' to me. Another thing is that one of these days if I get the chance I'm goin' to give you a beatin' that'll keep you perpendickler for about six years."

I turn away an' I go out, an' as I get over the doorstep she throws her handbag at me, an' it hits me on the back of the head. I spin around, pick it up an' throw it back at her, an' it busts open an' everything spills out which makes me laugh. I slam the door an' go down the stairs to the lift.

It looks to me like this interview has been very successful because I reckon that if these guys have got anything ready to spring they are goin' to spring it good an' quick.

An' I hope it will be good for me, because, between you an' me an' the post box, it looks like this Carlotta is out for my blood an' I reckon that she has got nerve enough to pull a very fast one if she wanted to.

CHAPTER SIX
THE BLONDE BABY

WHEN I wake up next morning I have got a definite idea in my head that there is business in the air, you know the sorta feelin' that you get when somethin' hot is on the grill.

I get up an' I have a very good breakfast an' I do not think about anythin' at all very much because it looks to me like there is not very much to think about; all of which will show you that I am a philosopher—or whatever they call it.

About eleven o'clock I go around to the Hotel Court an' I ask the reception clerk if anything has been poppin' around there, an' he tells me yes an' gives me an envelope which he says that some guy who was half cut at the time has left with the night clerk about four o'clock last night.

Now I reckon that this must be Hangover, so it looks as if he was around there just about half an hour after I was there gettin' the reply from Washington to my wire.

I slip this guy five bucks an' tell him to keep his eyes skinned for me an' if anybody comes around askin' for me not to let 'em know that I have left this hotel but to sorta give 'em the idea that I am just out for an airin' an' will be back pretty soon.

I then go into some quick lunch an' have a cup of coffee an' bust open this envelope. It is from Hangover an' it says:

Dear Perry,

Oh boy, oh boy, have I got the laugh on you because believe me it looks to me right now that I am doin' very much better at this game than you are.

There is a lot of reasons why I cannot write down here all the things that I have got wise to but believe me I have worked up a lot of information which added on to what you told me about this gold snatch makes this job look like one of the biggest bits of racket stuff that was ever pulled in this man's country.

In point of fact it is so hot that I am seriously considering giving up rye altogether for the time being just so I do not miss anything.

Perry, I am very sorry but I am going to do you dirt and hold out on you, but pal, I want you to realise that I am indulging in this holding out process just because I have got to do this because there isn't any other way for me to handle this business, but I reckon anyhow that you and I are going to meet pretty soon and that I can do all the talking that is necessary and that there will still be time for you to do a big act in the way that I know you would want to. However I can give you the low-down on a certain amount and here is the way it is:

In the first place you will remember that I told you that I did not think that Willie the Goop's real name was Charles Frene. Well I was right here because this stiff is Charles Velas Chayse and he is the adopted son of a big Wall Street guy by the name of Harberry Velas Chayse. Now I have seen this Harberry Chayse and he is burned up considerable because in spite of the fact that Willie the Goop is a no good, the old man (who is about 65 and is not so well) is not at all pleased at having his adopted son bumped off, more especially as it looks as if these two have been having one hell of a row about one or two things which I will talk to you about in a minute.

The main point is this, that Harberry Chayse is fed up to the back of his neck with the fact that the New York coppers do not seem to be making any headway in finding out who did the bumping. He also says that he reckons that there is some dirty work flying about somewhere, but that he has got a method by which he himself is going to find out who the murderer is. I am going to tell you about this method in a minute and I promise you you will get a good laugh. I will now close down on this angle just for the time being to tell you that I have also contacted another dame who is a swell blonde, and when you see her you will agree with me and you are certainly going to see her because it looks to me by what I can hear that she is going to contact you just as soon as she can get set.

Now I am going to give you a tip-off about this blonde. I have told you before that Carlotta is a pretty warm proposition and that anybody who tries to make any funny business with her is liable to get himself into a mess, but I hope to tell you that this Mirabelle Gayford is to my mind even a little bit more dangerous than Carlotta even if it is in a different way.

This Mirabelle is a classy dame. She is about twenty-eight, and she comes from an old Connecticut family. Her Ma and Pa are both dead, but originally she is engaged to Willie the Goop. Now it looks as if she is pretty stuck on Willie because she has got plenty of money of her own and I don't think that she is after his. It also looks to me as if Harberry Chayse was very keen on this marriage going through because he thinks that this Mirabelle who is a determined sort of dame is just the right sort of girl to make Willie take a pull at himself.

Anyhow it looks as if everything was hunky-dory until not so long ago Willie starts playing around Carlotta, after which Mirabelle begins to get fed up with everybody and starts making herself annoying all round.

Now here's where the big act comes. It looks like this guy Harberry Chayse is one of those guys who are a bit nuts on the occult, and no matter how amusing you may think it is that a guy who is running a big Wall Street combine should be interested in this sort of stuff, the fact remains that it is so, and it seems

that this Harberry Chayse has got some sort of pet seer or clairvoyant, or whatever you like to call him, whom he calls in from
time to time to get advised on different things that he is doing.

So when the police tell the old boy that they cannot get a line
on the murder of Willie down at Joe Madrigaul's place, a fact
which the old boy does not believe because it is a stone ginger
that one of about four or five people shot Willie, he sends for
this clairvoyant guy, who is a fellow of about fifty years of age
with piercing eyes and a grey beard, and this guy gets busy
and starts using his occult powers, as a result of which he tells
Harberry as follows:

He says that in order for him to find out who murdered
Willie, that the scene in which the murder took place should be
re-created, but that it should be re-created, in some place that
is away from all antagonistic influences, and that exactly the
same circumstances as near as possible to those happening at
the time of the murder should also be arranged.

Old man Chayse falls for this like a ton of coal, and right
pronto he has a photograph of Joe Madrigaul's club and suggests
to this occulist, whose name is San Reima, that he will build
up the exact scene of Joe Madrigaul's Club in the saloon of his
yacht 'Atlantic Witch' which is lying down at New London, and
that he will try and get down on this boat the people who were
around Willie the Goop at the time he was bumped off, which
as you will realise beings you into this story.

This San Reima says that it is only necessary to have the
people who could have shot Willie the Goop down on this yacht,
and that he will get the band playing the same music and he
will duplicate the lighting and everything, and that if the yacht
is taken three four miles off the coast so as the astral influences
can get busy then he will put his finger on the murderer.

All of which looks to me like a first-class pipe-dream except,
and I feel I ought to tell you this, that there is no doubt that this
guy San Reima is a very weird cuss because the first time I saw
him he told me a lot of things about myself which nobody knew
but me, and therefore although it looks a bit screwy this guy
might be able to do something about this.

To cut a long story short old man Chayse has got a list of all the guys who were around Willie when he was killed, and is going to offer them all five grand each to go down to his yacht, and it looks as if he will get them down there because he says he is going to tell each and every one of them that if they are decent honest citizens they will not mind cashing in and giving him a chance to find out who bumped off Willie, and that if they will not do so then it is only because they have got something to hide.

Now I have told you, Perry, that this looks to me like a pipe-dream. At the same time I reckon that there might be a line in it that you are looking for, and knowing your faculty for following your nose on jobs like this where there aren't any clues, possibly you will get something out of it.

Now to return to Mirabelle, after I had this talk with Harberry and his guy San Reima I saw this Mirabelle, and she tells me that she thinks this idea is a whole lot of hooey. She also tells me that in her opinion this bump-off of Willie the Goop is a job put up between Saltierra and Carlotta, and as I have told you before she is about as fond of this Carlotta dame as a bunch of rattlesnakes.

Now listen, Perry, I have got an idea in my head. Its just an idea and I've got nothing to support it, but I have a sneaky sort of feeling that this blonde Mirabelle Gayford is about sixteen times as dangerous as Carlotta ever was. First of all she is a swell looking piece and I cannot make out why Willie the Goop should have chucked himself at Carlotta like he did unless he had found something out about Mirabelle which wasn't so good.

The second thing is that I know Harberry Chayse is not quite so stuck on this Mirabelle at the present time as he was, which makes it look as if he had found something out about her. The third thing is that I saw this dame having a very quiet and confidential conversation with Rudy Saltierra round at the back entrance of Joe Madrigaul's place just when I was leaving there tonight, and the fourth thing, and this is an important thing, is that this Mirabelle has got a cousin who is very stuck on her who has got some job in the U.S. Assay Office which makes it look to me as if this dame might be the one who supplied the original dope about the bullion.

So there you are. Now I have got a couple of other lines that I am working on and I am going to get busy on them. I promised you that I would not break with this story in any newspaper.

Well, so long, Perry, keep your eyes skinned and don't forget what I told you. You watch out for Mirabelle.

Yours till the cows come home,

HANGOVER.

Now this looks to me like a pretty good sort of letter, and it looks too as if this business is goin' to get a little bit more involved than I thought it was goin' to be, although to tell you the truth I am not particularly surprised at Hangover goin' off to check up on these other lines that he says he has got.

Anyhow maybe this Harberry Chayse an' this Mirabelle Gayford will be comin' around some time or tryin' to contact me somehow, so I wise up the reception clerk at the Hotel Court to call me through at the Delamere if anybody comes an' asks for me but to keep my address there quiet an' not to tell a soul. I sweeten this guy with another ten bucks an' he says that he will look after that O.K. for me.

I then go back to the Delamere an' read through the Hangover letter again an' do a lotta quiet thinkin' because in a funny sorta way I am beginnin' to make sense outa this thing.

About four o'clock in the afternoon the reception clerk at the Hotel Court comes through an' he tells me that there has been a telephone call for me from Miss Mirabelle Gayford, an' this Miss Gayford says that she would be very much obliged if Mr. Perry Rice would call an' see her at an address in Brooklyn that she has left. She says this business is in connection with the Charles Frene killin' an' that it may be well worth my while to go along. She also says that she will be around until five o'clock that evenin' an' that maybe I will be savin' myself a lotta bother if I go around. This message looks to me like one of those things—you know, if I go maybe it's goin' to be worth my while an' if I don't maybe it ain't goin' to be so good for me!

However, this don't worry me very much because I would not miss goin' for a lot.

The reception clerk also tells me that there is a letter for me that is marked 'Very Urgent' an' that this has been brought round by some guy from Mrs. Harberry Chayse, an' I tell the clerk that I will send a messenger round to pick it up.

Altogether it looks like something is goin' to happen, an' I go out an' I drop in at a drug store nearby an' get the clerk to send the despatch boy around to the Court an' pick up the letter for me an' take it round an' leave it for me at the Delamere as I reckon I will deal with this after I have seen this Mirabelle Gayford.

I go over to Brooklyn pronto an' after a bit I find this place where I am supposed to meet this dame. It is a very ordinary four-storey buildin', a sorta commuters apartment house, an' when I ask the janitor for Miss Gayford he tells me that I will find this apartment No. 12 on the third floor an' I proceed to do some climbin', there being no lift.

Apartment No. 12 is at the end of a dark passage an' does not look quite so hot to me neither does it look like a dump where a dame with money would live. I have a sneakin' idea in my head that it might have been wise to bring the Luger with me because I have got an idea that this Mirabelle might pull somethin' fast, but anyway I have left it behind, and I am not a guy for carryin' a gun when I go to see a woman anyhow.

I knock at the door an' after a minute somebody opens it. It is a bit dark inside owin' to the fact that the window blinds are pulled down an' it takes me a minute to get a look at the guy who has opened the door. He is a big guy with a derby hat an' he is smilin' an' lookin' as happy as a sandboy.

"Mr. Perry Rice?" he says, an' when I say yes, he motions that I should go in.

I go into this room an' take a look around. One window blind is up an' by the light that is comin' in I can see that the apartment is empty of furniture except for a coupla packing cases that are stuck about.

The guy shuts the door behind him an' when I turn round I can see that he is lookin' at me very old-fashioned.

"Now see here, Mr. Rice," he says. "You sit down on one of them boxes an' listen to me. I reckon that you got as much intelligence as the next feller, an' I reckon that you don't want to run yourself into any trouble, do you?"

I grin at him, an' I sit myself down on the box on the other side of the room.

"I wouldn't know smarty," I say. "But I didn't come here to see you. I came here to see Miss Gayford, an' where is she an' who are you anyhow?"

Just as I say this the apartment door opens an' another guy, a very big guy, comes in. He don't say anythin', he just nods to the first guy and sits down on another box. This feller looks like a muscle man to me.

"Looky Rice," says the first guy, "you ain't goin' to do yourself no good by bein' fresh. I reckon you'll see Miss Gayford when the time's right. In the meantime we wanta ask you a few questions."

I grin some more.

"You don't say," I crack back. "An' who is *we* anyhow?"

He puts his hand in his coat pocket an' he brings out a badge.

"We're the Davance Detective Agency," he says, "an' we're representin' Miss Gayford, an' I reckon that we don't wanta waste any more time, Rice. So let's get busy."

"Listen, mug," I tell him. "Why don't you be your age instead of talkin' that way. You an' your Davance Agency make me sick an' as a detective I reckon you'd make a helluva success as a roadmender. If Miss Gayford is around here you produce her pronto otherwise I'm goin'."

He looks serious.

"We don't wanta get tough with you, Rice," he says. "Now you be good an' talk nice."

I am sittin' on this box with my hands behind me an' suddenly my fingers touch somethin' hard. It is the sledge hammer that somebody is goin' to use to open these packin' cases with. An' it looks as if it is goin' to be plenty useful.

"Listen punk," I tell him. "You go an' give yourself a shower. Your brain's dusty."

He gets up.

"Come on," he says to the other guy.

They start comin' towards me an' I reckon that it is time I did something about these guys. I pick up the hammer an' I throw it good an' hard at the shins of the guy who has been doin' all the talkin'. It connects an' he lets out a howl like a hyena an' flops on to the floor. The other guy rushes me an' I drop my head an' it gets him in the guts an' we proceed to mix up.

Luckily for me the first guy is hurt an' is sittin' in the corner feelin' if his leg is all there, but this other palooka is a real tough an' he is givin' me all I can take.

I am not doin' so well because he contacts me with a swing to the jaw that makes me see about a million stars an' as I go over he jumps on top of me. He knocks every bit of breath out of me, an' I roll over an' drag him with me. This guy is strugglin' to get on top an' I want him to because we have rolled over near to the big packin' case an' I reckon that if this guy will roll on top of me maybe I can smack him up against the case good an' hard because I want to finish with him before the other feller comes into action again.

It works. As he swings to get on top of me I let him, an' as he arrived I stick my foot against the floor an' push. He smacks up against the side of the case an' he is so surprised because he didn't know that it was there that he relaxes for a second an' during that second I hit him smack between the eyes an' knock his head back against the case. He goes right out.

I get up an' go across to the other guy who is still not feelin' so good an' who starts scramblin' to his feet. I yank this guy up by his coat collar an' I smack him across the puss with a heavy flathander that sends him skyrocketing across the room to where his pal is. I then pick up the hammer an' sit down on one of the boxes.

"Now listen, sweetheart," I tell him. "Supposin' you tell me a few things because otherwise I'm goin' to get really rough with you guys. You gotta understand that I never did like rough tactics especially from private detective agencies an' if you ain't the mug I take you for you're goin' to behave an' like it."

He don't say anything but I can see that he is lookin' behind me at the door. I peep over my shoulder and I see the door openin' an' into the room comes a dame that woulda knocked your eye out.

She is a blonde an' can she wear clothes or can she? Everything she wears is Park Avenue an' she makes 'em look worth double. This dame is about thirty. She has got sex-appeal an' knows it an' she walks with a sorta insolence that takes about five generations of high hats to manufacture. She has got a haughty sorta expression on a face that is naturally durn pretty. In fact she looks so good to me that if I was wrecked on some desert island with this dame I wouldn't even wave to a passin' ship. I would just stay put an' pick cocoanuts.

She is holdin' a handbag in front of her with both hands an' when she lets go with one of 'em I see that she has got a little automatic pistol, the sorta thing you use for killin' gnats with.

She points this at me an' she starts talkin'. She has got, a pretty voice that is younger than she is an' she speaks like somebody who has learned how.

"Mr. Rice, I believe," she says, an' then she smiles a little bit. "It looks as if you were in command of the situation, but I think I should tell you that if you attempt to move I shall kill you."

"Sarsaparilla to you, honey," I crack at her. "You're the Gayford dame, I suppose. Well, lady, you must have been readin' some very heavy fiction if you think that you can get away with this sorta stuff. Another thing, if you think that you can start anything around here with that pop-gun you squeeze it an' see what happens. This place would be lousy with cops before you could wink an' what good that is goin' to do you or me I don't know."

I get off the box and I walk towards her. I am still grinnin' and I can see that this dame is burned up because I am not standin' for this bluff. As I watch her she casts an appealin' sorta look at the two other guys but they are not startin' anythin' else. They are sorta tired.

"It is no good, Mirabelle," I say, takin' the gun outa her hand an' puttin' it in my pocket, "neither of these guys feel like any more children's hour stuff. The big feller is just beginnin' to come back again an' the other feller has been hit on the shin bone with a sledge hammer which is not a very nice thing. I reckon when they send you their bill in it will cost you plenty.

"Another thing," I say, "a dame who is as swell as you are with a pretty name like Mirabelle should not employ a bunch of cheap private dicks to go leapin' around tryin' to bust information outa me because I am not at all an easy guy in that way."

She don't say anything at all, she just stands there glarin' at me an' not knowin' what to do.

"Say, honeybunch," I tell her, "if you wanted to talk to me why didn't you come here an' meet me? Why do you have to have a coupla short arm merchants like these frontin' for you. Now I gotta a big suggestion to make. You come out with me and maybe we'll go some place an' get a drink and talk this thing over nice an' quiet."

She stands there an' she hesitates for a moment, an' while she is doin' that I walk across an' I take her by the arm and I lead her outa the room an' down the passage. She comes because she is undecided an' don't know really what she wants to do. When we get at the top of the stairs I tell her to wait for a minute an' I go an' stick my head round the door an' I tell those two near detectives to go home an' get themselves a coupla hot baths because I think they need 'em, an' I also tell 'em that the next time I see 'em kickin' around I am goin' to measure 'em for straight-jackets. I then go back to the dame an' we go downstairs.

Parked outside the place is a big car with a chauffeur. When I ask her if this car belongs to her, she says yes, so we get inside an' she tells the man to drive to some club near Park Avenue. I don't say anything for a bit, I am just watchin' this dame, an' I am wonderin' just how much she is puttin' on an act an' just how much she is sincere, because I'm tellin' you that by the looks of her this Mirabelle is a rather nice piece of femme, an' I think that maybe Hangover has not been right in what he said in his letter.

Still I am not a guy to take chances, so I think I will hear what she has got to say. I offer her a cigarette but she won't have one, so I just smoke quietly till we get to this club place. This is a pretty swell sorta dump, an' when we go inside she orders some tea for herself an' a cocktail for me, after which she opens her handbag, takes out a cigarette, lights it an' starts in.

"Mr. Rice," she says, "maybe I have been misinformed about you, but the Davance Detective Agency who have been working for me on this business told me that you were a very rough sort of individual and that their method was the only possible one for getting information from you. It seems that they have failed."

"That's O.K. by me, sister," I say. "Let's forget all that, but what's the information?"

"Mr. Rice," she says, "I was engaged to Charles Chayse who called himself Charles Frene, and who I believe was nicknamed Willie the Goop. I have very good reason to believe that he was killed either by you, Saltierra, or that Carlotta woman, and I am going to move heaven and earth to prove it.

"If you are innocent in this matter then maybe you can be of help to me."

I nod, although I must say that this business sounds screwy to me, but I tell her that I quite understand the situation, and I also tell her that I certainly did not kill Willie the Goop, because that was my first night in New York an' I had never even seen or heard of him in my life.

From this she goes on talking about what happened that night at Joe Madrigaul's place, an' it is quite obvious to me that she is tryin' to pump me good an' hard. I say nothin' but I lead this dame on to talk as much as I can. After a bit I ask her just how Harberry Chayse is takin' Willie's death, an' whether he is pleased with the way the police are investigatin' this business, an' by the way she talks about the old man it is a cinch that she has had some sorta row with him, an' it begins to look to me as if this dame is playin' some game of her own.

I also reckon that havin' regard to the fact that she hired these two tough guys to sock some information outa me in the empty apartment in Brooklyn that this dame thinks I have got hold of somethin' that she wants to know, an' she wants to know it pretty good an' quick, otherwise she would have tried an easier method. I reckon that she is goin' to try that now.

An' I am pretty right here because when I have had another cocktail she asks me if I have heard anything from Harberry Chayse, an' when I ask her why he should try to contact me she says she don't know, but she had an idea that maybe he would want to know if I could give any information about the murder.

Then I get it. It is stickin' out a foot that this dame knows that Harberry Chayse has written me a letter. It is stickin' out a foot that she hired this detective agency to wait for me at the apartment in Brooklyn, because they thought I would be carryin' it with me. Well this is one time that the job didn't come off.

But all this new business is a help to me. Things are beginnin' to shape in my head. I have gotta hunch that the original idea that came to me when I went back to Joe Madrigaul's place an' found Saltierra's tuxedo, an' went an' sat in the dark club room an' watched the broken paper streamers lyin' across the floor, was right.

Sittin' there I gotta kick. I reckon that you guys know that bein' a "G" man ain't so hot sometimes. You have to take the rough with the smooth, but I'm tellin' you that it's mostly rough, but, as the dame said when her husband fell off Santiago pier, life has its compensations, an' just now I'm gettin' one of 'em.

I realise that all I gotta do is to sit pretty an' let all these wise an' clever people get ahead an' pull their stuff on Lemmy.

Why? Because there never was a crook who could play a game through without trippin' himself up some place.

Give a smart guy or a clever dame enough rope, an' they'll send themselves to the chair an' take their pals along too.

Somehow, I gotta hunch that I am goin' to get some place with this job soon.

CHAPTER SEVEN
MIRABELLE

I SIT there lookin' at this dame. Mind you I suppose I am the sorta guy that folks would describe as tough, but I have always got a great deal of pleasure in my life through lookin' at dames and wonderin' about 'em; wonderin' what they are thinkin' an' what they are really tryin' to get at because it is a cinch that whatever way a dame is lookin' she is always thinking somethin' different, like some Spanish woman in the Philippines who handed me a posy of flowers with a smile with one hand an' bust me on the nut with an iron bar with the other. You never know where you are with 'em.

But lookin' sideways at this Mirabelle she is a nice baby. She is wearin' a very swell suit an' the shirt she has on is made of little lines of frilly tucks an' there is a big sorta jabot round her neck sorta framin' her white face. She is wearin' a little tailormade hat an' the guy who does her hair certainly knows his business because under the side of this hat is all little gold waves and tendrils. I have known plenty fellows would have left home for a dame like Mirabelle, but just how she is breakin' in on this business I do not know, although it looks to me that I had better find out good an' quick because one way an' another you will agree with me that this bezuzus is beginnin' to get slightly involved.

I think I will try some frank stuff, so I talk to her nice an' quiet.

"Listen, lady," I tell her, "I don't know what you are doin' in this business but I reckon that you are all burned up because somebody has bumped off this fiancé of yours. I know you wanta ask me a lotta questions, but maybe you an' me can get some place quicker if I ask you some.

"First of all let me tell you how I break in on this job. I am a bond salesman. I come from Mason City an' I've been savin' up for years to have a vacation in New York. About three four hours after I got down here some guy tells me I oughta go around to Joe Madrigaul's. He says it is a good spot an' I go.

"All right. Somebody gets bumped off, an' I happen to be standin' near this guy an' I'm roped in an' taken, down to headquarters an' grilled. Two things are lucky so far as I am concerned. The first thing is that I ain't carryin' a gun an' never have carried one, an' the second thing is that a friend of mine, a crime reporter, happens to be stickin' around an' can identify me an' tell the cops all about me, so they let me go, an' that's all I know.

"Mine you I ain't sayin' that I am not interested in this business. I am; like hell I am. I reckon if you go up to Mason City, the Chief of Police there who is a sorta uncle of mine by marriage will tell you that I am reckoned in the neighbourhood to be better at solvin' mysteries than any other guy, an' this is the only reason why I am interested in this thing.

"I am a guy who is always interested in a thing I cannot understand, an' what is troublin' me at the moment is why a dame like you, a swell dame"—an' I lean over close to her an' I look at her as if I was struck dumb with admiration—"who is so lovely an' sweet, well it looks a bit funny that such a dame should be worryin' about a guy like Willie the Goop."

She spins round.

"There was nothin' the matter with Charles," she says. "Charles was a good fellow once, an' I happened to love him. Maybe," she says, "you've even heard of women who love men knowing that they wasn't so good."

I grin.

"You're tellin' me," I say, "I can remember a dame who fell for me in France. . . ."

"Were you in France?" she says.

"Have a look at me lady," I tell her, "what would the Marines have done without me?"

"Charles was in France too," she says. "They tell me he was a great man in those days."

"O.K." I say, "will you tell me this? If Charles was such a good guy an' he had a dame like you, what's he want to go kickin' around these night clubs for, contactin' women like Carlotta?"

I pause to see what happens when I mention this dame. I see her mouth tighten.

"He was a fool," she says after a minute. "He was sorta disappointed. He was all right and then suddenly he went to pieces."

She turns round an' she looks at me again.

"Listen, Mr. Rice," she says, "may be I am going to trust you a little bit. Maybe I am in so bad on this thing that I've got to trust somebody. I reckon that whoever shot Charles did it because he knew something."

I look surprised.

"You don't say," I say. "What do you think he knew?"

"I don't know," she says, "that's just it."

She looks round the club an' then she sinks her voice a little.

"This man they found in the telephone box," she says, "the man they say was Harvest V. Mellander. Do you know, Mr. Rice, that this man was a Federal Agent, a 'G' man?"

I whistle.

"You ain't askin' me to believe that, are you, lady?" I say. "Just fancy! So he was a 'G' man. Well, what was he doin' gettin' himself shot in a telephone box. It looks to me as if he wasn't a very good sorta 'G' man."

"I don't know what he was doing," she said. "Charles and I had quarrelled. We hadn't talked to each other for some time, but he telephoned me on the day he was shot. He told me that he realised he had been a fool. He told me that he was going to turn over a new leaf, but he said that he had something to do first. I questioned him. I asked him what he meant, but he wouldn't say. All he would say was that he had to meet a Federal Agent that night, a man he'd seen before.

"Since he was shot I've checked up on everybody in that club and it seems that the only persons that Charles had been seen around with or talking to during the days previous to the shooting, were Rudy Saltierra and this man Mellander. Well everybody knows that Saltierra is a racketeer, so it looks as if Mellander must have been the 'G' man."

"It just shows you, don't it?" I say. "An' they say romance is dead. Well," I go on, "I think this is all very interestin' an' I am certainly gettin' a kick out of it, but it don't get us no place. Listen," I say, "you tell me somethin', what's your idea in usin' these two mugs from this Davance Detective Agency, an' what was they tryin' to find out?"

"I'll tell you," she says. "When I was having that conversation on the telephone with Charles, he told me he'd written somebody a letter, that everything depended on that letter. After he was shot and the police seemed to be doing nothing about it, I went to the Agency to see if they could help me. You were the person they suspected most, and they said if they could get you around some place where they could get at you, they'd probably discover something."

She smiled.

"Well it seems they weren't quite so efficient as I thought they were," she says.

"I don't know about that," I say, "that tough guy certainly gave me a coupla wallops, but as far as I am concerned I haven't got any letter from anybody."

I try a new line.

"Look here, lady," I say, "I don't know anything about this, but this is how it looks to me. It looks to me like this Charles of yours finds out somethin'. Whatever it is he finds out burns him up. He feels he's got to do somethin', so he writes somebody a letter, this letter being a very important document. We don't know who he wrote that letter to (I wink to myself as I say this because I reckon the letter she's talkin' about is the one that Willie the Goop wrote to Carlotta, the one she gave to Saltierra, the one I found in the tuxedo pocket at the Club), an' you reckon he wrote this letter to this guy Mellander, who you think was a Federal Agent? Well, where do we go from there, ain't you worryin' yourself unnecessarily? What does it matter to you what letters Willie the Goop wrote? He's dead anyhow, an' you can't get him back again. Mark you," I go on, "it's a cinch mat you want to find out who bumped him off, that you wanta have this guy fried. I reckon I'd be feelin' the same way myself, but what's the good of you stirrin' up all this stuff?"

She don't say anything, because she ain't got any answer.

I'm in a funny position about this dame. I'm half ready to believe that she's told the truth, an' yet when I look at her, it looks as if she might be holdin' out on somethin'.

After a minute she turns round again, an' she goes on:

"Maybe there is something I can't tell you, Mr. Rice," she says, "maybe I'll be able to tell them to you some time, and then you'll know more about it."

"Why don't you cash in, lady?" I say. "Two heads are always better than one maybe. After all, I got brains. Maybe I can advise you."

She shakes her head.

"I'm trustin' nobody at the moment," she says.

I tried a fast one.

"Not even that cousin of yours," I say, "the guy who's in the U.S. Assay Office?"

She looks at me like I was bats.

"I don't know what you're talking about," she says.

She sorta clamps down. She sets her lips an' I reckon she ain't talkin' any more.

"O.K. Miss Gayford," I say. "Well, all you've gotta remember is this. There ain't anybody can say that Perry C. Rice wouldn't give a woman a hand if she needed one. I gotta go now, but you give me your telephone number, maybe I'll call you; maybe you an' me can have another little talk some time."

She nods her head, an' she gives me the number. Then I finish my drink an' I shake hands with her an' I scram, because it looks to me that there ain't any more business doin' around here. Outside I have a look around just to make certain I haven't got anybody on my tail. I get a cab an' I drive round a bit, then I tell the driver to go on to the Hotel Delamere.

When I get there, up in my room I find the letter from old man Harberry Chayse. Here it is, an' it looks a honey to me:

> *The Mulberry Arms,*
> *Park Avenue.*

Dear Mr. Rice,

> *I am sure you will forgive me for writing to you over a matter in which I believe you have already been put to some trouble. My excuse is that the feelings of a father whose son has been brutally murdered in cold blood are such that any process for bringing the murderer to justice is excusable.*

> *I do not have to recount the circumstances in which my adopted son was shot to death in Joe Madrigaul's Club Select. You were present. You were I believe one of the individuals in*

his direct vicinity at the time of the shooting and you were one of the people taken down in the patrol wagon by Police Lieutenant Riessler to Headquarters for the purpose of being questioned.

When I had got over the first shock of hearing of the death of my adopted son, it occurred to me that the apprehension of his murderer would be a matter only of hours. He must have been shot by somebody standing within fifteen to twenty feet of the table, in other words one of these people:—Miss Carlotta de la Rue, yourself, one of the two waiters standing behind the line of tables on the top right hand side of the club, the electrician Skendall who was in charge of the lights and who was stationed on the perch behind the wall above the pass door leading from the club to back-stage. The man Saltierra was also taken to headquarters, but it seems an alibi was put forward in his case by the electrician Skendall, who—and I must say this—could hardly have been the murderer inasmuch as he would not have had time to descend from his perch, pass through the door, dispose of the weapon and regain his position. Also as the spot light on Miss de la Rue was actually moving and being worked by this Skendall this practically eliminates him from the list of suspects.

There were as you know eight or nine other people who were sitting at tables nearest that at which my adopted son was killed, and whilst I agree that any one of these people could have fired the shot yet enquiries have elicited the fact that none of them even knew him.

Apparently so far as the police are concerned the position is a stalemate. My enquiries at police headquarters receive one reply only—the matter is still being investigated and there is nothing to report. I have therefore decided if possible to evolve some system under which the murderer may be indicated, and for this purpose I have been forced outside the realm of practical thought.

I ask you not to be amused when I tell you that I have been for years a believer in certain occult forces and that an individual by the name of San Reima, who has on many occasions given me proof of his extraordinary powers, has told me that under *certain circumstances he would be in a position definitely to nominate the murderer of my boy. The circumstances are these:*

San Reima suggests that a seance should be arranged in the saloon of my yacht 'Atlantic Witch.' He suggests this venue because if the boat were taken a short distance out to sea he says he would be sufficiently far removed from any earthly influence in order to successfully carry out his part in the business.

He has ordained that a replica of Joe Madrigaul's Club Select should be built in the saloon of my yacht and that the persons intimately concerned with this business should be present under the same circumstances as nearly as possible as obtained at the time of the murder.

I should tell you that the other persons concerned in this matter have agreed to be present and I ask you in the name of justice and humanity to throw out of your mind any disbelief in the powers of this man and to proceed immediately you receive this letter to the Guyle Wharf, New London, Connecticut where the 'Atlantic Witch' is lying.

I enclose herewith five one thousand dollars bills to cover your immediate expense. On arrival a further sum of the same amount will be paid over to you. If you are an innocent man you will take part in this seance. If not your non-arrival will at least indicate that you have something to hide, possibly that you are the murderer.

> *I am, Yours sincerely,*
> *HARBERRY V. CHAYSE.*

I read this letter an' then I sit down an' think about it. It looks like the old man is pretty good an' burned up about Willie the Goop bein' bumped, an' I can see his point of view because, havin' just had a bit of a schlmozzle with Willie—over dough I suppose—he feels all the more sore because Willie was ironed out before he had time to make it up, which just goes to show that a lotta people would not be so tough if they thought that the people they was bein' tough with was goin' to get a coupla slugs put into 'em soon afterwards.

I look at my watch an' it is seven o'clock. I reckon that the sooner I get down to this Guyle Wharf place an' get aboard this *Atlantic Witch* the better it is goin' to be for me because here's the way I look at it:

Supposin' this San Reima guy pulls a fast one an' spots somebody as bein' the murderer of Willie. Well this is goin' to create a situation of some sort and the accused guy—supposin' he is tied up with the people who did fix the shootin'—is going to shoot his mouth. I reckon that it is goin' to be very funny if this guy puts his finger on somebody else instead of Rudy Saltierra who, as I know, was the one who bumped Willie.

Mind you I reckon that all this clairvoyance an' occult stuff is a lotta hooey, but at the same time there is a lot more things flyin' about than we know of an' you never know this San Reima palooka may be an honest to goodness best bet.

But it is stickin' outa mile that my main reason for goin' down is to see if Rudy is goin' to be there an' Carlotta, an' it looks to me that they have agreed to go as otherwise this Harberry Chayse would not have got in touch with me.

After a bit I put the letter in my pocket an' I go downstairs an' I have a little talk with the reception clerk who is a nice sorta cuss. I ask him if there is any people stayin' in this Hotel Delamere who come from Connecticut an' he tells me yes, there is a travellin' salesman called Sam Yarthers who is along in the bar. I get along an' buy myself some rye an' after a bit I pick a casual sorta conversation with this Yarthers an' I do a lotta stuff an' get him interested an' then I get him talkin' about Connecticut. After a bit I ask him if he knows anything about some family called the Gayfords an' he knows a lot an' proceeds to shoot his mouth.

It looks like Mirabelle is pretty well known in that State an' that she is the big social bet around there an' is absolutely stuck so full of dough that she don't know what to do with it.

This Yarthers guy also knows about the fact that she was engaged to Charles Chayse, but of course he don't know that the Charles Chayse he is talkin' about is Willie the Goop who was bumped.

Altogether I get a pretty good mental picture of this Mirabelle before I am through with this travellin' salesman, after which we have just one little one for the road together an' then I say so long an' go back to my room. I pack my bag an' stick the Luger in its holster under my left arm, after which I scram downstairs an' pay my bill. The reception clerk tips me off where I can hire a fast roadster an' puts a call through to the garage to send it round pronto.

Then I sit around down in the hall lounge an' smoke a cigarette an' do a little quiet thinkin'. After a bit the roadster comes around an' I go an' take a look at this car an' see that she is right for the road because I reckon that I have got to step on it plenty.

Then I go back into the hotel an' I go into the call box near the reception an' I put a call through to Mirabelle Gayford at the number she gave me.

A dame who sounds like a French maid answers, an' when I tell her that I am Perry Rice she tells me to hang on an' while I am waiting I am doin' some very rapid thinkin' an' wonderin' whether I am entitled to take the chance that I am proposin' to take.

But it looks to me that you have just gotta take a chance sometimes an' in this case it is worth it because if it goes the way I think it will then I am goin' to prove something that I want to prove right now.

Just then Mirabelle comes through. Has that dame gotta swell voice or has she? Carlotta's voice is low an' rich an' sorta soothin' but Mirabelle's is a sorta young voice with a lilt in it.

"An' what can I do for Mr. Rice?" she says.

"Listen, honeybunch," I tell her. "This is Perry Rice comin' to you by the courtesy of faith hope an' charity with bells on. An' he is goin' to tell you a little bedtime story that is guaranteed to make you think plenty."

She laughs.

"Sometimes I think I like you, Mr. Rice," she says. "I think that you're most amusing. And what is the bedtime story?"

"So you think I'm nice," I crack back. "Well for a dame who's wondering most of the time about whether I bumped her late boy friend off I think that ain't so bad."

I get serious.

"Now listen," I say, "I been thinkin' about things an' I reckon that I can advise you up on one or two late developments in this little game of blind poker that we're all playin'.

"First of all—since you are so keen on knowin' all about who bumped Willie, have you thought this: Whoever shot that guy did it with a gun, didn't he? Alright; now listen to this one. When we was all taken down to police headquarters after the shootin' nobody had a gun, an' that means that they musta got rid of it somewhere. It might interest you to know that I went back to Joe Madrigaul's place late that night an' searched it good an' plenty an' there wasn't no gun anywhere, although I found enough evidence to fry Rudy Saltierra for shootin' your young man because, sweetheart, you can take it from me that it was Rudy who did it.

"Well, what does that mean? It means just this. It means that after Rudy Saltierra had bumped off Willie he went back-stage an' he passed that gun to somebody who was out there an' who scrammed outa the club by the back way before Joe called everybody up an' closed the doors.

"So if you wanta help you just do a little investigatin' into who was hanging around the back-stage entrance to the club just before the shootin' took place. Have you got that?"

"I've got it," she says. "An' so you say it was Rudy Saltierra who shot Charles?"

"That's right," I say, "but I ain't goin' to produce any evidence to that effect until I want to, so don't start gettin' excited an' don't ask a lotta questions because I am in a great hurry.

"Now the next thing is this. I gotta letter from old man Harberry Chayse, an' he tells me that he has got some palooka on board his yacht the *Atlantic Witch*, who is goin' to do a big fortune tellin' act an' then tell us all who the murderer was. It looks like the old guy has got everybody concerned down there at some dump near New London by payin' 'em five grand—the same as he sent me—to go down there an' be looked over by this big occult guy. Well, I am just on my way so I reckoned

that I'd wise you up just so that you could sorta keep your eye on things around Joe Madrigaul's place while I am gone.

An' if you're payin' good money to those imitation flat-feet, the Davance Agency, tell 'em to stick around that club an' keep their eye on what's poppin'.

"Well . . . so long, Mirabelle," I crack. "Be a good girl an' don't do anything you wouldn't like your Uncle Perry to know about, an' maybe I'll be seein' you some time."

Does that dame get excited, or does she?

"Listen, Mr. Rice," she calls. "Listen. . . . You can't go down to New London . . . you can't . . . !"

I hang up.

It looks like it has worked.

I grab my bag and scram out to the car. I start her up an' I whiz. I shoot about half a dozen traffic lights an' get away with it, an' in half an hour I have settled down to some nice steady drivin' an' I can do quite a lot of peaceful thinkin'.

It is one o'clock an' a nice cold night when I blow in to the outskirts of this New London. I stop for some gas at a gas station an' they tell me that this Guyle's Wharf is about five miles out on the Groten road, an' the guy looks at me as if I was a bit screwy. I ask him what's eatin' him, an' he tells me that plenty guys have been askin' the way to this Guyle's Wharf place, an' that it looks as if there is goin' to be a party or something an' that they ain't used to such a lotta company around this part of the world.

I move on, an' presently the road narrows down an' pretty soon it begins to be just a sorta asphalt track. I can see plenty car marks on it though. Away through the trees I can see the sea glimmerin' an' I reckon I am gettin' pretty near this Guyle's Wharf.

All of a sudden the headlights pick up a tree that is lyin' dead across the track in front of me. I stick on the brakes like hell an' pull the car up dead, an' I am just makin' a grab for the Luger when a guy steps out of the trees at the side.

He has gotta sawn off shotgun pointin' pretty near my head an' he is wearin' a sorta jersey like a sea-goin' guy wears.

"Say, are you Perry Rice?" he drawls.

"Dead right first time," I tell him. "Say what is this. Are you huntin' or do you always meet guys with a shotgun?"

He grins.

"Take it easy," he says, "an' get outa the car an' come along quietly. Nobody ain't goin' to hurt you so long as you just play ball. But if you start anything I reckon I'm goin' to fill you so full of holes that you'll think you was a nutmeg grater."

I get outa the car an' right then two other guys come outa the trees at the side of the track. One of these guys is an old sorta guy with gray hair an' a face tanned like your best shoes an' the other is a little feller—very strong he looks too. They are all wearin' these blue jerseys an' they walk like they was an advertisement for a winter cruise.

"Take him along to the cabin," says the old guy.

He looks at me an' he grins.

"I reckon you'll be right smart if you just stick around nice an' quiet," he says. "You won't come to no harm so long as you just keep that way, but if you try anything then Hiram here will surely shoot you up an' I reckon he don't wanta do that."

"That's O.K. by me," I say. "Here is one thing that Hiram an' me both don't want."

I start to get outa the car an' I am takin' my time about it. The palooka with the shotgun is standin' facin' the door of the car—the one I am goin' to get out by.

"Say Eph," says the old guy to the little one. "You get right along an' get on the wire an' just say that everythin's O.K."

"Okey doke, Paw," says the little guy.

By this time I have opened the door an' I start to get out. As I am gettin' out I lean over the dash an' make that I am turnin' off the ignition key. Doin' this I have got my back turned to the guy with the gun. I do a little mental calculation an' I hope that I am goin' to be right an' as I make out to step backwards outa the car I shoot my leg out hard an' I find that my arithmetic was right because I kick the guy with the gun right clean in the face an' he don't like it any neither.

Before he has time to have a meetin' with himself about this I spin around with the Luger in my hand.

"Put 'em up, sailors," I say, "an' let me tell you that you are the worst lotta stick-up men that never heisted a bank. Just take it nice an' easy an' don't move till I tell you otherwise you'll think the anchor's hit you."

I take the shotgun away from the feller with the bust nose, an' I sit down by the side of the track.

"Now listen, boys," I tell 'em, "just put in a little heavy work an' move that tree outa the way so that I can proceed good an' quick to my destination. Otherwise I am goin' to give you the works. When you've done that I'll give you some further instructions."

They get busy. The old guy is cussin' his head off to himself an' the others don't look so pleased.

While they are movin' this tree I look at 'em. They are all nice lookin' guys with rough serge pants an' big boots. One of 'em has gotta snake tattooed on one arm an' "I love Cora" on the other.

When they have moved the tree I get back into the car an' switch on. I throw the shotgun in the back.

"O.K. brothers," I say. "That was nice work, an' one day I'll let you come an' play boats with me. In the meantime Paw," I say to the old man, "I'm goin' to repeat your instructions to Eph."

"Eph"—I turn to the little guy—"you get along an' do like Paw told you. You get on the wire an' tell Miss Mirabelle Gayford that everything is hunky-dory an' that Mr. Rice sent her his compliments an' says that when he sees her he'll buy her a big raspberry ice cream.

"An' if you can remember it, Eph, you can say that if she used that pretty little head of hers she can work out that the reason that I got through to her before I left New York was just to see if she'd try a fast one like this.

"An' if she gives you the air for fallin' down on this job remember boys that the Navy needs guys like you."

With this crack I put my foot down on the gas an' I shoot off. I turn back an' look at 'em, an' they was standin' in a row in the middle of the track lookin' after me. All except the old guy an' he was tellin' the feller with the bust nose where he got off the tram.

I reckon they was three good guys, but it looks to me that they was just three nice sea-goin' sailors.

As hold-up men they was merely a big pain in the neck.

Chapter Eight
THE PROPHET GETS HIS

I DRIVE on down this track. When I have done about another half mile I can see that the track branches off through the trees to my left, and then there is a clearin', an' then I see a sorta wooden pier. Tied up to this pier is a big yacht an' I reckon this is the *Atlantic Witch*.

I slow down an' pull the car in among the trees, then I get out an' I start gumshoein' back, keepin' well off the track, to the place where I left these three sailor guys. After a bit I see 'em. Paw an' Hiram are sittin' down by the side of the track talkin' to Eph who is standin' up an' not lookin' so pleased with himself.

Presently Eph pulls some turnip watch outa his trousers pocket an' looks at it an' walks off. He passes just a few yards ahead of where I am standin' behind a tree. I go after him. We walk pretty considerable until we come to a gate in a stone wall. He goes through this an' I go after him.

On the other side of the gate I see we are in a sorta park. Way back is a big colonial house. There are two three carriage drives leadin' up to this house an' on one of 'em facin' the entrance gates which are away on my right I can see the headlights of a car.

Eph starts walkin' across the rolling lawns to this car an' I stick around in the shade of the wall. Presently I start easin' down to the right keeping close to the shrubs and the wall doin' this. I come to a place where there is some trees so that I can start movin' up until I get near enough to see the car.

Inside it at the wheel I see Mirabelle talkin' to Eph. After a bit she starts up the car an' Eph goes off, but he remembers somethin' an' comes back. I reckon that when she goes she is goin' out from the main iron gates way down on my right, so I run over there pretty quick an' stand in the shade by the side of 'em. The gates are shut so I reckon she has got to slow down anyway to open them. After a bit she comes down; when she gets to the gates she stops the car an' I step out.

"Hulloa, Mirabelle," I say, "how're you making out?"

Is that dame surprised?

"Aren't you funny, Mr. Rice?" she says. "You're always jumping out of corners."

I grin.

"I suppose you're sorta relieved to see me," I say, "aren't you, seein' that you took such a lotta trouble to stop me gettin' on that boat? The worst of it is," I tell her, "these sailors are no good at stick-ups, they ain't experienced enough. Anyhow I reckon it was nice of you. What did you do it for?"

She don't say anythin', she just sits lookin' at the steerin' wheel in front of her.

"Listen here, Miss Gayford," I say, "why don't you come clean, why don't you shoot the works? This here business is a serious business, you know, an' maybe you know more about it than you've told."

She looks up, then she takes a gold cigarette case outa her coat pocket an' lights herself one. She looks at me through a puff of smoke an' her eyes are sorta half closed. I reckon she is weighin' me up.

"Exactly what are you talking about?" she says.

"What do you think?" I tell her. "Are you interested in anything else except Willie the Goop being bumped off, because if you are I am. Look here," I say, "what do I have to think about you? You are the dame who was engaged to this guy who has got himself shot. You hire detectives to try muscle stuff with me in order to get information out of me. When I come through to you on the telephone to tell you I am comin' down here to go aboard this yacht an' do this seance stuff, you get excited an' tell me I ought not to go. Why?"

I go over to her an' I lean on the side of the car.

"Listen, Mirabelle," I say, "I reckon you're going to shoot the works an' like it."

She blows another cloud of smoke.

"Am I," she says, "and why?"

I put my hand in my secret pocket inside my waistcoat, an' I take out my Federal badge an' I open the case an' shot it to her.

"That's why, sweetheart," I say. "My name's Lemmy Caution, Special Agent, Federal Bureau of Investigation, United States Department of Justice."

She sorta smiles.

"I'm not particularly surprised," she says.

"That's O.K. by me," I tell her. "Life is sometimes not very surprisin', but the point is there's been too much jumpin' around in the dark. I wanta know why you didn't want me to go aboard that boat."

She gives me a cigarette an' lights it with a little gold lighter. Her attitude is sorta changed towards me since she has seen I am a "G" man.

"I suppose you know the truth about Harvest Mellander," she says. "You know whether or not he was a 'G' man too."

"Yeah," I tell her, "his name was Myras Duncan. He was a 'G' man all right. So what?"

"Is that all you know?" she says.

"Pretty well," I say. "If you can tell me anything else I am listenin'."

"You know what he was workin' on?"

I nod.

"This gold snatch, an' what do you know about it?"

She looks serious.

"I don't *know* anything about it," she says, "but I think something. I think that Charles was mixed up in it. I think he had something to do with it, and I think that's why they shot him.

"You see," she says, and she looks sorta sad. "I feel in a way that maybe I was responsible for Charles getting mixed up in this thing. He was a funny sort of man. He was a spendthrift and his old man wouldn't let him have any more money, so he came to me and he asked me to lend him a large sum. I refused. Maybe that's how he got mixed up with this ridiculous business.

"Well, that wasn't really the thing that was worrying me," she goes on, "you see the point is this. I saw his father Harberry Chayse yesterday morning. He told me all about this idea which had been suggested to him, this idea of getting this clairvoyant man to go down on the boat and to try and find the murderer. I told him that it was ridiculous and foolish and even if it was successful it wouldn't do any good. I almost thought I had talked him out of it. You can imagine how surprised I was when you called me on the telephone and told me that you'd heard from him asking you to go down, because it means that he must have written that letter to you very soon after I'd left him. At the time I left him he was decided that he wouldn't do it."

"That's O.K." I say, "an' there is a perfectly good explanation for that. You see I gotta pal workin' on this job with me, a crime reporter, an' I reckon he must have contacted Harberry Chayse some time when he had this idea in his mind. Maybe he saw him after you did. Maybe he persuaded him to go through with it, which is just the sorta thing he would do because you know what newspaper men are, they'll do anything for a story, and another thing I reckon that if this guy talked Harberry into goin' through with the scheme he knew what he was doin'.

"An' where do we go from there?" I say. "Listen lady, I don't know very much about this besuzuz, but I've got my job to do, an' I reckon the only way I am goin' to go through with it is by goin' on that boat an' seein' what's poppin'. You see," I tell her, "a lotta this stuff you read in detective books is a lot of punk, there ain't many detectives who solve anything by sittin' around the fireside, an' the only way I've ever got next to anythin' is by just followin' my nose.

"I reckon that somebody—an' it don't matter who it is—has persuaded old man Chayse to go through with this job of havin' this seance on this boat, an' it looks like I've got to stick around because I don't see anything else to do, so that's that."

She nods her head.

"It looks rather like that," she says.

Then she goes on to spiel a lotta stuff about she wishes that I wouldn't go on the boat. When I ask her just why she says that it ain't so mucha matter of knowin' anything but that it is a matter of instinct an' that she has gotta idea in her head that maybe I can do just as much by stickin' around on shore as I can by goin' to this seance.

I try everything I know, but I cannot get anything else outa this dame. She sits there lookin' straight in front of her with her little mouth shut as tight as a clam. I reckon that this little dame knows plenty if she would only spill it; but for some reason she is holdin' out on me.

"O.K." I say. "Well it looks to me as if the best thing you can do is to go home to bed an' mix yourself a little toddy an' drink my very good health. The other thing you can do for me is just to go on behavin' nice an' normal an' not start doin' any big acts tryin' to stick people up or something, otherwise when I get around to you next time I'm goin' to be tough."

She shrugs her shoulders.

"Alright," she says. "You're the boss. But when this seance thing is over I'd like you to come up to the house an' see me."

"That's nice of you, sister," I say. "But what do you want to see me for—you're seein' me now."

"I'd like to hear about that seance," she says. "I wish you'd let me come along with you."

"Hooey," I say. "You do what I tell you. You scram outa here good an' quick an' behave yourself. You ain't doin' any good by tryin' to make me do somethin' I don't want to do or by tryin' to muscle in on this job. You got that?"

"I've got it," she says.

She puts the car in reverse, then she puts her hand out.

"Good luck, Mr. Caution," she says.

I shake hands with her.

"Good luck, lady," I tell her. "Maybe I'll be seeing you. I hope so."

She backs the car up the drive an' turns it round. I walk back over the grass along the wall until I come to the gate. I cut through an' I go back to the place where I left my car. I get in an' I drive down to the wharf.

This wharf is a desolate sorta place. It is on the left side of a little bay an' there is a long wooden pier on timber piles. Lyin' up against this pier is the *Atlantic Witch*. She is a big long boat an' I bet she cost a bundle of dough. There don't seem to be anybody about to me, although here an' there where a porthole ain't quite closed I can see lights glimmerin'.

I pull up on the side of the pier an' get out, an' walk towards where I can just see a gangway onto the boat. When I get near a guy comes over. He comes up to me, an' he shines an electric torch at me. Then he looks at a paper he has got in his hand.

"Are you Mr. Rice?" he says, an' when I tell him yes he tells me that I should go along with him, an' we cross the gangway an' walk along the deck. After a bit we go down a companion way an' he knocks on the door of a cabin at the bottom.

Somebody says to come in, an' this guy stands on one side an' motions me to go first. When I am inside he shuts the door behind me an' scrams.

I am in a fair sized cabin that has got a lotta books around it. There is a desk in the middle an' a shaded lamp on it, an' sittin' at the desk is some guy. He moves an' when the light falls across his face it looks to me that this palooka is the San Reima guy.

An' I am quite right here.

"Please you take a seat, Mr. Rice," he says.

He speaks in a foreign accent an' he has got the funniest pair of eyes that I have ever seen. They sorta change colour an' they glitter like a snake's eyes. I sit down an' he pushes a box of cigarettes over to me an' starts a long spiel about what all the business is for an' how, under the right circumstances, he reckons that he is goin' to nominate the murderer.

"An' it won't be you, Mr. Rice," he says quietly, lookin' at me full in the eyes, "because I see now that you are not the man who killed this unfortunate young man. I can see that you have not the aura of a murderer."

"That's O.K. by me," I tell him, "but even if I ain't got the aura of a murderer I have got one helluva thirst at the moment, an' where can I get a little drink?"

He laughs and rings the bell on the table, an' some steward in a white coat comes along an' takes me along a passage an' shows me into a big cabin that is rigged up like a bar.

An' they are all there! There is Rudy Saltierra an' Carlotta an' a bunch of other guys, but I notice that the people who was sittin' around Willie the Goop at Joe Madrigaul's place when Willie was shot are missin', an' there are a bunch of people, includin' some women in evenin' clothes that I ain't ever seen before.

I take a look at Carlotta. She is sittin' in a corner on a lounge seat drinkin' a highball, an' she is lookin' at me with a peculiar sorta smile that might mean anything you like.

"Hey, Rice," says Rudy Saltierra. "I reckon I'm glad to see you. Have a little drink."

He goes around behind the bar, an' he mixes me a stiff highball. I walk down to the end of the bar where there ain't any people an' he comes down there with the drink.

"I'm sorta actin' as bar tender around here," he says. "Now you've come I reckon that maybe they will get goin'. This oughta be a funny sorta evenin'."

"Yeah," I tell him. "It might be at that . . . an'," I go on, "it might not be so durn funny for you either. . . ."

"Meanin' what?" he says.

"Meanin' that you bumped Willie the Goop an' you know it, sour-puss," I say. "An' if this palooka San Reima puts the finger on you you can bet your last nickel that old man Chayse will never have a good night's rest till he's got you fried for it."

He looks at me like a snake. He is wearin' a tuxedo with diamond and ruby studs an' cuff links, an' his eyes are as hard as the stones. His hand that is lyin' on the bar with the fingers around his glass is long an' thin, but the fingers look like steel hooks, an' I reckon that he could squeeze a mean windpipe with anybody if he wanted to—an' I reckon he wanted to just then.

"Oh yeah," he says. "I forgot you was the little amateur Sherlock Holmes, still stickin' your nose into things that ain't your concern. You take a tip from me, Rice," he goes on, "an' keep a civil tongue in your head. Otherwise I might start somethin' with you."

"Sarsaparilla," I tell him. "You couldn't start anything with a box of wooden soldiers, Saltierra, so don't get funny, an' just be your age."

He is just goin' to crack back at me when the door opens an' in comes some feller.

He is wearin' a ship's officer's uniform, but it don't fit him too well, an' he looks like he's been hittin' up a bottle some place.

"Everybody who ain't in this seance thing off the ship," he bellows. "Only those ladies an' gentlemen who are takin' part in this thought readin' stuff can stick around. Everybody else scram!"

Two or three women get up an' go out, an' a coupla the men. I hear this ship's officer guy goin' along the passage bellowin' this stuff about people who ain't concerned gettin' off the boat, so I reckon that there are plenty people on this boat.

I ease over to where Carlotta is sittin'. She is wearing a suit an' believe me it is cut swell. It is a black suit an' she is wearin' a sorta lace shirt that just goes with her general set-up. I believe I have told you before that this dame is a honey—to look at anyway.

"How're you makin' out, Carlotta?" I say—an' outa the corner of my eye I can see Rudy Saltierra watchin' me like a snake. "How's the little Poison Ivy an' is business good. Are you still takin' 'em?"

She looks at me like I was something that crawled out from under a rock.

"Listen, big shot," she says. "You may be somethin' to your mammy, but to me you're just a heel. Another thing," she goes on, "I ain't forgotten about your last act with me. You're pretty good at tellin' ladies where they get off, ain't you? I suppose you think you're the big guy."

"Yea," I crack at her. "Well, sweetheart, if you're a lady than I'm the King of Siam gettin' himself elected President of Cuba in a snowstorm. But don't let me worry you any, because I can see that your boy friend Rudy is about to come across here an' pull one of his big heroic acts, an' when he does that I always like to lay off everything else so that I can go on laughin' without interruptin' myself."

Saltierra comes over. He is livid with rage. This guy is so burned up that he coulda torn a hole in me with an axe an' liked it.

"You keep your head shut, Rice," he says. "You don't have to talk to Miss de la Rue because she don't like it an' I don't like it—"

"An' I don't like it, nor her nor you either," I bust in, "but this is a free country an' maybe if I wanta talk to her I'm goin' to. If I like to tell her that she's nothin' but an oversize in stuffed olives—an' I don't like olives—then I'm goin' to say so, an' as for you when I wanta think up some description of you I'll just lay off for a day so's I can look up a lotta new words."

He says something that ain't in the dictionary, an' he picks up a bottle of rye by the neck. Just then I pull a fast one I learned in Cuba. I sidestep, feint that I am goin' to smack him in the puss, an' as he brings the bottle up to sock me I swing around an' give him a cut with the edge of my hand right across the hip joint at the back where the nerve is. He goes over like a skittle with his face twisted up with pain an' his eyes lookin' at me like all the devils in hell.

A coupla other guys get up an' it looks like there is goin' to be merry times for all, when the door opens an' standin' there lookin' at everybody with a smile on his face is this guy San Reima.

He speaks nice an' soft in his foreign way, an' he sorta quiets things down just by standin' there an' lookin'.

"Ladies and gentlemen," he says, "don't you think that it is wrong to make quarrels at a time like this?"

He smiles round at us and strokes his silky gray beard with his fingers.

Everybody gets quiet. Me, I am beginnin' to like this guy San Reima a bit. He looks to me as if maybe he has got some clairvoyance or whatever they call it, an' maybe he can see what happened, or what's goin' to happen.

But just at that moment I am thinkin' of something else. We're movin', an' we're movin' fast. I reckon that while I was havin' that bit of a schlmozzle with Rudy, we cast off. The vibration of this boat is just nobody's business, an' I reckon she is fairly tearin' through the water, which is a bit odd when you come to think that all this guy San Reima wanted to do was to just get two three miles off shore.

He goes on talkin'.

"I have altered the arrangements a little bit," he says. "Along the passage is the big saloon. The other people are already there. That is I believe everybody who was sitting around this young man when he was killed. The saloon is in darkness except for a little tiny dim light which will let you see where your places are.

"You will find that there is a circle of chairs. I want everybody to sit down on a chair. I want them to put their hands on their knees. Then I am going to sit in a chair facing the circle. We shall all sit there and a few minutes afterwards I shall tell you who murdered Charles Chayse."

Nobody says anything for a minute, then Rudy pulls one.

"O.K. Professor," he says, "that sounds swell to me, there is just one little thing. I don't know who this murderer is. You're goin' to tell us that, but I reckon he knows who he is, an' I reckon we've got a pretty good idea who he is."

He looks at me an' grins, an' I see Carlotta lookin' at me too.

"We reckon this guy Rice was the guy who bumped off Willie the Goop," says Rudy, "an' I reckon he's carryin' a gun now. I think we oughta have it off him."

I get up, but before I can say anything the tough lookin' ship's officer guy who has come along an' is standin' behind San Reima comes around him an' over to me.

"That's right," he says, "there ain't no reason for anybody to be carryin' a gun in this boat. If you've got one hand it over."

There ain't nothing to be done, so I hand over the gun an' believe me I have never been so sorry at partin' with that Luger in my life.

When I have done this we all follow this San Reima guy down the passage. There is a door at the end an' beyond that I can see there is a big saloon. Upstairs on deck I can hear people movin' about. As I have told you the speed this ship is makin' is nobody's business.

When we get inside the room there are two three guys there in white jackets who show us the chairs where we're to sit down. Way back right at the end of the saloon sittin' in front of the curtains, which look as if they might have been rigged up like the curtains was in Joe Madrigaul's place, I see a big lookin' guy sittin' in a chair, an' I think maybe that this is this Harberry Chayse.

After a minute we have all sat down. We have all got our hands on our knees like this San Reima said. He sits down in the chair facin' the circle an' he looks straight in front of him.

"If you please to put out the lights," he says.

Somebody turns off the one solitary shaded light that was going at the other end of the saloon.

It was pitch dark, you couldn't hear a thing. There was just a little bit of breathin' goin' on, that's all. Nothing happens for about two three minutes then we hear San Reima start to talk.

"I see this place," he says. "I see this Joe Madrigaul's Club. I see and I hear Miss de la Rue singing her song. I see behind the curtain is a man coming from the passage where there are dressing rooms. He is a thin man. He is a very cruel man. He is wearing a white carnation in his buttonhole.

"In his right hand is a pistol. He walks across the left hand side of the stage behind the curtain and he says something to the man who is sitting up on a perch, the man who works the lights. He looks at the pistol in his hand, then he puts it in his coat pocket. He goes through the pass-door. He walks five or six paces and he is now about six paces away from the young man who is sitting at the table listening to the singer. The man with the white carnation shoots through his pocket."

He stops. Nobody moves.

"Please put up the lights," says this guy San Reima.

Somebody puts the lights up. San Reima is sitting in the chair lookin' straight in front of him. He is in a sorta daze. After a bit he pulls himself together. He sorta comes back to earth. All the lights in the saloon are up. I see round the doorway three or four fellows, stewards I suppose, in white jackets, and behind them other guys—the crew I expect—lookin' on.

San Reima points to Rudy Saltierra.

"That is the man," he says. "That is the man who shot Charles Chayse."

I look around. Nobody is movin' an' nobody seems very disturbed. Saltierra gets up. He put his hand in his hip pocket an' he brings out a gun.

"Listen, prophet," he says, "ain't you the berries? You're just about the best guy at solvin' murders that I ever struck in my life, an' I'll tell you somethin'—you're dead right. I bumped Willie the Goop, because I don't like guys stickin' around who know too much."

I think it is time I took a hand in this mother's meetin'.

"Just a minute Rudy." I say. I turn around to the rest of 'em.

"I don't know if there are any honest to goodness guys around here," I tell 'em, "but if there is then I call on 'em to witness that this here Saltierra has just confessed to the murder of this Willie the Goop, otherwise Charles Chayse an' . . . ."

Rudy interrupts. He swings around with his gun.

"Can it, punk!" he says. "Nobody wants to hear you talk. I'll get around to you presently."

He speaks to San Reima again.

"I reckon you're a pretty good clairvoyant prophet," he says . . . "too durn good. But tell me somethin', did you get any big ideas about this business before you came here to-night?"

This San Reima smiles. I like this guy—he ain't frightened a bit an' he ain't so young neither.

"I knew," he said. "I knew because I saw all this yesterday. . . . I did not have to come here to know it."

He stands there still smilin'.

Rudy grins. He looks like a wolf that has found a rabbit.

"I reckon you know too much," he says.

He raises the gun.

"Maybe you saw this too?"

He was sneerin' at the old guy.

San Reima smiles. He looks as placid as a stream in the summer.

"I saw that too—murderer. . . ."

He don't say any more, because Rudy stepped forward an' pulled the trigger an' went on pullin' it. He sent half a dozen bullets into San Reima, an' liked doin' it. He was grinnin' like a hyena. Even when the old guy was lyin' on the floor, Rudy let him have a couple more. He was a nice piece of work I'm tellin' you.

Then he throws the gun away an' turns around to me. I look about an' see that everybody around here is grinnin' at me. I see that round the doorway are some guys in white jackets—the guys who I thought was stewards—an' behind them some more thugs.

"Well folks," he says. "May I present to you one of the shinin' lights of the U.S. Department of Justice"—he waves towards me—"Mr. Lemmy Caution the original gift to the Federal flatfeet—the little 'G' man complete with badge an' everything."

He stands there laughin'. They all join in. It was like bein' in the snake house.

"Well," he says. "An' what do we do with this mug?"

CHAPTER NINE
SHOW DOWN FOR LEMMY

IT'S A funny thing but whenever there's a good chance of my bein' bumped off I start thinkin' of all sorts of durn silly things. I'm like that.

Just at this moment I am thinkin' that Carlotta has got nice ankles. She is standin' there lookin' out at one of the portholes that she has opened, smokin' a cigarette. She is a cool cuss.

I come back to earth again an' take a peek at Rudy. He is standin' there lookin' at me like all the devils in hell. He is grinnin' like a fiend an' is he enjoyin' the situation. I reckon Rudy was a real killer. He didn't kill because he was scared or because he had to; he was the sorta guy who liked bumpin' people. He got a kick out of it.

An' it looked as if I had mine comin' to me, because it was a cinch that he was goin' to give me the works, an' all I wanted to do was just to get at him for one minute so's to let him have a really good one before he got busy on me. I reckon I've seen a few guys bumped off in my time, but I was pretty good an' burned up about seein' this San Reima ironed out for nothin' at all—poor sap.

I put my hands in my pockets an' nodded my head towards where the body was lyin'.

"O.K. Rudy," I said, grinnin' pretty at him, "but there's just one little thing I'd like to point out to you—something you forgot."

I take my right hand outa my pocket an' I point towards the stiff on the floor. Sure as a gun Rudy looks towards it an' I jump for the dirty so-an'-so.

I made it. I got my fingers round his throat an' then I let go with my right hand an' smashed him between the eyes with every bit of weight I got. I hit him twice before the rest of 'em arrived, an' I had the pleasure of hearin' him yelp when he started swallowin' his own teeth.

Then they was on to me. I reckon I've been in some rough spots in my time, but what that hell-club did to me was just nobody's business. If ever a guy got the works it was me. I tell you that these guys just pushed each other outa the way in order to bust me about like nobody ever was, an' when they was finished with me it looked like all I needed was a nice tombstone with "he did his best" on it.

My left eye was all washed up. Somebody had closed it with a bottle, an' I reckoned that if all my ribs wasn't broke through kickin' it was only because they'd elected to twist 'em instead. My right arm was paralysed from a smash on the nerve with a stool an' my nose felt like a piece of india rubber that had just been put through a mincin' machine.

Then Rudy spoke to 'em an' they stopped an' stood off. Lyin' on the floor where they'd left me I could see him outa my good eye an' he wasn't so pleased neither. I'd only hit him twice but both socks had been honeys. Half his pretty teeth was gone an' one eye was closed an' goin' black. An' he still had the marks of my left hand on his throat.

I tried to get up but I couldn't make it. He walked over to me an' he kicked me in the face, an' if you ever been kicked in the face by a feller like Rudy you will realise that it hurts considerable.

Then he started in. He couldn't speak very well because he was havin' a bit of trouble with his lips which were swellin' up pretty good. I got a kick outa that.

"O.K. Caution," he says. "So you're tough, huh? So you wanta play around here do you? Alright. Listen you sap, I was just goin' to kill you nice an' quick but now I'm goin' to have a big time with you. I'm goin' to think up somethin' really nice an' pretty for you right now. Before I'm through with you you'd give something just to get yourself shot quick. Pick him up boys!"

Some guys yank me to my feet an' they stand there holdin' me up. I am not feelin' so good an' the saloon is lookin' misty an' the walls are sorta openin' an' shuttin', but I can see well enough to watch Carlotta walk across an' speak to Saltierra, then she walks over to me an' stands in front of me with her hands on her hips, lookin' at me like a green snake.

"Well, well, well," she says smilin'. "Just fancy the great Lemmy Caution's got himself smacked down just like a naughty little boy."

She turns to Saltierra.

"Throw him some place, Rudy," she says, "while we think up something for him. Right now," she goes on, "here's something for him to remember *me* by . . . something just to even up that clever stuff he handed out to me."

She smacks me on the puss. An' when I grin back at her she does it again. Then she walks off.

"O.K. boys," says Rudy, wipin' his face with a handkerchief. "Throw that punk in the calaboose. Put some irons on him or tie him up an' don't worry about bein' gentle with him. We'll have a game with him later on, an' somebody fetch me a drink an' some cold water."

Two of these guys drag me along outa this saloon. They take me along the passage an' down another—a short one—at right angles. Then one of 'em goes off an' comes back in a minute with a pair of steel bracelets. They fix my hands behind my back with these an' then they take me along open another door. In front of me is some steps leadin' down to some black hole that looks like it is in the bowels of this ship. One of these guys steps back an' takes a good kick at me an' I go down—head first, an' when I arrive at the bottom I don't know nothin' at all. Life was just one big, beautiful wallop.

How long I am lyin' down in this hole I don't know, but when I come to I am not feelin' so good. Every time I try an' move it feels as if somebody is pullin' me to pieces. My head is singin', one eye is closed up an' altogether I am not feelin' so hot about anything.

This boat is goin' like hell. The engines are throbbin' an' I reckon that, wherever we are goin' to, Rudy's in a hurry.

I stretch myself out although believe me it is not very comfortable when your wrists are handcuffed behind your back, so eventually I turn over on my face an' find it's a bit better that way.

Although I don't think it matters very much, I cannot get this business at all. What Rudy is doin' on this boat an' how he managed to snatch it the way he has is too much for me, an' it looks to me that anyway it don't matter because it is a cinch that just as soon as he thinks of me Saltierra will certainly give it to me an' throw me overboard afterwards.

I lie in this place for a long time an' the door opens an' a coupla guys come down. They pick me up an' they take me along to a cabin. Rudy is sittin' at the table with a bottle of rye in front of him. He has got a piece of raw steak over one eye an' his face looks like a sunset—all blues an' reds.

"O.K. boys," he says, "you can take those bracelets off him, he couldn't do a thing to anybody."

I'm telling you he was right. If anybody had paid me a grand to smack a fly down, I don't think I could have done it. They take these bracelets off me, an' I am able to stretch myself a bit. I flop down on a seat. Saltierra pushes the bottle across the table.

"Have a drink," he says, "maybe you'll feel better. You see, Caution," he goes on, "I want you to feel good for a bit, I want you to have all your brains about you just so as you can realise what a big punk you are."

I pick up the bottle, although believe me or not it hurts me even to do this, an' I take a swig. It is good rye an' my head clears a bit, but I don't let Rudy see this. I just sit there lookin' dopey. I take a look at this guy. He's wearin' a nice lounge suit an' a silk shirt, so I reckon it is daytime the next day. I cannot see whether I am right or not because the porthole is closed an' there is a curtain over it an' the lights are on. He has got his chair tilted back an' he's lookin' at me as if he's very pleased with himself. I get a hunch that this guy's long suit is conceit.

Every crook has got somethin' that he slips up on an' whilst it don't look to me that I have gotta chance anyhow, I am still goin' to play along an' do the best I can for myself an' everybody else. I reckon I will play up to this guy.

"O.K. Saltierra," I tell him, "you win, but believe me, you been clever. I don't know how you do it."

He grins. Then he sticks one thumb in the armhole of his vest. I reckon this dope I am pullin' on him is workin' a bit.

"You're right, copper," he says, "it wasn't so bad. You know, you guys ain't got all the brains."

"That's the way it's beginnin' to look to me," I say, "but how you knew about Mellander I don't know."

He laughs an' has another wallop at the bottle.

"You don't know nothing," he says.

He looks at me sorta quizzin'.

"I'm a bit sorry for you, Caution," he says. "You're a tough guy, ain't you, at least you was. You're the copper who bust the Siegella crowd, huh? I knew Ferdie Siegella once. He was a smart guy, but he hadn't got brains like I got. This is where you slip up."

"You're tellin' me," I say. "You don't have to prove that, I know it. Say listen," I go on, "it don't mean a thing now so there ain't any reason why you can't talk about it, but this is a nice bit of work. Where do we go from here?"

I look at him again.

"What's the voyage about," I say, "what is this, a summer cruise or just an exploration of the North Pole? Listen," I tell him, "hark at those engines goin'. This boat's movin' some. Do I know where we're goin' before I get mine, Saltierra?"

He leans across the table an' he pushes the bottle over to me again.

"Give yourself another drink, sap, make yourself comfortable an' I'll make you laugh."

I take the bottle an' I make out I am drinkin', but I don't. I think that maybe I will let him do the drinkin'. When I put the bottle back, he lights himself a cigarette.

"We're goin' to England, fly cop," he says, "an' how do you like that? You was the clever little Sherlock, wasn't you? You an' Myras Duncan knew everything, at least you thought you did, an' you thought that we was goin' to be mugs enough to try an' pull that gold snatch in America. You come up for air, sweetheart, because there's something wrong with your brains."

He sticks his head across the table over towards me. He's so pleased with himself he just don't know.

"Listen, Caution," he says, "we're goin' to snatch that gold in England, an' I'll tell you somethin' else. You're goin' to help too."

He gives himself another drink, a big one this time, an' I can see that this rye is beginnin' to take effect. It looks to me like Rudy has been doin' a spot of drinkin' before I came along, an' I think maybe that if I annoy him enough he will do a bit more talkin'.

"That's a clever idea, Saltierra," I say, "swell, if you can pull it off, but you know it ain't easy to pinch bar gold, an' if you think you can get away with that sorta racket in England you'll find they are pretty hot over there. They got coppers too—did they tell you? What are you goin' to do, blow up the Bank of England? You make me laugh!"

He grins.

"We ain't goin' near no banks," he says, "this is no bank hoistin' job. If you had any sense in your head," he goes on, "if you was anything except a lousy copper, you'd know that the easiest place in the world to pinch gold is in England if you do it the right way. Why . . ." an' he leans over the table, "do you know they deliver gold in London in a van that drives up to the bank an' a coupla clerks hand it in. It almost don't seem possible that people could be such mugs," he goes on.

I nod.

"So you're goin' to stick a van up, are you?" I say. "That's swell, but you know Rudy, when you get it where you are goin' to take it. You got to get outa the country with it."

"Aw, shut up, punk," he says, "you make me sick. We're not stickin' up any vans."

I grin. I grin in a sorta way that suggests he's talkin' hooey. He gulps down another drink an' then he takes some more.

"Just how we're goin' to get it an' just how we ain't goin' to get it is nobody's business," he says, "but I'll tell you one thing, you guys have been helpin' us, an' you've been helpin' us right from the first. The best thing that ever happened to us was when I crowned that mug with a bottle an' he started talkin' down at the Bellevue Hospital. We didn't know he was goin' to do it, but my was it good? An' you all thought that we were goin' to try a gold snatch in the U.S. an' you did all the things we wanted you to, swoppin' over boats, doin' every durn thing that would give us a hand. Say, look at this."

He fumbles about in his pocket an' he brings out a piece of paper which is folded up very small. He chucks this across the table to me, an' I read it. It is in typescript, an' here is what it says:

As you know there have been huge flights of capital to America in the last two years, partly due to the investors anxious to profit by business recovery over there (New York's stock and bond prices have roughly doubled in the last nine months), and partly due to scares of a war with Italy, to scares over the re-occupation of the Rhine or to scares of franc de-valuation.

These are all of course major issues for all the owners of the enormous mass of liquid capital in the greatest countries in the world. Yet only three times in the last two years have the weekly exports of gold from the whole of Europe touched twenty million pounds.

Under the new Tripartite Agreement movements of gold will be only by way of reducing 'earmarks,' balances between the three exchange equalisation accounts, that is the English, French, American accounts will be supplied by 'earmarking' gold in the country where it is sold for account of the country who buys it. Only when earmarks become unreasonably large will gold probably be shifted. Movements will therefore not be connected in any way with exchange rates.

Under these circumstances our operation must be planned at a time when information reaches us that 'earmarks' become unreasonably large.

We know that American Insurance Underwriters insist so far as possible on small shipments in fast liners, nearly all of which have special bullion rooms; but in winter when transatlantic passenger traffic is thin many first-class liners are taken off the route. In consequence there is a tendency to use boats without proper bullion rooms or to crowd large consignments on the few fast liners available.

Therefore if for some reason or other the Federal Authorities were to suspect an intention to operate in some way against a bullion carrying ship they would no doubt arrange for the transfer of the bullion at the last moment to another boat, and if the time were carefully planned the only boats which might be available would be trans-atlantic cargo passenger boats which are slow and which would give us time to put our scheme properly into execution.

It must be noted therefore that if the attempt is to be made on a shipment of roughly two million pounds the weight of the actual gold will be somewhere in the region of eight tons. Probably most of this shipment will be in U.S. Mint bars of four hundred troy ounces each, possibly an awkward weight. Remember that a 14.1" cube of fine gold weighs roughly one long ton, so that the mint bars measuring 3½" by 6¾" by1¾" will each be as heavy approximately as a good solid suitcase. Under these circumstances you must arrange for each man at the other end of the operation to make not more than six journeys between the gold and the lorries in order that the time angle for clearing the gold may not be unduly extended.

I read this very quick, but I pretend to be readin' it slow, an' I also make out that I cannot see the words very distinctly because of the fact that one of my eyes is closed up. Also, in the middle of readin' I reach out for the bottle an' make out that I am takin' another drink, all of which gives me time to come to some very interestin' conclusions about this paper I am readin'.

I get to one place where I make out I cannot see at all, an' I pick the paper up an' hold it up to the light an' oh boy, am I pleased with myself!

This paper is a piece of good quality linen-faced foolscap an' the typin' is very small and with some small spacin' in order to get the stuff on, but the thing that interests me is just this.

This sheet of paper hasn't got any headin'. It is quite plain, an' the watermark in it which I see when I hold it up to the light is the same as the watermark on the foolscap letter paper that came from Harberry Chayse's apartment on Park Avenue. In other words this piece of paper is a follow-on sheet.

I just go on pretendin' to read, but I am doin' some heavy thinkin'. I am rememberin' what Mirabelle told me, that Harberry Chayse hadn't made up his mind about having the seance, that he had said that maybe he wouldn't have it. Well it looks as if somebody had pinched that notepaper from the Chayse apartment, and the follow-on sheets at the same time, or else they had ordered some to be made so as to be able to send out phoney letters when they wanted to.

Then I remember again that Mirabelle had said that Willie the Goop was mixed up in this gold snatch an' it looks as if he was mixed up a durn sight more than she knew. I am beginning to think that Willie was in on this job from the start an' maybe got cold feet when he found that Myras Duncan was hangin' around.

Supposin' I am right, then here is a first-class explanation for the letter that Willie wrote to Carlotta, the one I found in the pocket of Rudy Saltierra's tuxedo. Willie was stuck on Carlotta an' he was goin' to give her the tip-off that Myras Duncan was gumshoein' around lookin' as if he might put his finger on somethin' in a minute, an' that it looked as if the best thing for Willie to do was to blow the whole gaff to Myras an' so save his own skin. He wanted to see her that night to tell her to get out while the goin' was good before Myras had heard the truth an' started pinchin' people.

Now I am beginnin' to see what was in Duncan's mind when he had the palaver with me down in Moksie's bar. He didn't know just what Willie the Goop was goin' to come across with, but he knew he was goin' to spill the works about something an' so all he wanted to do was to put Willie on to me so's I could get ahead with the business from that point.

Willie was gettin' all stewed up about Carlotta. He knew that if he wanted to save her skin he'd got to contact her an' tell her to scram out of it before Duncan started grillin' people. Maybe Willie was goin' to arrange some story with Carlotta that would explain her bein' in on the job an' would yet sorta let her out when it came to layin' criminal charges.

Lookin' at it from this angle everything sorta begins to clear itself up in my mind. At last it looks like I am seein' a spot of daylight. The tough thing is that it looks like it is a spot too late.

While I am thinkin' all this stuff I have got my hand held up to my head an' am sittin' lookin' hard at the letter. Outa the corner of my eye I am watching Rudy an' wonderin' just what is comin' next.

After a bit I fold up the paper an' I hand it back to him. I am glad to say that my right arm is beginnin' to ease up a bit but I don't let him know this, I give it back with my left hand, an' then I flop back in my chair like I was all out for nothin'.

He gives a big horse laugh. I tell you this Rudy was good an' pleased with himself.

"Well, copper," he says, "you see we got some brains runnin' this racket an' you ain't heard the half of it. Now then,"—he draws himself up like he was goin' to say somethin' really good—"I'm goin' to make a proposition to you, an' I don't care whether you take it or not, but I'm goin' to give you the chance."

He lights himself a cigarette an' looks at me through the flame of the lighter with his lousy snakes' eyes, an' he keeps 'em on me while he shoves the cigarettes over to me.

"Here's the way it is, sap," he says. "I'm goin' to tell you the whole works so you know what you're doin'. The gold shipment all youse guys is worryin' about so much left New York about ten hours ago on the *Maybury*, an' once she was to sea I reckon the Federal Government just breathed a hearty sigh of relief an' thought that everything was hunky dory. Well, it ain't, because it might interest you to know that we're goin' to snatch that gold an' it's goin' to be so simple that you just don't know."

He helps himself to another drink an' gulps it down, watchin' me all the time. This guy is beginnin' to interest me.

"So what?" he goes on . . . "So just this, what you guys ain't realised is that this racket is an international racket. This is the first time that we got boys workin' on both sides of the Atlantic on the same job. You police palookas reckon you got organisation. Well, so have we.

"The *Maybury* is about as fast as a hearse. They might just as well have got a wind jammer to take that gold over. This boat you're on is as fast as they make 'em, an' in a couple of days we're goin' to be hangin' on the tail of the *Maybury*. But we don't do a thing . . . not a little thing.

"So what. . . . Why, when the *Maybury* gets to Southampton, England, we just stick around out to sea, just sorta hangin' around, an' then they're goin' to take the gold shipment off the *Maybury* an' put it through the Customs, an' that gold is scheduled to go up to London on a special night train. Our English mob have got that all doped out.

"O.K. Now let's get down to real business. When they're stickin' that gold on the train we're standin' off between Selsey Bill an' Chichester. We got the place all charted an' we can stand right in close to the shore.

"Soon after the train leaves Southampton she passes through the right spot, an' then what happens. Well,"—he grins at the joke—"the boys on the other side are goin' to stick up that train. There ain't ever been a train stick up in England before an' they'll be so surprised they'll wonder what's hit 'em.

"The engine driver of that bullion train is goin' to find something big across the track. He's goin' to pull up, ain't he? An' the next thing he knows is that somebody pulled a gun on him. We got forty boys stickin' that train up an' they know their stuff. The nearest signal box will be heisted too an' one of these British palookas who knows his railway stuff is goin' to close the line for traffic.

"We got it scheduled that we'll have the gold bars taken off that train an' shipped into lorries drawn up on a road alongside the rail track inside twelve minutes, and then the lorries are goin' to shoot across country through some place called Havant to the coast. When they get there they signal us an' we stand in an' take delivery of the gold in two launches pullin' collapsible rafts that we're goin' to send ashore.

"We're allowin' fifteen minutes to get that gold aboard, an' then we're scrammin'. Got it."

"By the time the news of this snatch has trickled out the English coppers will be lookin' around for the gold in England. They'll find the lorries left all over the place on country roads where the English mob leave 'em after we've got the stuff. It's a cinch they'll never think that somebody had enough brains to snatch the stuff on to a boat. An' how do you like that?"

How do I like it? I reckon this is a good one, an' it looks as if these thugs can get away with this thing. It looks to me as if this time the Federal Government has played right into their hands by thinkin' that whoever tried to snatch this gold was goin' to do it in the States. This way the fact that this brother of Skendall's—the guy who Rudy smacks over the head with the bottle—shoots his mouth off while he is dyin', is absolutely a help to the mob because it makes the Government take the gold shipment off the original boat an' stick it on the *Maybury* which bein' a slow boat just helps these guys along considerable.

Another thing, what Rudy says about it being easy to snatch the gold in England is right. If anybody wanted to do a stick-up job England is the place to do it, because nobody ever thinks that anybody is goin' to stick anybody else up in that man's country. I don't mean that the English cops are saps because believe me those babies know their stuff, but crooks ain't fools enough to do stick-up jobs in England because although they might pull 'em off they can't get away when they've done the job, the country's too small and the police check-up on the ports, roads, an' airports is too hot.

But combined with the scheme for stickin' up the gold train, closin' the line so that nobody ain't goin' to know what's happenin' before it's all over, gettin' the gold across country in lorries an' then meetin' it with a boat an' scrammin' off with it, is such a darned bit of horse cheek that it looks as if it would come off easy.

The English cops ain't goin' to know the gold's gone. They're goin' to think that some English mob have pinched it an' are stickin' around with it, an' a long time is goin' to elapse before somebody finds out that the stuff's been carried abroad.

An' it looks as if this job's been pretty well organised, an' in this respect anyhow I gotta hand it to Rudy because I didn't know he'd got the brains to organise a thing like that, although I do know that mobs have been workin' together in Europe for a long time an' that crooks are learnin' to be international just as easy as coppers, an' because coppers have to organise against what the crooks do, they got to wait till the crooks do it first, which makes the mobs one jump ahead of the coppers all the time, although they usually lose in the long run.

The only thing that's goin' to worry 'em is when Harberry Chayse finds that somebody's pinched his boat in order to pull a gold snatch. Directly he gets good an' busy an' finds out what has been done this guy is goin' to the cops an' the cops are goin' to get wise. They're goin' to smell a rat an' try to find out what's happened to the *Atlantic Witch*, an' it won't be very long before some bright guy puts two an' two together an' guesses what's been goin' on.

Even this way the Saltierra mob have got a lot of time to make their getaway. They got a fast boat, an' the world before 'em, an' I reckon that there's plenty places they can make an' land the stuff at before somebody starts gettin' the Navy to work.

Altogether it looks to me like a darn good lay-out. I gotta hand it to these crooks. They are pretty good this time, an' it looks as if I'm goin' to hand in my dinner pail this journey.

There's only one thing in my mind. I can't expect any help from nobody. The Feds don't know where I am an' I'm all washed up, but maybe somehow there's just a chance that I can pull a fast one, an' if I have to hand in my pay-sheet an' shuffle off to wherever it is "G" men go to when they're bumped, then I reckon that I'm goin' to try an' take this Saltierra crook with me, and that goes for Carlotta too, because of all the lousy crooks I ever met, an' I've met a few, I reckon I got it in for these two more than anybody I ever contacted.

Well . . . this is where I play along. I look at Rudy, an' I screw up my face as if I was sufferin' great pain.

"I give up," I tell him. "I'm all washed up an' I know it. What's the good of my arguin' with you. You got the low-down on me Saltierra, an' I know it.

"What's your proposition? I'm playing ball."

CHAPTER TEN
PAUSE FOR EFFECT

"OKEY doke," he says. "Well, there it is."

He gets up an' he opens the porthole behind me. Then he motions with his head for me to look out. Outside I can see the Atlantic—just a big sweep of sea stretchin' for miles. It don't look so hot to me neither. It is cold and gray an' sorta clammy.

"I had a swell idea about you this mornin'," he said. "One of the sailor guys on this boat tells me they used to work a big idea on cusses they didn't like in the old days. When a guy got fresh they tied a rope under his armpits, made the other end fast to the stern rail an' chucked him overboard. This guy got dragged through the sea considerable an' every time he was about to fade out through cold or exhaustion or something they pulled him up an' gave him some hot liquor, sorta made a fuss of him just till he felt good again, then they chucked him overboard some more. This guy eventually got tired of this business an' sorta died; but it took plenty time an' it wasn't so hot while he was doin' it. How d'ya like that?"

"I ain't very partial," I tell him. "So what? Where do we go from there?"

He grins. This Rudy looks like a coupla tigers who don't like each other—an' then he gets up.

"I think it's a swell idea," he says, "an' up to the minute that's the idea we got for you, an' you can just stick around an' think about it. Maybe we'll do it to-morrow an' maybe we'll do it the day after, an' maybe we'll start in tonight. In the meantime I'm goin' to move you to a cabin an' sorta look after you—fattenin' you up so's we can get a bigger laugh out of a punk copper who thought he'd got all the brains."

He goes out an' in come the two guys, an' they take me along to some cabin an' chuck me in. They handcuff my hands in front of me this time which ain't quite so bad. Then they lock the door an' scram.

I lie there an' do some heavy thinkin'. But it looks to me like I can go on thinkin' all day an' all night, but it's goin' to take a bit more than that an' a whole lotta luck to get me outa this jam. I reckon that I'm goin' to live just so long until Rudy takes an extra shot of liquor an' thinks that he'd like a little cheap amusement, after which he will start doin' this performin' seal act with me over the stern rail, an' havin' regard to the look I had at the sea it won't be so nice neither—for me I mean.

Then I get to thinkin' just what chance there is of this gold snatch bein' short circuited, an' it looks to me that they got a good chance of pullin' it off, that is if they got the English end of the job laid out as well as they had the other end. The idea about takin' the gold outa the country after they snatched it is swell, because if they go through with the actual pinch without some copper gettin' wise to them, then everybody will think that this gold is somewhere in England. They will never think that it's been taken off abroad pronto.

But there's one way they can slip up. Supposin' Harberry Chayse finds out that somebody's snatched his boat, well, he's goin' to do something about it, ain't he? He's goin' to the Connecticut State police an' it's just possible that they might contact some New York copper who knows about the proposed gold snatch an' links the two things up, but it's a long shot and I don't think there's much chance of it coming off. First of all because there ain't any real reason why anybody should link up the yacht stealin' episode with the gold, an' secondly I reckon that when that gold was stored aboard the *Maybury*, the U.S. Government patted themselves on the back an' told each other that everything was hunky-dory. They ain't goin' to be worried about the stuff bein' stolen on the high seas—that is supposin' they thought that was goin' to be done—because that's the marine insurance people's bother, an' anyhow they have got to know that it has been stolen before they do anything about it.

Altogether takin' everything by an' large it looks as if Rudy had gotta good chance of gettin' away with everything including bumping me off, which he is certainly goin' to do because I know too durn much.

Another thing that is worryin' me is why they worried to get this guy San Reima on the boat. If they was just plannin' to get their hooks on me they mighta known that when I got the letter tellin' me about the seance that I would fall for it an' go down. Well if I do this all they gotta do is to grab me when I get aboard an' chuck me in the calaboose an' wait till the boat's at sea an' then give me the works an' throw me overboard. I do not see why they have to have San Reima on the boat an' go through with all this seance business when every durn guy aboard knows just who killed Willie the Goop, an' is in on the gold-snatchin' scheme.

I lie on my back on this berth lookin' at the ceilin' an' wonderin' about this an' that. Maybe you will think that I am a bit screwy to be goin' on this way when any minute these thugs are comin' in to give me the works, but to tell the truth I have been in some very tough spots before durin' the time that I have been workin' for the Federal Government, an' I've been in jams that looked maybe as hopeless as this one does an' still I have managed to break out of 'em somehow. I'm one of them guys who believes that while there's life there's hope, an' I am therefore goin' to amuse myself while I am still livin', in tryin' to get this thing worked out.

I would like very much to know just what it was that Hangover found out that sent him sky-rocketin' off some place without even tellin' me or givin' me a hint—even if it was all wrong—as to what he was at. I can understand him sendin' me the letter tellin' me about the seance because it looks to me that what has happened is just this:

In the first place Hangover goes along to see Harberry Chayse an' starts talkin' about Willie's bump off. The old man then tells Hangover about this guy San Reima, an' says that if the police don't do somethin' he is goin' to have this seance an' try to find out that way. Hangover probably talks him into sayin' that he will get ahead with this seance business right away an' then dashes off an' writes an' tells me what is goin' to be done. But maybe, soon after Hangover leaves the old man, Mirabelle arrives an' Harberry Chayse tells her the big idea. She probably tells him that it's a lotta punk an' that supposin' this San Reima does put his finger on the murderer—well then what? It's one thing gettin' some prophet to tell you who's bumped somebody an' another thing provin' a charge of murder against the guy that the prophet picks.

Mirabelle probably tells him all this an' maybe either Harberry Chayse believes her an' changes his mind, or else he gets fed up with her planning the scheme an' just tells her that he won't do it or he will put it off so as to keep her quiet, or—an' this looks more likely to me—so as to stop her from askin' to be down there on the boat when it happens, because it looks as if by what I have heard that she an' the old man ain't so friendly as they have been, although what the reason is I do not know.

Alright, well, supposin' that Harberry has planned to go through with the thing, an' it looks as if he had—even if the letter that was written to me was phoney an' he never wrote it—then where is he? San Reima got down on the boat alright. Why didn't Harberry Chayse?

But then again I don't know that Harberry Chayse ain't on this boat. He might be—or maybe they have given him the works on his way down an' he is bumped off an' nobody knows it. It stands to reason that if these guys have gone to the trouble of ironin' out the son they ain't goin' to be too particular about givin' the old man his.

If I am right here there ain't a dog's chance for anybody, because the only person who can start something is Harberry Chayse if he is alive, an' before he does it he has gotta find out that his boat has been snatched, an' he has gotta go to somebody with sufficient horse-sense to tie up the boat snatch with the gold snatch, an' as there ain't nobody except the Feds who know about the gold business, then even that chance looks pretty slim to me.

I lie there thinkin' an' thinkin', but I can't make any sense outa this thing, an' I go on doin' it for five more days an' still it don't make sense.

They treat me pretty good an' they bring me three good meals a day an' some cigarettes, although I gotta admit that every time the door opens I think it is Rudy comin' to tell me that I am to get set for the performin' seal act.

I can't find out a thing, an' the steward—or maybe I should say the thug in the white jacket—who brings in my meals don't say a word when I speak to him. He just grins like he was nuts.

It is somewhere in the evenin' of the fifth day, an' I have just finished eatin', which is a difficult business if you have a pair of steel cuffs on, when the door opens and Rudy busts in. He has been drinkin' considerable an' looks very pleased with everything.

"Well, you big 'G' man, how you makin' out?" he says. "You gotta admit I've given you a very nice little run. How're you feelin' about doin' that stern rail act. It's a nice cold evenin' an' I'd like to hear you howlin'.'"

"Can it, Saltierra," I tell him. "If you wanta get busy, get busy but don't talk so much—you give me a pain in the ear."

"Yeah," he says, "so you're still tough, huh?"

He sits himself down on the opposite berth, an' lights a big cigar.

"Say, you punk," he cracks. "I'm goin' to make a proposition to you, an' if you're a wise guy you'll say yes an' like it. Or maybe you'd like the idea of goin' over the stern here an' now."

"I don't like it," I tell him. "So what's the proposition? I'm listenin'.'"

"Well," he says, "it's this way. I reckon that sooner or later somebody's goin' to discover about this boat bein' gone, ain't they, an' then they're goin' to ask themselves a lotta questions about it.

"Now Carlotta wises me up that some of you Federal dicks are trained in wireless. Does that go for you?"

I nod.

"Yeah," I tell him, "I know wireless, so what?"

"Just this," he says. "If you want to keep some life in your lousy carcass for a coupla days more—well, you can do it, an' here's how. I reckon the day after tomorrow will see this job done an' the gold aboard. Alright, directly we got it we're goin' to stand away from the shore an' run some place—never mind where. Well, here's where you come in. You gotta code number haven't you—your Federal code number. Alright, when we get away with the gold you're goin' to listen in for any wireless that's flyin' about an' let me know what the messages are, an' when you done that you're goin' to send out a radio an' give your code number an' say that you're a prisoner aboard this boat an' that you've bust into the wireless room an' that everybody's so drunk they can't even stand up an' that you heard that we're goin' to make a run for it to Mizantla in Vera Cruz, after which you'll sign off good an' quick.

"It's a cinch that some boat is goin' to pick up an' relay this message, an' in a day or so they will be chasin' after this boat with the idea that she's goin' to the Gulf of Mexico which will lead 'em nicely up the garden."

"An' allow you to make a getaway somewhere else," I say. "Well, I'm fond of livin' an' I'm glad Carlotta got the idea. It's O.K. by me because there ain't anything else I can do. But," I go on, "what happens to me after I done this wireless act?"

"I'm goin' to shoot you like the lousy copper you are," he says, "an' chuck you overboard. But anyway, that'll be quick, or maybe," he says with a yawn, "you'd rather try the flyin' dive act over the stern rail with a rope round your waist."

"No thank you, Rudy," I say. "I never did like water. I'll take the bullet if you don't mind, an' see you shoot straight, else I'll get annoyed with you."

"You're a wise guy," he says. "O.K. Well, that's fixed."

"Just a minute, Rudy," I say. "I've been thinking. I'm a naturally curious cuss an' I was interested in hearin' the story of how you planned this snatch. It looks pretty good to me, but there is one thing that I ain't on to. How did Willie the Goop come in this thing, an' what did you bump him for?"

He grins.

"So you'd like to know," he says. "Well, I reckon he knew too much. Willie the Goop wasn't such a fool as a lotta people like to make out. That was one thing, an' the other thing was he was a bit too stuck on Carlotta for my liking, an' Carlotta's my property, at least she's goin' to be directly I can get her to listen to reason.

"Willie the Goop!" He laughs. "You know," he says, "I'm goin' to tell you something. If I hadn't found out what that guy was up to, you still might have got away with something. Somebody must have opened their mouth," says Rudy, "because it looks like this Willie the Goop was gettin' all burned up about something an' wanted to start talkin'.

"It looks as if he was goin' to shoot his mouth about something, but the mug was silly enough to write a letter to Carlotta to tell her he wanted to talk with her. When I saw that," he goes on, "it looked to me as if the thing to do was to take Willie the Goop outa the way nice an' quiet so that whether he knew something or whether he didn't he'd be safe."

I put on a look of surprise.

"Why, wasn't he in on this job with you, Rudy?" I say. "I thought maybe seein' that he was hard up he was playin' in with you."

He gives a big horse laugh.

"Don't be a mug," he says. "What would we want with a punk like him. He was just hangin' around after Carlotta, that's all."

I do some quick thinkin'.

"Well, ain't life funny?" I say. "So it looks as if he might have come across to Myras Duncan if you hadn't shot him, then we'd have got the lot of you."

He nods.

"Maybe you're right, copper. You'd have had a good chance to anyway. It was just lucky I found him out."

"It was a near thing, Rudy," I say. "Tell me something. When did you make up your mind to bump him, because if he'd had a coupla hours more, the fat would have been in the fire as far as you're concerned."

He grins again.

"You're right, Caution," he says. "It was a pretty near thing. I found out what he was doin' early in the evenin'—about seven o'clock—an' I made up my mind that he wasn't goin' to talk to nobody, an' he'd got to get his that night, an' I gave it to him."

"If I hadn't," he says, lookin' very pleased with himself, "it might have been the other way round. I might have had those handcuffs on right now instead of you."

I don't say a word. He sticks around for a few more minutes gloatin' over me an' tellin' me what a big guy he is an' then he scrams out of it.

I lie there lookin' up at the ceilin' and thinking, because I have got a very very funny idea in my head. I am beginnin' to switch around on all the conclusions that I came to on this job, an' I'm beginnin' to realise what a funny business the whole of this gold snatch thing is because directly I make up my mind on one line of country I find I am all wrong to blazes an' have to start over again.

All along I been figurin' out that Willie the Goop was in on this business from the start an' that he got cold feet at the end an' wanted to shoot his mouth, but now Rudy says that Willie was nothin' to do with anything, an' there ain't any reason at all why Rudy should lie about it because Willie is dead an' it looks that pretty soon I am goin' to be too.

An' it looks as if Rudy didn't know anything at all about Willie until seven o'clock on the night he shot him, which means that that was the time that Carlotta showed him the letter an' told him that Willie knew something.

But at last I have got an idea that looks like it might mean something. Rudy sayin' that the Willie the Goop bump off was not a planned thing, but just done on the spur of the moment, has put an idea into my head that is so big that it almost makes me gasp, an' I am not a guy given to gaspin'.

So I take it easy an' I start workin' this thing out from an entirely different angle, an' believe it or not, everything begins to match up, an' I realise that the cleverest thing I ever did was to come down an' get aboard this boat, from one angle, an' the darndest silliest bit of business from the other, although the way things are now nothin' ain't goin' to be very much use to me.

I told you, way back at the beginnin', at the time when I went back to Joe Madrigaul's place, after I had been released from Police Headquarters the night that Myras Duncan and Willie got bumped, that I sat down there at a table an' sorta got a funny idea. Well, that was O.K., but by itself it didn't tell me a helluva lot, but now I got another idea, one that sorta matches up with the first one, an' if I could get outa this jam I reckon I would do myself a bit of good over this besuzuz.

Nothin' happens until the next evenin', when I can feel that the boat has slowed down considerable an' seems to be sorta hangin' about. It is about ten minutes after the steward guy has taken my tray away when the door opens and Carlotta looks in with a pretty smile playin' over her face. She looks like she has just found a million dollars an' is certainly pleased with somethin'.

With her is the thug in the ship's officer's uniform an' he looks good an' stewed to me. I reckon that they have been givin' themselves a swell dinner an' pattin' themselves on the back about the way this job is goin'.

I am sittin' on the edge of the bunk an' they come in an' look at me.

"Good evenin', Carlotta," I say, "an' how's it goin' with you. What you want around here? Come in to play with the animals?"

She smiles. I have seen some good teeth in my time, but I don't think I ever saw teeth like hers, an' she has a mouth that woulda made temperamental guys go chasin' themselves round in circles.

"Why don't you behave," she says. "I reckon you oughta to be very pleased with me. If it wasn't for me you'd be a shark's meal by now somewhere way back in the Atlantic Ocean!"

"Lady," I say, "you're right an' I thank you from the bottom of my heart. That was a nice little idea of yours about my bein' wireless operator aboard this floatin' thugs' club, even if it was only because it let me live for a few days longer."

"That's O.K. by me," she says, "an' I'll tell you something else. We don't want any screwy business over that wireless act either. All you gotta do is to listen for any messages that are flyin' about in connection with this ship, an' weigh in with 'em good an' quick, an' you can keep your hands off the instrument key until somebody tells you to use it. We don't want any funny business from you, otherwise we can still get tough."

"O.K., lady," I say, "I'm bein' good, but is there any reason why I can't have a little bottle of rye in here, I ain't had a drink to-day, an' I was beginnin' to think I was gettin' in bad with the steward or whoever it is keeps the liquor store aboard this ship. Another thing," I say, "seein' that I'm bein' so good an' behavin' myself so nice, wouldn't you be a little sweetheart an' take these handcuffs off my wrists for just about five minutes. You gotta realise," I go on, "I've had these things on for days an' they ain't a bit comfortable."

"That's all right," she says, "maybe we'll find you a bottle an' I'll check up with Rudy about taking those cuffs off you for a bit, he's the boss around here."

She goes off leavin' me with this other guy, who is leanin' up against the wall lookin' very stewed, I reckon this guy must have drunk gallons. In a coupla minutes she comes back. She has got a little bottle of rye an' some glasses on a tray. She puts this on the table an' then she comes over to me an' unlocks the handcuffs.

I slip 'em off, an' believe me it was a relief.

"You wouldn't try and start anything funny, would you," she says, "just because you've got those bracelets off, because Kertz here has got a gun, an' he can use it."

Kertz looks at me an' taps himself under the left armpit, an' I reckon by the look on his face he'd have paid to have a shot at me.

"Don't worry, lady," I say, "I'm not tryin' anythin'. Now what about a little drink?"

I get up, an' I go over to the table, an' I pour out three shots of rye. She is standin' at the end of the table near the door, an' she has put the handcuff key on the table in front of her. Just in front of me at my end of the table on the right of the tray with the glasses is a story magazine, an' just on the right of that is an ash tray. Now I have gotta big idea in my head. If I can push the ash tray over the handcuff key so that she can't see it, an' I can then somehow manage to get her all steamed up, there's just a chance she is goin' to forget it if she goes outa the cabin in a huff. I know they're goin' to stick the cuffs on me again before they go, but these bracelets are self-lockin'. This Kertz guy is so shot away that he ain't goin' to notice anythin'.

So I start talkin' an' I go on bein' very nice an' quiet an' amiable. I make out that the one idea I have is to play along with these guys so as to keep myself alive as long as I can, an' I start an argument with this Kertz guy about how fast a boat like this can travel. I contradict him an' he gets a bit excited. Carlotta don't take any notice. She is leanin' up against the doorway watchin' both our faces an' smilin'. So it is a pretty easy matter for me to start the magazine movin' with my elbow. The magazine pushes the ash tray an' in about five seconds I have got the edge of the ash tray over the handcuff key. So far so good.

Then Carlotta breaks in.

"Say listen," she says, "why don't you two guys shut up? You don't know what you're talking about, Caution, you're a dick not a sailor, an' as for you Kertz you've drunk so much rye to-day that you don't know whether it's Italy or Thursday. Why don't you two shut up? I'm tired of you."

Here's my cue.

"Oh yeah," I say, "an' I suppose nobody is tired of you, you sour-faced cat. I suppose you think you look pretty good leanin' up against that doorpost, just showin' the world what a swell figure you've got, flashin' them cheap teeth of yours an' generally bein' the little mobsters' pet.

"Listen, Carlotta," I tell her, "I've seen better things than you crawlin' out from under sticks when the spring season starts. You make me tired. It's dames like you who make rats like this"—I point to Kertz—"You're the sorta swell classy baby that makes a cheap mobster like Rudy Saltierra think he's clever an' try somethin' big, but where does it get you? It don't get you no place.

"You're all pattin' yourselves on the back. You're all feelin' good. You think you've pulled a good job. O.K. Well, I'm tellin' you something. You can't win. You bumped off some coppers in New York, you bumped off Myras Duncan—a first-class guy—an' you gave Willie the Goop his. All right, an' you're goin' to give me mine. But I tell you, you still can't win.

"You know as well as I do that the Feds are goin' to get you before you're through. They'll fry the whole durn lot of you."

Her face goes livid with rage.

"An' I'd like to be there when they do it," I say. "I'd like to see them bring you along from the death house with only one stockin' on an' your skirt slit one side so that they can fix the electrode against your bare flesh. I'd like to see 'em strap you in that old chair an' I'd like to see that little whisp of smoke that comes outa the top of the head cap after they've fried you. I reckon if I was there I'd go off an' buy myself a big drink just outa sheer pleasure."

She looks at me like all the devils in hell.

"Go an' put them bracelets on him, Kertz," she says, "an' smack him across the puss for me."

I get up. Kertz pulls the gun from under his armpit.

"Take it easy, feller," he says. "One crack outa you an' I'll present you with a coupla pounds of lead. Put your hands in them cuffs."

I put my hands in the cuffs, an' he clicks 'em shut. Then he puts the gun away an' smacks me hard across the mouth. I fall back on the bunk. As I do so I grab hold of the pillow with my handcuffed hands an' swing it at Carlotta as hard as I can. It hits her. She goes back against the door. She spits out a nasty word at me an'—it works!

Kertz walks outa the cabin laughin', an' she goes after him, slams the door an' locks it.

An' she has left the handcuff key behind.

Chapter Eleven
COLD BATH FOR ONE

I GET back on the bunk, an' I lie there listenin'. There is plenty noise goin' on in this boat. Overhead I can hear people runnin' around, an' I imagine something is now gain' to happen. I stick around like this for about five minutes until I have concluded that neither Carlotta nor this Kertz guy is coming back; that Carlotta has not remembered anythin' about the key.

Then I get outa the bunk an' go over to the table an' I grab the handcuff key from under the ash tray. On the other side of the cabin is a little chest of drawers an' I stick one end of the key in between a drawer an' the framework. By doin' this I can work the key into the lock. I then twist my wrists an' the cuffs open.

I take the cuffs off, then I get a coupla matchsticks outa the ash tray on the table. I break the end off 'em an' I plug 'em down into the handcuff lock. By doin' this I can put the handcuffs on again an' push down the cuff where it fits into the lock so it stays like that an' looks as if it is locked, but with one jerk of my wrist I can get it open. Then I put the key in the cuff of my pants an' get back into the bunk.

I stick around there for about half an hour. Things have quietened down considerably. The *Atlantic Witch* is practically not movin' at all. I can hear the sea goin' plop against her sides. Then somebody unlocks the door an' opens it an' Rudy comes in.

He is all keyed up. His eyes are glitterin' an' I can see his hands tremblin'. It looks like he's had a shot of dope.

"Well, well, Rudy," I say, "I thought you was big enough to go through with it on your own. What's on your mind? Have you had a shot of morphia or been usin' a little nose candy?"

"Shut up, copper," he says, "an' don't get fresh, or you'll get hurt."

He puts his hands in his pocket an' he looks at me. This guy is so pleased with himself that I reckon he thinks he's the Napoleon of crime.

"Now you big punk," he says, pullin' out a gun, "I'm goin' to show you somethin'. I'm goin' to show you organisation. I'm goin' to show you that here is one time when we get you all beat to the works. Get outa that bunk an' walk in front of me, an' one move outa you that ain't legitimate, an' I'll blast your spine in."

"O.K., Rudy," I say, "I always did like watching fireworks. So you're goin' to pull the big job, huh?"

I get outa the bunk an' I walk through the cabin door an' along the passage an' up the companion-way. Rudy is close behind me. In a minute we are on the deck.

An' was it good? After being cooped up in that lousy cabin with the porthole shut for days, to stand out there an' breathe some real honest to goodness air, was worth a million bucks. I look around me. It is a pretty dark night, but nevertheless I can see that we are standin' in about a mile off the coast. I can see white cliffs.

I walk to the side of the boat, put my arms on the rail an' lean over.

"It is a swell night for it, Rudy," I say.

"You betcha," he says, "but it's goin' to be sweller before we're through. I'll tell you how swell it is goin' to be. It's goin' to be swell to the extent of ten million dollars, an' if you wants see how it's done, just watch."

"I am watchin'," I say.

I look at Rudy, an' he is standin' there lookin' all sorta sentimental.

"I always wanted dough," he says, "plenty dough. Pikers money is no good to me. I want the big stuff or nothin' at all."

He looks at me, an' he grins.

"Just think, copper," he says, "if you've got anythin' left to think with, in a month's time you'll be inside fishes' bellies with three slugs outa this pistol in you, an' I shall be way down in South America or maybe Mexico, livin' in a swell white *hacienda* with a dame that is the biggest eye-full you ever saw in your life."

"You don't say," I tell him. "I suppose that's Carlotta? An' so you two guys are goin' to get married, are you?"

He looks offended.

"You bet we're goin' to get married, an' who's goin' to stop us?"

"Well, it won't be me," I crack. "It looks to me I'll be married to a fish by that time. But," I tell him, "don't you think you're goin' to have a good time, Rudy, because you ain't. You an' Carlotta is goin' to have a swell time! Hear me laugh. A coupla cheap killers kickin' around in a white house down in Mexico. Rudy," I say, "you give me just one big horse laugh. The next thing you'll be tellin' me that you an' this little lady love of yours will be gettin' up good an' early in this little white love nest so that you can watch the sun rise, because you love beauty.

"Look," I tell him, "it is pretty easy for you with that gun in your mitt to give me mine, but you're still a punk. An' as for Carlotta, she's about the biggest ache I've ever seen in my life. Listen, unconscious," I go on, "she played around with Willie the Goop, didn't she? An' I bet she took him for plenty. Now it looks like she's transferred her affections to you, an' for what? Just because it looks like you're goin' to have plenty dough.

"An' you think she's goin' on that way, you're goin' to marry her. Well, well, well," I say, "ain't life funny? There's only one thing I wish I could go on livin' for an' that's so's I could stick around an' see the time when Carlotta gets somebody to give you yours, an' get you outa the way. That's when she's good an' tired of you, or maybe when she's found some other guy who has got more dough than you've got. Rudy, you make me sick."

He laughs.

"Aw, shut up, copper," he says, "I don't mind you tryin' to ride me. I've got the upper hand. Carlotta's for me because I'm a big guy, an' you know it."

He looks at me sorta quizzical.

"Maybe you was interested in her one time," he says, "although what chance you thought you'd got with your Federal dick's pay with a dame like Carlotta, I don't know. Anyway," he says, "keep your trap shut. I'm goin' to be busy, an' don't move or I'll give it to you."

I look around. Everybody on this boat is crowdin' to this side of the ship. There is Rudy, Carlotta, Kertz—who seems to be in charge of the ship—an' about twenty-five other thugs, an' believe me Rudy had picked 'em good. They was one of the toughest lotta babies I've ever wanted to see fried.

We stand there waitin'. After about fifteen minutes Kertz gives a yelp.

"Say, there it is, Rudy," he says, "right ahead. Take a look for yourself."

We look where he is pointin'. Way on the cliff top there is a little light. It twinkles, then it goes out. It goes on an' off five or six times, then there is a pause, then it starts again. Then it stops. I have seen a light like that before; some guy has got an electric flash lamp put in one end of an iron tube so it can be seen out to sea but nowhere else.

"O.K.," says Rudy, "here we go, boys, an' make it snappy."

I move, an' as I do so I feel a gun barrel in my back.

"That don't go for you, copper," says Rudy. "You stay just where you are an' don't try anything. Otherwise this cannon's goin' to go off."

About twelve of the crew have run forward. I look after 'em, an' I see already swung out on the davits on the port an' starboard side of the boat are two motor launches. The boat crews divide an' half go into each, an' in a minute the launches begin to drop way down to the sea.

The one on the starboard side starts up, circles back around the back of the *Atlantic Witch* an' eases up alongside the first one.

While this is goin' on some more guys have pulled two collapsible rafts down the deck. They open up these rafts, pump the air
into the sides of 'em an' chuck 'em overboard, an' the motorboat
crews make a raft fast behind each motorboat.

I reckon I have got the scheme. The railway stick-up has come
off. These guys have got the gold. The motorboats an' rafts from
the *Atlantic Witch* are pullin' in to pick it up, an' it looks to me
as if they have got away with this job. This don't surprise me
because I reckon that the only place they might fall down would
be the railway stick-up. Smuggling is pretty easy these days, an'
there's plenty of it goin' on both in Britain an' the U.S. There is
too much coast to be watched an' on a night like this nobody can
see a thing much.

I look at Rudy. I can see that the hand that is holdin' the gun
is tremblin' with excitement. Standin' just behind him is Carlotta
an' on the other side of her is this Kertz. I reckon that I'm goin'
to do something now or not at all.

They're all lookin' towards the motor launches. I drop my
hands, yank the handcuffs open an' spin round. As I do this Rudy
gets it, but he's too late. Before he can do a thing I hit him once
between the eyes an' he goes down like he was poleaxed. I drop
my head an' butt Carlotta I hit her right in the middle good an'
hard. She gasps, bumps Kertz an' they both go over on the deck.

Then before anybody is on to what is goin' on I scram across
the deck an' shoot over the starboard rail. Was that sea cold, or
was it cold? I reckon this is one cold bath I don't like. I also know
that the one thing I must not do is come to the top anywhere
where I can be seen because they will bump me from the deck
pronto, so when I hit the water I turn right an' swim underneath
at a slant till I feel the side of the *Atlantic Witch*. I turn over on
my back, get my nose above water an' push myself down until I
am under the stern.

Up on the deck I can hear bawlin' an' hollerin' going on. After
a minute one of the motorboats that has evidently got rid of the
collapsible raft comes shootin' round thirty or forty yards off the
stern of the *Atlantic Witch*. In a minute I can see the other one
come round the other way. These two launches are lookin' for me,

but those guys have thought what I thought they would think. They thought I am swimmin' towards the shore. They don't think I am such a mug as to paddle about under the stern.

When these two launches are well away from the ship, I swim round the starboard side an' start swimmin' under water towards the bows of the boat. I make it without bein' seen. When I get to the anchor chain I get hold of the chain an' pull myself right down under water with just my nose an' one eye stickin' out. I reckon I am pretty safe here.

After a bit one of the launches comes back an' I pull myself right down under the water to let her pass. I can feel the wash as she goes past me an' I reckon she couldn't have been more than three or four feet away.

These boats are kickin' around for about ten minutes, then I see one of 'em pass me again in the dark an' ease up towards the side of the boat. I think it is time I got outa this.

Hangin' on with one hand to the chain, I get my shoes off, then I do a somersault dive an' get my coat off. My waistcoat is easy. Then I push off. I start swimmin' away from the boat at an angle out to sea, the way I reckon they wouldn't look. In any event they cannot see very far on a night like this. There is a strong tide runnin'. It is runnin' diagonally towards the shore an' I reckon it's goin' to be pretty easy for me to make it when I go that way.

I battle on against this tide until I reckon I have put about a hundred yards between me an' the *Atlantic Witch*. Then I turn over on my back an' float an' go with the tide. It is as cold as an icehouse. I reckon if I ever make the shore I will need thawin' out.

After a bit I turn over an' start swimmin'. I do a strong breast stroke just to keep the circulation goin' an' all the time I am listenin'. I am listenin' to hear the noise of the motor launches, but I can't hear a thing. Then I look back. I can just see the *Atlantic Witch* although she is not showing any light at all, an' I can see a sorta white blob movin' up on her side. I grin to myself because it looks to me like Rudy is havin' the launches pulled aboard again. It looks to me like he has got the wind up.

Do I get a kick outa this? It looks like just because I got away off that boat that Rudy has got the wind up an' cancelled the snatch. I get my head up an' look towards the shore an' I can see the light on the cliffs blinkin' away. Then there is a long pause, then it blinks again, then it stops an' stays that way. It looks to me that these guys ashore on the cliff top have seen that there is nothin' doin', an' maybe they can hear like I can the anchor bein' weighed on the *Atlantic Witch.*

Even while I am swimmin', gettin' mouthfuls of salt water an' feelin' it's lucky there ain't no sharks around England, I am wonderin' just why it is that Rudy didn't go through with that job. He would have had plenty time to get that gold aboard before I could have got ashore even supposin' I made it, which is doubtful, an' got away with it.

After a bit I come to the conclusion that it's no good indulgin' in these reflections. I don't know how far away the shore is. I just go on swimmin'. I don't have to bother about this very much because there is a marvellous tide an' for every stroke I take I can feel myself being pushed two or three. I reckon if the tide had been against me it would have been all over with Lemmy.

The other thing that I am worryin' about is if I do make it, to land some place as far away as possible from these guys who are hangin' about on the shore, because I reckon that the fellers who have got the gold will be down on the beach itself, havin' left some of the mob to do the signallin' business from the cliff top, so while I let myself go with the tide I swim hard off to the right the whole time so as to land as far away as possible from this spot.

I get down to it. I swim like I was a scared fish, still thankin' my stars all the time that the tide is with me, because otherwise, although I have always been reckoned to be an ace at this swim stuff, I do not think that I would ever have made the shore.

But I make it. How long it took me an' what I felt like when I crawled up the foreshore was nobody's business, but I make it.

I look out to sea an' suddenly I see some lights go on. I guess this is the *Atlantic Witch* showing navigation lights an' it look as if she has decided to scram out of it.

I get up an' I start runnin'. I run along the beach until I come to some sorta cut path up the cliff. I'm tellin' you that path is hurtin' my feet like hell, but all I wanta do is to keep myself warm.

But I am feelin' good. I am one up on Rudy, an' I have spoiled his game good an' proper. It is easy to see that directly I went overboard off that boat an' they couldn't find me, that Rudy did some quick thinkin'. He knew durn well that if I reached shore alright an' blew the works about this *Atlantic Witch* havin' the gold aboard that he wouldn't have a dog's chance. He knew that the English police would send out a world wireless an' that the boat would have been picked up in a matter of days. Another thing is that he was reckoning to get stores from some place because I remember that Carlotta said that there wasn't much liquor aboard an' I can't fancy that mob of thugs goin' anywhere without liquor.

Scramblin' up this path I get another big idea: If Rudy has changed his plans, left the gold an' scrammed all because there was a chance of my reachin' shore, then it's a cinch that if I hadn't escaped an' he went through with his original scheme, that he didn't expect anybody would know anything about the *Atlantic Witch* for some time. In other words he coulda sailed that boat up an' down the coast an' nobody would have had any idea that it had the gold aboard. He woulda been as safe as safe.

I get to the top of the cliff an' look around. I can't see nobody or a thing. I look out to sea an' I can still see the ridin' lights of the *Atlantic Witch* gettin' fainter an' fainter. Rudy is surely on the run.

I start walkin'. I go pretty carefully because, although I have landed in a different place to where the signal lights showed, where Rudy was goin' to pick up the gold, still I reckon that some of this English bunch may still be hangin' around wonderin' what has suddenly decided Rudy to cut an' run for it, while they are waitin' around with a ten million dollar steal.

I reckon that they soon sorta get tired of this, an' would begin to worry about the English cops, who, by that time, must be makin' considerable noise about the train stick-up. I think out what they will do. They will stick that gold aboard the lorries or cars or whatever it is they have got an' they will scram with it some place. They gotta have some sort of headquarters somewhere in England where they will scram. Or maybe they will leave the gold somewhere split up an' fix to collect it later when they have found out what all this besuzuz is about.

I start runnin' inland, an' my brain is workin' like an engine. I reckon that I am not through with this gold snatch yet an' that maybe I can still pull a coupla fast ones.

Presently I see a light, an' when I get nearer I see it is a sorta cottage. By this time my teeth are chatterin' an' I am very nearly blue with cold, but beyond this I am alright. Anyhow I am better off the way I am than floatin' about out there somewhere with a coupla slugs in me from Rudy's gun.

I ease up to this cottage an' take a peek through the window at the back. There is some dame an' an old guy playin' patience with a big teapot on a little table at the side. You can always know when you're in England by the teapots. They have 'em around all the time.

I go round to the front an' I start bangin' on the door. Pretty soon the old guy comes out. He looks at me, an' he says:

"You're very wet, aren't you. Have you been in the sea?" Which I think is a good one.

I tell him yes. I tell him that I have fell overboard from some boat, an' I ask him if he has gotta telephone an' if I can use it.

He says sure, come in, an' I go in after him, an' he shows me the telephone in the hall. While I am waitin' for the operator to wake up from a heavy sleep which he is apparently enjoyin', the old lady brings me out a cup of tea which is swell.

After a bit the telephone operator comes up for air, an' I ask for long-distance Whitehall 1212, which is Scotland Yard, an' when I get it I get the information room an' say that I gotta speak to Chief Detective Inspector Herrick—who is the guy who worked with me on the van Zelden case. The guy at the other end says that he ain't there an' what can he do for me, to which I crack back that he can give me some dry pants if he was here, but in the meantime I gotta speak to Herrick an' that if they have heard anything about a bullion train bein' stuck up lately they might like to give me a little service because I can tell 'em plenty, but I ain't talkin' to nobody but Herrick.

This guy takes the number of the telephone I am talkin' on an' says he will ring me back, an' in ten minutes the call comes through an' I hear Herrick at the other end.

Is he surprised or is he? When I tell him that I am Lemmy Caution in a wet shirt talkin' from some place on the coast, an' prove it by tellin' him one or two inside things about our last job together, he nearly has a coupla fits. Then we get down to it. We start organisin' an' I tell Herrick my idea for the break-off an' he says O.K.

We fix that I am to stay in this cottage drinkin' all the hot tea an' anything else I can get my mitts on until Herrick telephones through to the Bognor Police an' gets them to send a car an' some dry pants for me. Then I am goin' straight off to Southampton to a little hotel called the Silver Grid an' stick around until Herrick shows up, an' he reckons that he is comin' down good an' quick.

Now all this sounds very swell to me an' when the old guy comes out I tell him that some friends of mine are comin' around for me, an' he takes me in by the fire an' gives me a blanket an' hot whisky an' more tea which believe me is a very nice thing to have when you are feelin' like a sick fish.

The old dame is a sweetheart too, an' they start to teach me to play three-handed bridge, which woulda been swell if my pants seat wasn't stickin' to the chair the whole durn time.

Just when I am beginnin' to feel like one big sneeze these guys from Bognor arrive. They rush me off to some place near Chichester where I get some dry clothes that don't fit me, some food an' when I say I am feelin' O.K. we go off some more.

It is half-past three in the mornin' when we arrive at this Silver Grid Hotel at Southampton. The guys who run this dump are expectin' me an' they have got a bedroom an' a big fire fixed for me. I have a hot bath an' then get myself into some pyjamas an' a dressin' gown that I get from the manager an' stick around an' wait. At half-past four Herrick arrives with some other guys.

Believe me I am glad to see this guy. If you take a quick look at him you would think he is anything but a copper. He looks like a coal agent or an insurance guy or something. He is a thin fellow, tall, with sorta luminous eyes an' he wears a derby hat right on the back of his head. It always looks to me that the only thing that keeps his hat on his head is his ears. But as a copper he is definitely good.

He don't get excited an' he has got brains. I like this guy.

We get down in front of the fire an' we talk. I tell him the whole business as I see it from beginnin' to end, an' I tell him what I guess is goin' to happen now.

First of all it is a cinch that the gold is still in this country—they have took it off somewhere. But there is one thing that I don't say anythin' to Herrick about, somethin' I am keepin' in the back of my mind just because it looks so big that I wouldn't like to make a fool of myself by blowin' it too soon.

Maybe you are on to it too. It's the thing that I thought when I was scramblin' up that path up the cliffs before I found the house where I telephoned. It is just this an' I cannot get over it. Rudy Saltierra altered his plans an' scrammed out of it good an' quick because I went overboard. In other words he was forced to abandon the gold snatch just when the job was nearly pulled off, just because one guy might manage to reach shore an' know that the boat that had the gold on it was the *Atlantic Witch*.

This is the point an' it makes me think plenty. I reckon that I am not lettin' Herrick down by not tellin' him about this idea I have got in my head, because in any event it just don't matter at the moment.

Anyhow we ain't got anythin' to worry about right now. We reckon the gold is in England, cached in some place where these guys have taken it. Maybe we'll find it, maybe we won't, but I reckon if my ideas come off we've got a good chance an' I reckon we'll find out plenty else besides.

We sit there for two hours plannin' the whole thing, workin' out the story an' our line of operations, an' when we have done this Herrick goes downstairs an' puts in some heavy phonin'. He comes back an' says goodnight an' scrams off back to London. Before he goes he leaves me some English dough an' gives me a police identification pass.

When he has gone I go back an' I stand lookin' in the fire. I reckon this case is the funniest job I ever had, because I have had plenty jobs before that was screwy but never a job where there were so many odd things turnin' up. Lookin' back I see that there has been plenty brains behind this gold snatch. I see that this job has been worked out to the last inch, but even so somebody had to make a mistake, an' it is a funny thing that no matter how clever crooks think they are, they always do make a mistake, an' that's why they don't ever win in the long run, although I ain't sayin' that Rudy an' his bunch ain't going to win out over on this job yet.

Then I get thinkin' about Carlotta. Are dames funny? You're tellin' me. Here is a dame who can sing like anythin', who is a swell looker with a swell figure an' personality. But with all these things she prefers to kick around with a guy like Rudy Saltierra, who is just a thug, an ordinary mobster an' a dope, the usual sorta nose candy king who likes bumpin' guys when he's had a sniff of cocaine.

All of which will show you that dames are strange things. You never know which way to take 'em, but I am wise to one thing. When Rudy told me that it was Carlotta's idea that I should not be bumped off in the first place, but that I should be kept around to receive any wireless messages that came in, an' to send out some message with my code number in it givin' a false destination for this boat; now that was clever. Just at the time I didn't quite see how this idea was goin' to work out for them. Now I do see it.

An' so did Rudy. He knew durn well that if for some unforeseen reason somebody had accidentally seen that gold shipment goin' aboard the *Atlantic Witch* that night, my wireless message pushed out an hour or so later would have mixed things properly for anybody who was lookin' for the *Atlantic Witch*, although— an' I still cannot understand this—if there was nobody aboard the boat who knew wireless they would have a helluva chance of knowin' what I was sendin' out, whether I was sendin' out the right stuff or not, wouldn't they. Maybe they was playin' me for a sucker here. Maybe some guy did know.

Eventually I get tired of thinkin' about this business. I smoke a final cigarette an' go to bed, an' as I have told you before, bed is a very swell place for those guys who like it.

An' I like it!

Chapter Twelve
HOT NEWS

Next morning I sleep till ten o'clock an' then I have my breakfast
brought up, an' order the papers. They are all runnin' something
or other about the gold snatch, but I go for the *Daily Sketch* that
is printin' the report that I have fixed with Herrick. Here is what
it says:

Amazing Gold Robbery.

*Nothing in the annals of the most wild west-
ern "stick-up" romance can equal the story of the amazing and
sensational gold robbery which took place in the early hours of
the morning.*

*Gold ingots worth two million pounds which had been
despatched by the American Government under the Tripartite
Agreement were stolen from the special bullion train which was
bringing the gold from Southampton to London.*

*The train was held up by armed men. The doors of the bullion
train were blasted with the extract of nitro-glycerine known by
criminals as "soup"; the guards were overpowered and the gold
ingots transferred from the train to conveyances of some sort
which were stationed in the neighbourhood.*

*The method employed in this unique robbery shows that the
whole business was planned on a most extraordinary scale. The
rapidity with which the gold was removed from the train indicates that at least fifty men were employed. At the moment—so
excellent was the organisation—the police are without any clue
as to the identity of the railroad robbers or the destination to
which the gold was taken.*

*Chief Detective Inspector Herrick who is in charge of the
case is certain that members of the gang are experienced in railway organisation. The method used to bring the bullion train
to a standstill at a spot some three miles from the Havant level
crossing indicates this.*

*This amazing coup was achieved in the following manner.
The gold train, which was following a special route, was, it is*

calculated, some five miles from the Havant level crossing when two large lorries, one loaded with bricks and the other with heavy iron castings, collided whilst trying to pass each other on the level crossing track. The wheels became interlocked and the lighter lorry was overturned.

The time was one o'clock in the morning and the spot was deserted. The operator in the Havant signals box, realising that it would take some little time to remove the lorries from the crossing, put his signals at "danger," thereby stopping the gold train some four miles away from the crossing.

In the meantime both lorry drivers had disappeared.

During the time that the lorries and debris were being removed from the line the gold train was held up.

The driver of the train interviewed this morning told a sensational story.

I was about four miles from the Havant Crossing, he said, when the signals went against me, and I slowed down. The train had hardly come to a standstill when somebody shouted from the right hand side of the track. Both my fireman and myself looked over in the direction of the shout, and when we turned back into the cab of the engine we saw that a man had climbed on to the footplate on the other side of the train.

He held a heavy automatic in his hand and he ordered us to put our hands up and keep them there, otherwise he said he would shoot us like a pair of dogs. There was no doubt that he meant it. We should neither of us be able to recognise this man again. He was dressed in a long dark raincoat and had a ladies' black lisle stocking pulled over his face with small slits cut for his eyes. This man remained in the cab.

A great deal of noise was going on, and out of the corner of my eye I saw fifteen or twenty men approach the train from the coppice on the right of the track. It was also obvious that a number of men appeared from the other side. Within a few seconds we heard the noise of two muffled explosions, which I now know to have been caused by the blasting off of the bullion car locks with nitro-glycerine.

After about four or five minutes another man, also masked and with a pistol in his hand, appeared and spoke to the first man, who thereupon told us to drive straight on immediately the signals gave us permission; that any attempt to do otherwise would mean our instant death. He then leapt from the cab and disappeared."

A member of the bullion guard, which consisted of several men who were actually in the bullion van, corroborated the driver's story.

We felt the train slow down and stop, he said, but naturally we were not very surprised at this, as we knew that the bullion train was a special and was not taking the usual route. We were astounded when the front near side and the rear off side doors of the bullion van were blown in and several men appeared. They were all dressed in long raincoats, masked and armed.

They told us that the slightest move on our part would mean our instant death. Simultaneously, a large number of men, working in two parties, one on each side of the train, proceeded to shift the gold bars by throwing the boxes out to the track where they were picked up and removed by other men. The whole business was carried out so quickly and efficiently that it had obviously been rehearsed until every member of the gang was perfect in his part.

When the van was cleared, the man evidently in charge of the gang told us that the bullion van would remain covered from the woods on each side of the track, and that any move on our part from the train after they had left would mean that fire would be opened immediately.

A minute after this we heard the sound of heavy lorries being driven away. I made a move towards one of the open doors of the van and was immediately fired at from the side of the track, the bullet missing my head by a few inches and embedding itself in the woodwork inside the van."

This is the first time that a railway hold-up has ever taken place in this country, and it is this fact, together with the efficient organisation and element of surprise, which allowed the raid to be successfully carried out.

Police enquiries in the neighbourhood have elicited little information with reference to the mystery lorries which must have carted the gold away. Unfortunately for the success of these enquiries there is a large amount of night lorry traffic in this part of the country and such members of the public as are awake at that time are unlikely to notice such traffic.

Unluckily also the methods used in this robbery are unique and therefore do not point to being the work of any known criminal organisation in this country.

The police however are confident that the difficulties attendant on the disposing of such a large quantity of gold bars will provide definite clues which will lead to the apprehension of England's first train robbers.

I turn over to the stop press, and I see this:—

Exclusive to the Daily Sketch. Further to Gold Robbery report on page 1, the Daily Sketch learns that Mr. Lemuel H. Caution, United States Federal "G" man, assigned to investigation into a rumour of an attempt being made to steal the gold in America before shipment, escaped in the early hours this morning by jumping overboard from a private yacht stolen in America in which he had been held prisoner, and from which he escaped at the risk of his life.

Interviewed at the Silver Grid Hotel, Southampton, at which he is staying, Special Agent Caution said:

There is no doubt in my mind that this plot to snatch the gold is an international one. I am certain that but for my escape from the 'Atlantic Witch' last night the gold bars would have been by this time on their way to some foreign destination. I am staying on here in readiness to assist the English police authorities if called upon to do so."

Pirate Yacht Abandoned.

The s.s. "Washington Trader," a Trans-Atlantic cargo boat wirelessed early to-day that a yacht answering the description of the "Atlantic Witch" was sighted in the early hours of this morning on fire and apparently abandoned.

This looks O.K. to me, an' Herrick has got his report printed just like we fixed. There is nothin' to be done now except to stick around and wait until he gets a line on something an' wises me up to what is goin' to be done.

I take a stroll around Southampton an' buy myself a suit of clothes an' some other kit with the dough that Herrick has given me, an' I then put a long-distance from a call station through to the U.S. Embassy in London an' report where I am an' get their O.K. to get ahead with the job.

There is only one snag about this, an' this is that the Second Secretary—who is a guy I know—says that I had better get down an' amuse myself by writin' my report for the Director of the Federal Bureau of Investigation which, if you ask me, is a dirty crack, because I do not like writin' reports owin' to the fact that English is not my hot point an' when I do write a report I have a lotta trouble lookin' up dictionaries. Anyhow I say O.K. an' I go back to the Silver Grid.

I get myself a pad of writin' paper an' I borrow a dictionary off the guy who runs this dump, an' I go up to my room an' do I get one big surprise because sittin' in front of the fire with a whisky an' soda standin' by him is Hangover an' what is more he is sober.

He looks at me an' he grins an' waves his mitt.

"So what . . . you big slob," he says. "I bet you didn't expect to see me around here!"

Am I glad to see this guy. I reckon that this is the first time that I have shook hands with him in my life, but I gotta admit I do it. Then we have a little drink together, an' he starts to talk.

"Listen, Lemmy," he says. "I've felt plenty bad about you. I blew in here a couple hours ago on the *Minnetonka*, an' directly I read the papers an' saw that you was stuck here, did I run here or did I? I've been feelin' plenty bad about you, Lemmy, because when I realised that if it wasn't for me you might not have gone down to Connecticut an' got aboard the *Atlantic Witch*, an' when I saw how near you come to gettin' yours from that Saltierra bunch I didn't feel so good."

I give him another drink. "Cut out the soft stuff, baby," I tell him, "an' spill the beans."

"Here's the way it was, Lemmy," he says. "After I left you that night at Joe Madrigaul's place I was keen to get a line on this business—I wanted to pull a fast one on you an' see if I could weigh in with somethin' that really mattered. So I go spielin' around, an' I contact old man Harberry Chayse who is a good old guy, an' he tells me about this guy San Reima who he says has been seein' visions about Willie the Goop's bump-off. After a lotta hummin' around he makes up his mind that he will have this seance aboard the *Atlantic Witch*, which, he says, is what this San Reima wants. He says that the job has gotta be done right away an' that he is goin' to write an' ask you to come along because you are one of the suspects an' he reckons that you know more than you are lettin' on.

"So I get down an' right then I write you that letter tellin' you what he is goin' to do so that you could make any arrangements you wanted because I reckoned that you would be keen on gettin' down on this boat an' seein' what was breakin'.

"Late that evenin' I go to see the old boy again, an' it looks like in the meantime this dame Mirabelle Gayford has been along an' put him right off the scheme. First of all she says what is the good of it, because even if San Reima does put his finger on some guy that ain't evidence in a court, an' secondly she says that Harberry Chayse will make himself look a sap doin' a thing like that. So he says that he ain't goin' to do it.

"He also tells me that just after I saw him he has been on the wire to the Captain of the *Atlantic Witch* an' given him instruction an' that he will get through an' cancel 'em. When he tries to do this he finds out that the Captain ain't there an' neither are the skeleton crew who are supposed to be aboard the yacht.

"I smell that there is something screwy goin' on an' I find that somebody has been callin' all these guys on the telephone an' sayin' that Harberry Chayse wants 'em to report to some place at Long Island to take some other boat out. This stuff is all punk because I know that he ain't done anything of the sort. I get down to Long Island, an' see this Captain who is wandering around lookin' for this boat that don't exist an' I then see that somebody has framed the yacht crew so as to get 'em away from the boat. Right then I put a long-distance call through to you at the hotel an' they tell me that you have already left for Connecticut, so it looks like somebody is pullin' some funny business, because I know that Harberry Chayse ain't been in touch with you or sent you any letter to go down to the *Atlantic Witch*.

"But I'm stuck down there an' I can't do a thing until next morning', when I get along to New York good an' quick an' see the old boy an' tell him what has been goin' on. We grab a car an' we run down to New London like devils was after us, an' when we get there we find that the *Atlantic Witch* has sailed an' nobody knows where or who took her out.

"Then I get it. It looks like the old boy had sent off the letter to Saltierra—the one tellin' him the seance was to be held—an' then got through to him on the telephone an' cancelled it. It looks to me like Saltierra has jumped on to a great scheme for pinchin' the *Atlantic Witch* an' gettin' after the *Maybury*, an' I think that maybe he is goin' to try a little spot of bein' a pirate.

"But suddenly I getta hunch. Supposin' they was goin' to snatch this stuff over here, I think, an' pick it up with the *Atlantic Witch*—which is one of the fastest yachts in the world—an' scram off with it. Well, was I right or was I right?

"I tell all this to Harberry an' he is burned up? An' he is more burned up because he reckons that this business pins everything right on Rudy Saltierra, an' the old guy swears by all that is holy, an' a lot that ain't, that he's goin' to shoot this guy Saltierra like the dog he is because he reckons now that it is a cinch that it was Rudy who shot Willie the Goop.

"So we go back to New York an' when we get there the old guy gets some firm of enquiry agents to give the once over to Rudy's flat, an' they find a letter there, that Rudy has dropped in the fireplace but what ain't burned, settin' out some of the details about this business, an' in this letter is the address of some dump over here.

"O.K. Well now old Harberry starts goin' wild. He says he is comin' over here an' that he is goin' to get hold of Saltierra an' shoot the pants off him. He says he ain't goin' to have no arrestin' an' squared juries or bribery an' this guy gettin' off. He says he is goin' to shoot Saltierra an' nothin' on earth is goin' to stop him, an' do I want to come along an' sorta hold the bag.

"Do I? I ask you. With a story like this breakin'. But the old guy won't tell me what the address is he has got. I don't know where this place is that might be the Saltierra dump over here. Directly we blow in here we hear about this gold snatch an' while I am readin' the paper an' gettin' my land legs, Harberry blows. He scrams. He gets himself a car an' he goes off to London—at least that is what the garage who hired him the auto say.

"Now get this, Lemmy. I reckon that Harberry is goin' up to London an' park himself there for a bit an' then he is goin' to get out after this place he knows about an' try to find Saltierra. If he does he's goin' to bump that guy so sure as my name's Tierney because he sure hates his guts.

"So what? Well, if he goes to London he's got to stay some place ain't he, an' I reckon that he didn't want to lose me, he was just so excited about readin' about that gold snatch an' his boat that he just scrammed off out of it in a hurry. Here's my idea. I go up to London pronto. I find the old boy, because it's a cinch he'll pull up at one of the big hotels an' when I find him I don't leave him until I've got that address outa him. Directly I get it I get through to you wherever you are. How does that go?"

"It's O.K. by me," I tell him. "Listen, Hangover, you scram outa here an' get the first train up. An' you freeze on to that old geyser until you got that address. I'm stickin' around here an' directly you got it you come through to me on the telephone, an' if I could hear from you quick I'd be glad."

He looks at his watch.

"There's a fast train pretty soon," he says. "I'll be gettin' along. So long, Lemmy. I'll be seein' you. We'll be on to this bunch yet."

"You're tellin' me," I say. "An' don't do anything your Ma wouldn't like."

After he is gone I get down at the desk with this writin' pad an' the dictionary an' I start trying to work out this report. I'd like to tell you that I would be plenty happier fightin' with hyenas than writin' out reports because writin' is not a practice of mine if I can get outa it, an' I have often found that the guy who is swell at makin' out reports is not always so hot at the real job. However I gotta do it so here we go:

> *Silver Grid Hotel,*
> *Southampton,*
> *England.*

From: Special Agent Lemuel Henry Caution,
To: Director, Bureau of Investigation,
Federal Department of Justice,
Washington, U.S.A.
Sir,

On receipt of original operation instruction I contacted Special Agent Myras Duncan at Moksie's Cafe Waterfront as directed. Information received from him as to proposed activity regarding gold movement nil. Duncan made an appointment at Joe Madrigaul's Club Select for the same night in order to give me further information.

As you know this was impossible owing to Duncan being shot previous to my arrival. Charles Frene otherwise Charles Chayse, adopted son of Harberry Chayse, was also shot the same night.

After being released by the New York police I returned to Madrigaul's place and effected entry. Evidence found in the club showed that Chayse had been shot by Rudy Saltierra. I was not very interested in this murder at the time as I considered that the Myras Duncan killing was the more important and more closely tied up with the proposed gold attempt. I also realised that it was improbable that Duncan had been shot by Saltierra.

I had previously had an idea as to the probable method by which the Duncan killing had been effected, and I had taken a step to check on this as far as was possible for me to do. The result of my check confirmed my suspicion.

I then created further situations in order to (a) check reactions from suspected killer, and (b) definitely tie up Rudy Saltierra, Carlotta de la Rue and others both in connection with the Myras Duncan Charles Chayse killings, and also in definite connection with the gold attempt. These situations were partially success-ful, and . . .

Just at this minute there is a knock at the door an' when I say come a guy comes in. He is a very nice quiet sorta guy an' he shows me his police warrant that makes him a detective-sergeant, an' he hands me a suitcase an' a letter from Herrick, after which he scrams. I am very glad at any interruption that is goin' to stop me sortin' out words for this Director's report an' so I go over to the fire an' I read the letter from John Herrick that says:

Dear Lemmy,

The arrangements we made have been carried out in detail as follows:

1. Two selected plain clothes men—both good, good shots will be permanently on duty outside your hotel. If and when you go out they will follow you if you are wearing the white silk scarf which is in the suitcase sent herewith. If not they will remain on duty and not bother you.

2. Squad car arrangements as follows: Three squad cars will be cruising in the Southampton District from the time you receive this. These cars will be in continuous touch with the wireless officer at Southampton Police Station. A telephone call from you to him giving the code number 32/B4 will concentrate these cars or any of them at any spot nominated by you. Should operations take you into Sussex the services of a further two cars organised by the Chief Constable of that county may be secured through Southampton Police wireless.

3. After a certain amount of trouble I have got you a Luger pistol. You will find it in the suitcase with two extra clips, only I hope that you won't have to use all the cartridges, and, my dear Lemmy, for the love of Mike, remember that you are now in England, and the Commissioner of Police does not like the countryside littered with corpses—even if the shooting is done by a police officer.

We prefer to arrest them here. If you want anything else you will get all the co-operation you ask for from Southampton.

The Commissioner asks to be remembered to you. He wants to thank you for the stone bottle of applejack you sent him after the van Zelden case was finished. He says it gave him a sore throat.

And I hope your little idea will come off. Personally I doubt it, but then I'm like that.

Yours ever,

John Herrick.

I open the suitcase an' inside I find the white silk scarf, an' also a Luger—like I am used to—with a coupla clips. The gun is in nice condition an' has been cleaned an' oiled which shows you that this John Herrick is a nice guy an' thinks of everything.

Well, I reckon that there is nothin' else to be done but for me to get down with this dictionary an' do some more of this durned report, so I start in again from where I left off:

. . . confirmed some of the ideas I had in the first place. The most important of these operations was in connection with the electrician of Joe Madrigaul's Club—the man Skendall. I suspected this man as being implicated in the Charles Chayse murder as he had obviously given a false alibi for Saltierra on which he secured his release from the New York police. I obtained the address of the man Skelton from Tierney a Chicago crime reporter who was familiar with the Madrigaul customers and staff and who had rendered me assistance in other cases.

I interviewed Skelton the same night and discovered that he was running, assisted by another man, a downtown garage that formed part of the Saltierra organisation. On leaving his place an attempt was made to machine gun me from a car. This attempt definitely proved to me that . . .

I stop again because the telephone in the corner of the bedroom has started ringing an' I am very glad of the interruption. I go over an' it is the Southampton Police callin' to confirm about the squad car organisation an' tellin' me that everything is hunky dory so far as they are concerned.

I say thank you very much an' after this I think that maybe I will go to sleep for a bit because there is nothing like a sleep when you have got to write a report, an' I guess that I must be tired because directly I lay down on the bed I go off like I have never had any sleep before.

"An' do I sleep or do I? I am woke up by the telephone ringing. It is ringing like hell an' when I open my eyes I see that it is dark an' that the fire is nearly out.

I jump up an' switch on the light. On my way to the phone I look at the clock on the overmantel an' I see that it is eleven o'clock. It looks like I have done some good sleepin'.

I grab the phone. An' do I get a kick? It is Hangover.

"Listen, buddy," he says, an' I can hear the excitement in his voice. "It's in the bag, Lemmy. I'm getting that address in an hour. Now get this. Here's what you gotta do. Meet me at twelve-thirty tonight at Felden's Garage. It's way out on the Botley Road. It stands fifty yards off the road. It ain't used now, it's been shut up for a year or so. I'll be along there at that time an' I'll bring the address with me an' give you the rest of the dope. So long, Lemmy, an' don't forget. Felden's Garage on the Botley Road at twelve-thirty."

"Right, sweetheart," I tell him. "I'll be there with bells on. Good work, Hangover, we'll make you a chief of police yet."

He don't say nothin'. He just hands me a raspberry over the telephone and hangs up.

CHAPTER THIRTEEN
CURTAINS FOR ONE

I RECKON that now things will be brightenin' up a bit because it looks like I was not very far wrong in my guess that Rudy's English boy friends would cache this gold somewhere around the neighbourhood.

It stands to reason that these guys, expectin' to put this gold aboard the *Atlantic Witch*, are goin' to be taken by surprise when the boat scrams off. It also looks a cinch that they musta had some organisation for hiding the gold supposin' that something went wrong between the time they stuck up the train an' the time they got the stuff down to the beach; an' in this case they would have some dump somewhere around a place like Southampton, where they could organise to get it away somewhere else if anything went wrong with the first scheme.

An' Hangover's message makes me think I am right about this. I reckon if he wants me to meet up with him at this garage place on the Botley Road then he is selectin' this spot because it is not too far from the address he has got from Harberry Chayse.

I give myself a cigarette an' I think out how I am goin' to handle this proposition. After a bit I am all set on this job. I call through to the Southampton Police an' I tell 'em that I want all the squad cars that they have got available to concentrate about two miles down the Botley Road beyond the garage. I want these cars to patrol around an' check up on any car movements in the neighbourhood. But they are not to let themselves be seen. They gotta lie low an' just report on what cars are movin' around' an where they are goin' to.

I say that if they see anything that looks excitin' around the neighbourhood they are to get through to Southampton police so that the police headquarters can send out any message that looks useful over the radio.

I then ask to have a police car fitted with a radio—for me to drive myself—sent around to this hotel in time to get me out to this Botley dump at twelve-thirty, after which I lie down some more because I am a big believer in havin' a rest when you can.

I get up pretty soon an' go downstairs an' see that the car has arrived. I send the guy who is in it away because I have got an idea that I am goin' to see this thing through on my own. Then I find out just where I have got to go an' just where this deserted garage place is.

After which I go upstairs an' stick the Luger in my pants waistband, an' I give myself a whisky and soda an' I go down, without any white scarves around my neck, an' get in the car an' drive off.

Drivin' along I get to considerin' the different angles on this job an' tryin' to work things out the way they might go from now on.

Life is a funny thing, an' all the things a guy thinks is goin' to happen don't always break. It looks to me that when you work something out, fate—or whatever it is that fixes the works—makes a point of arrangin' that something entirely different pops up. An' what can a guy do?

Pretty soon I am well away from Southampton an' on this Bodey Road. It is pretty deserted an' I drive not too fast keepin' my eye skinned for this garage place.

About ten miles down the road I come on it. It is a frame building, two storeys high, standin' well off the main road in a sort of clearin' amongst some trees. It looks as if there was a sort of in-an'-out drive off the main road to this place when it was workin', but now the grass has grown over the tracks an' the garage looks like it is standin' in the middle of a clearin' with a thick coppice of undergrowth an' trees at the back.

I pull the car on to the grass an' drive it into a dark patch by some trees well away to the left of the garage. Just as I do this the radio comes through an' I hear the Southampton Police talkin'.

"Southampton Police callin' squad cars," says the message. "All cars are now concentrated fifteen to seventeen miles down the Botley road. They are coverin' all exits from the road leadin' to main an' secondary roads. Up to this time there is nothin' to report."

I scram outa the car an' start walkin' towards the garage. The clock on the car dashboard tells me that it is five an' twenty past twelve an' I reckon that I am a bit early so maybe I will take a look around.

I go up to this garage place by the back way. There is a door at the back an' I go through. I find that I am now on the main garage floor. The big doors leadin' through the front way are closed, but there is a big shutter on one side open an' the moonlight is comin' through so that I can see pretty well.

There ain't anything to be seen except some old junk lyin' about this main floor. Away on the right hand side at the far end of the garage there is an inclined run leadin' up to the floor above. This is so cars can run up, an' I walk up this an' find myself on a first floor that looks like it has been used for a workshop. There is glass windows here, an' although they are dirty there is enough light comin' through to show me that there ain't anybody or anything here.

In the right hand corner on this floor, matchin' up with the floor below is a flight of steps leadin' up to the top floor which, I reckon, was probably the offices in the old days.

There ain't a sound to be heard. I go over to the window an' I look out on to the main road which is about sixty yards away. There ain't a thing there, but the moonlight is lightin' up this road an' I reckon I can see when Hangover arrives, because it is a cinch that he is comin' from some place in a car.

I wait for another five minutes but nothin' happens. Then I think that maybe I will walk down to the ground floor an' out on to the road an' have a look-see if this guy Hangover is anywhere around, because I reckon that if he said he would be here at twelve-thirty he would be here, an' I ain't feelin' too good about stickin' around just at this time.

So I walk across the floor an' start walkin' down the runway that leads down to the ground floor, an' I have just got to the bottom when I hear a noise.

This noise comes from somewhere outside an' it sounds like some guy pullin' up a car an' putting a squeaky handbrake on. I scram over to the door at the back of the garage, an' I go out an' take a look, but I cannot see anything, an' although I wait around there for two-three minutes nothin' happens.

I go back into the garage an' I decide that I will walk over to the front wall an' look out where one of the big doors is a bit open. I am walkin' across the floor when suddenly, right outa the darkness, comes the pop of two quick shots.

I spin around. I look across the garage, an' I see Hangover staggerin' down the runway from the floor above. I can see that he is hit bad. He is holdin' one arm across his body. As I look he drops a gun he is carryin'. The gun bounces over the side of the runway an' falls down on to the main floor.

He sorta looks after it—stupid—just like a guy looks who has been on the liquor for about three weeks. Then he staggers back from the edge an' bumps himself against the wall. His hat falls off. He stands there lookin' at it just as if he'd never seen a hat before.

Then he stands sorta wavin' about an' lookin' after the gun, an' then he takes a step forward an' slips. He falls over the edge of the runway an' flops down to the floor after the gun. He is lyin' there on his face an' as I run over to him he turns over an' starts crawlin' towards the gun which is about four feet away.

I walk over to the gun an' pick it up an' put it in my pocket.

"Take it easy, kid," I tell him. "I'll be back in a minute."

He grins.

"Yeah?" he says. "Maybe you'll be too late. I'm handin' in my checks, Lemmy. I'm goin' home."

"You don't say," I tell him. "So what do I do? Get excited? The only thing that's wrong with you is that you oughta died before you was born. I'll talk to you in a minute."

I scram out through the back door an' race around to the front of the garage.

I am just in time to see a gray racin' car shoot off down the road. I reckon that I am not worryin' very much about this car because it is a cinch that the squad cars are goin' to pick this up.

I go back into the garage. Hangover is lyin' where I left him. I pull him up against the side of the runway an' prop him up there. He looks pretty bad. I feel in his pocket an' find his usual flask an' I prise open his mouth an' give him a shot of his own liquor.

There is an old wooden box around on the floor an' I get this an' sit down. I sit there watchin' him. I reckon that there is durn little to be done for him. One bullet has ripped right through the guts an' the other has plugged clean through the chest. I reckon that it is a matter of minutes.

After a minute he opens his eyes an' looks at me an' grins.

I slip him a little drop more out of the flask. I wanta keep this guy alive as long as I can.

"Well, copper," he says, sorta husky, "how're you goin' . . .?"

I look at him.

"Listen punk," I tell him. "You're goin' home, ain't you? Ain't you made enough trouble, Hangover? Why don't you come clean? That was a sweet job the way you shot Myras Duncan."

He grins some more.

"How'd you know I done it, Lemmy?" he says. "I thought that was a nice job. I thought I'd got you beat that time. You know, copper," he goes on, "I'm beginnin' to think you're smart. Howd'ya find out I shot Duncan."

"Don't be a mug," I tell him. "I ain't dead from the neck up. Didn't I tell you the first night at Joe Madrigaul's to go an' put that call through for me to Moksie's dive? Well . . . what did you do? You passed two empty telephone booths on your way to the one at the end of the passage. What did you wanta go to the one at the end of the passage for, when you could see that it had an 'Out of Order' notice on the door? I'll tell you why. Because you wondered why the hell somebody had put that notice on a booth that had a stiff in it. You just had to see if anybody had been to the booth, an' if the body was still there. If you hadn't known about Duncan bein' shot you'd have gone into the first booth you come to. You shot him just before I come in.

"I didn't get it at first, but I got it when I went back to Joe Madrigaul's that night an' checked up that Rudy had shot Willie the Goop. Then I knew you was playin' along with Rudy.

"You ain't a good crook, Hangover. You oughta stuck to crime reportin'. I had you again when Rudy tried to have me machine-gunned the night I went down an' beat up Skendall. Nobody knew that I was goin' down to Skendall's but you—you was the guy who gave me the address—an' Rudy couldn't have had me followed because I'd altered my hotel—none of you knew where I was. It musta been you blew the works to Rudy an' you gave yourself away doin' it.

"You're all washed up an' you're through. Why didn't you have more sense. Ain't you ever heard of guys who play around with the mobs an' get sucked in an' get theirs—the way you have?"

He gasps a bit.

"Aw shut up, copper," he says. "You're smart, but they'll get you too. I ain't the only one who's winnin' some lead over this. They'll crease you, Caution."

"Okey doke," I say, "maybe they will. Maybe they'll get me. That's alright, I'm drawin' down pay for bein' bumped an' if I don't get bumped then I'm lucky. But I'm tellin' you one thing, before I'm through with this besuzuz I'm goin' to get my hooks into some of them hot pertato palookas that is doin' the big ironin' out acts, an' maybe with a bitta luck I'll get them before they get me."

He groans. Then he opens his eyes again.

"Aw, hooey," he says, "you're all washed up, they'll get you first, copper. You don't know nothin'."

"Shucks," I tell him. "Listen, Hangover," I go on, "you ain't got much time around here, why don't you spill it? Come clean. Where do we go from here? You know what's goin' on around here an' so do I. But maybe you can help. Talk . . . an' talk fast."

He grins again—this time very weak.

"Be your age, Lemmy," he says. "I ain't talkin'. You got the low-down on me, that's all, but I ain't talkin'. You find out for yourself . . ."

His voice sorta tails off.

I lean over him.

"Listen, you goop," I say. "Who gave it to you. Who shot you? Come on . . . wise me up. . . ."

He opens his eyes again. They are startin' to glaze over. "She done it," he whispers . . . "that durn Carlotta . . . that Poison Ivy . . . the . . ."

He goes out.

I close his eyes an' I straighten up. You could have smacked me down with a piece of fluff. So Carlotta had been around an' ironed this guy out . . . she done it . . . !

I stand there just for one minute thinkin', an' then do I whizz or do I? I rush outside an' I start up the car. I run her on to the road an' I put my foot down an' I go down this Botley Road like all the devils in hell was bein' paid overtime to get me.

All the time I am listenin' to see if any police wireless is comin' through, an' after a minute I hear it, an' is it music?

"Southampton Police callin'." it says. "The gray Cadillac racing car that proceeded down the Botley Road some ten minutes ago is behaving in a strange manner. This car drove for five miles at high speed, then checked down to fifteen miles an hour for two miles, then accelerated to fifty for three miles. It is now proceeding straight down the road at a rate of about twenty-five miles an hour."

I put my foot down an' I whizz. I have got it! At last I have got it! All this time I have been guessin' around the place an' I am the biggest punk detective that ever signed a contract with Uncle Sam.

I am goin' at about seventy an' this car can certainly run, an' not knowin' the road I have one or two near twists, especially as I am drivin' on the left of the road, a business that I am not used to.

Pretty soon I catch up. Way ahead I can see the rear lights of the car I am chasin'—the gray Cadillac. I check down an' take it easy. As the car in front of me goes round a bend half a mile ahead, one of the squad cars shoots out a side turnin'.

I pull up. Inside is Herrick.

"Well, baby," I crack at him, "it looks like I am right, don't it. Just stick behind me but not too close, an' if I break in some place don't rush anything. Just stick around until I ask you to do something about it."

He grins.

"Alright, Lemmy," he says. "It's your funeral!"

I put my foot down some more. When I get round the bend I see the gray car about the same distance in front of me. It slows down an' I do the same. Then it pulls off the road, an' eases in among the trees, an' I can see that it is makin' for some house that stands about a quarter of a mile off the road, in a sorta park.

I go down the road for about another quarter of a mile an' then I pull off the road over the grass at the side. I drive the car in an' out amongst the trees, gettin' nearer to this house, an' when I am close to the wall that goes around it I pull up.

Twenty or thirty yards from me, pulled up by a gate in the wall is the gray car, standin' there with its lights out.

I ease over to it. It is empty, but there is a woman's glove lyin' on the drivin' seat. I pick it up an' smell it. I get the perfume at once. It is Carlotta's glove an' the scent is the same as I sniffed when I was turnin' over her dressin' room at Joe Madrigaul's.

I grin to myself.

"I got you this time, Poison Ivy," I say.

I search this car as well as I can in the dark. I poke my fingers all over it but I cannot find a thing, an' after a bit I go back to my own car an' sit down an' proceed to have a meetin' with myself. It looks to me that there has gotta be some very fast work from now on.

I am worried because I am tryin' to do two or three things at once. First of all I reckon that I have gotta get my hooks on this gold which is the thing I am paid to look after an' at the same time I am hot to get in an' mix in with this Carlotta.

I am also annoyed with myself that I did not run the rule over Hangover before I left him lyin' in the garage; not that I expect that any guys have been around there since I left, but it looks like I have got to get back there, which means more time, an' I reckon that time is goin' to be good an' precious from now on.

I start up the car; turn around an' get back on to the road. There is a bit of moon comin' up, an' the English countryside is lookin' swell. Once I get on to the road I drive like I was nuts back to the garage.

While I am speedin' along I am thinkin' about this act that Carlotta has put up while she was drivin' the car after she left the garage. I reckon she was doin' this act—drivin' fast an' then easin' down so as to give me time to catch up with her—so as to draw me on into the house, where I reckon that there was goin' to be swell reception committee to meet me, a committee that is liable to fill me so fulla lead that I would sink in a reservoir even if I was wearin' a cork suit. I gotta hand it to this dame Carlotta that she has gotta a wow of a nerve.

Well I am not goin' to show up for a bit. I am not goin' to show up there until I have fixed one or two things that I wanta fix, because I am havin' a sorta bet with myself that I am goin' to clean this job up tonight good an' plenty so's it stays cleaned up.

I come to the garage. I leave the car just off the road an' I walk over. I lamp around first just to see that there ain't any other guys hangin' around waitin' to iron me out an' then I go in.

I go in the back way an' I ease over to where I left this guy Hangover lyin'. The moonlight has shifted some an' the place where he was is dark an' in the shadows now.

I switch on the flash an' look around. He is still lyin' there propped up against the side of the runway like I left him, an' it looks to me that he is grinnin' a little bit like he knew he had still got me guessin'.

I go over him. I search through the linin's of his coat, an' everything else. I walk up the runway an' pick up his hat where it has fallen off when he was staggerin' about, an' I rip out the linin' an' see if I can find anything there, but there is just nothin'.

I reckon that I am beat, but I think that maybe there is just a chance of somethin' being in the office place right at the top, the place he musta been hidin' in when I went upstairs to the first floor.

I go up the runway an' across the floor an' up the stone steps to the top room, keepin' the flash lamp shinin' on the ground in front of me.

I get to the top room. It is dark an' damp. Way over in the corner I can see a sorta bench an' there is something on it. I go over an' look—it is a pair of gloves—new ones.

By the side of these gloves is an empty .38 automatic shell. I take the gun outa my pocket—the one Hangover reckoned to use on me, an' I check up on the clip. There is one shell missin', an' I reckon this is the one an' that he cleared it from the gun while he was waitin' for me.

Then I look at the gloves. He didn't use to wear gloves but maybe he was thinkin' of fingerprints. They are new an' when I turn 'em inside out I get one helluva kick because stamped inside is the name of "Greenes, Gentlemen's Outfitters, Romsey."

Maybe this will give me what I am lookin' for.

I scram down the steps an' down the runway on the floor below, outa the garage, an' back into the car. I drive down the road until I come to a side turnin' with a signpost which says that it is the way to Romsey, an' I start doin' some more heavy drivin'.

I do not see anything of the squad cars an' I do not particularly want to because I reckon that if Herrick does what I have asked him to he will hang around the place where Carlotta was doin' the big act, an' will stay there until I show up like I told him. Maybe I am a mug to be doin' this because perhaps I would like some of these boys around pretty soon, but I am a guy who is used to workin' by himself an' I get all jittery if there is a lotta flatfeet hangin' around me when I am tryin' to work.

Another reason I have for wantin' to be solo is that some of my methods are inclined to be a bit tough, an' I have got an idea that these English coppers are not so pleased with any strong-arm stuff, but I have found very often that the best way to make some guy talk quick an' plenty is to smack him down first of all an' then start gettin' nice with him afterwards. All the guys who don't believe in force are the guys who cause all the trouble in the long run because there is only one way to deal with mobsters any place in the world an' that is with a good sock in the puss in a quiet corner.

On the outskirts of this Romsey place I pull up. I pull up because I see a white cottage with some arms over the door an' Hampshire Constabulary written on it. I get out an' start bangin' on the door—there bein' no bell—an' after about five minutes of this some guy sticks his head outa the window upstairs an' says what do I want an' what do I think I am doin' anyhow at this time of night.

This guy is the Hampshire Constabulary an' I reckon that if I tell him what is really goin' on around here he is probably comin' down to start something which I do not want started, because I have found that if you tell people the truth they will very often not believe you.

I say that I am an American who has just arrived at South-ampton, an' I am lookin' for an uncle of mine who has taken a place somewhere around here near Romsey an' I thought that maybe he could help me because it is a matter of life or death if I do not connect this uncle.

This copper is a good guy even if he is a bit rural, an' he puts some pants on an' comes downstairs an' does a big head scratchin' act an' goes into a huddle with himself. Durin' this process I slip him a pound note an' after a bit he remembers that there is a distinguished lookin' guy has taken a dump called Playne Place, which is a nice sorta house about four miles off. He tells me where this house is an' how I get to it.

I then ask him if the guy who has taken this house is doin' any furnishin', because I reckon my uncle would be doin' a spot of furnishin', an' the copper says that this is funny because this is just what is goin' on, an' that there is a lotta stuff stored at some other dump a mile or so from Playne Place in a farmhouse which has been for rent, an' which has been hired to store this furniture which is now bein' moved.

I getta big kick outa this because it looks as if I am strikin' somewhere around the right alley. I then get the whereabouts of this farmhouse outa this guy an' slip him another pound note an' then I tell him that I have left my brother—by the name of John Herrick—waitin' for me at the Southampton Police Station an' that I would take it as a great personal favour if he would put a call through to the Southampton police an' ask them to tell my brother John Herrick that I am goin' to the farmhouse an' that I would be very pleased if he could cash around there in about an hour's time from the time he gets the call.

I reckon that this way the Southampton police will send out a radio an' Herrick will pick it up an' will send out one of the cars to hang around this farmhouse an' await instructions which is what the poets would call a comfortin' thought.

I then say good-night to this guy an' step on it some more.

Pretty soon I come to a fork in the road, an' away up on the right I can see the farmhouse, which is a long flat sorta buildin'. I stick the car in the hedge an' I do not walk towards the farmhouse. I walk straight up the road in front of me for about a quarter mile an' then I turn right across the fields an' start workin' around slowly towards the back of this dump.

When I get near it I feel pretty pleased, because outside in the yard at the back I can see a big lorry, an' when I get near I can hear the engine runnin'.

I keep in the shadow of the hedge an' I get up good an' close. There are three guys carryin' stuff out from the back of the farm an' loadin' it up on this lorry.

I wait my chance an' scram across the yard until I am behind a tool-shed where I can watch easy.

After a bit they get through with this job. One of these guys gets up in the driver's seat an' switches on the drivin' lights. This leaves two, an' one of 'em gets in the back of the lorry an' the other guy closes up the back an' stands there while the lorry starts to move off.

It drives outa the yard away around the front of the farmhouse on the fork road, an' this guy stands there watchin' it. Then after a bit he sticks his hands in his pants' pockets an' moves towards the door at the back.

He is whistlin' to himself an' he seems very happy. He goes past the end of the shed—which is a sorta lean-to place against the wail—where I am hidin' an' just as he passes me I let him have it.

I smack him one short sharp yudo clip just where the neck joins the bottom of the skull an' he goes down like he was pole-axed. I grab hold of him by the collar an' I drag him across the yard into the field beyond. There is a sorta ditch there an' I chuck him in this an' just sit around an' wait until he comes up for air.

Pretty soon he starts movin' an' I yank his head up an' pinch his nostrils until he is beginnin' to remember who he is. Then I pull out the Luger an' I show it to him.

"Listen kid," I tell him. "You an' me is goin' to have a nice little quiet talk without any interruption. An' you be good an' do your stuff otherwise I am goin' to paste seventeen different kinds of hell outa you.

"Now what are you doin'? Are you talkin' or are you talkin?"

He looks at me, an' he looks at the gun. Then he rubs the back of his neck an' says he is talkin'.

Chapter Fourteen
RUB OUT FOR THE BOSS

I GIVE this guy just a few minutes to sorta get a hold of himself an' then I tell him to take it nice an' easy an' just concentrate on what I am sayin'. I also tell him that if he don't come across with what I wanta know then I am goin' to give him the works.

He thinks this over an' comes to the conclusion that he is goin' to play ball with me, an' I then go over him an' find that he has gotta .32 Spanish automatic in his hip—one of them guns that when you squeeze the trigger either shoot the other fellow or explode an' blow your nose off, you're never certain which—an' I take this off him an' we are all set for the convention.

I ask him if he ever met up with a guy called Hangover an' he says yes he knows this guy an' that he was around early that mornin'. He says he don't know very much more about this because he is not the big guy on this job, but that the boss is way back in the farmhouse an' will start gettin' good an' burned up if he does not show up pretty soon.

He also says that the boxes they are loadin' are the gold boxes alright, an' that they arrived there the night before. He says that they are bein' moved to this Playne Place, an' that he does not know what is goin' to happen to them after they are handed over there. He says that the guy at Playne Place is a guy called Melford an' that he seems a very nice sorta cuss.

I ask him how much of this gold has gone over an' he says that there is only one more lorry load to go an' that the lorry will be back for it, because they are only usin' the one truck.

He says that they are workin' as fast an' as quiet as they can because there has been a slip up over this business owin' to the fact that the gold was supposed to be put on to some boat, but the boat scrammed off an' the English mob is not feelin' so good about things, they havin' done their job an' not wantin' to do very much more about it.

I next ask him what he is gettin' outa this an' he says they are all drawin' down the same, two hundred an' fifty pounds English money, an' that they are collectin' tonight from the guy Jack Marpella who is runnin' the English crowd who are workin' in on this thing.

I ask him about this Marpella palooka an' he says that he is plenty tough an' has gotta helluva record on this side.

I ask him some more stuff but it is stickin' out a foot that he don't know much more; that he is just one of the crowd who have been pulled in on this business.

"Alright, baby," I crack at him when he is done spielin'. "Now you get up an' walk back nice an' quiet an' get on with the loadin' business. But you don't go back into the farmhouse. Just go an' hang about in the yard an' whistle until that truck comes around again, an' remember this that I am stickin' around an' that I am goin' to keep you somewhere on the end of my gun sight, an' that if I see one screwy move outa you then I am goin' to give it to you good an' quick so's you'll be playin' angels' harps pronto. Now scram!"

He scrams an' I go after him. I watch him go back into the yard, an' as he gets there some other guy comes outa the farmhouse. This guy is a big sorta feller an' stands around like he was a big noise.

I work around until I get back in the shadow of this shed that is in the yard an' I stand there an' watch this pair. They stick around talkin' until they hear the noise of the truck comin' back.

It comes up the fork road an' backs into the yard an' then two more guys come outa the house an' they start loadin' it up. I notice that the guy I have been talkin' to is clever enough to keep himself well in the middle of the yard an' not try any nonsense.

Pretty soon they start takin' it easy an' I conclude that they are pretty near through. I ease away from the end of the shed an' begin to work along the farmhouse wall in the direction of the road. This way I reckon that the guy will still think that I am there an' will let everything go through like we arranged.

In a minute I get on the road an' I slip down it for about fifty yards an' then stand up behind some tree. Two three minutes afterwards the lorry comes down from the yard an' runs on to the road. I see that there are two guys up on the drivin' seat an' I reckon that maybe there will be one or two more on the back.

But I reckon that if the Hampshire Constabulary guy put the call through like I told him for John Herrick, then there is goin' to be a squad car operatin' somewhere around here an' with a bit of luck maybe this car will be near enough to give me a hand if I should want it, although I am not worryin' a helluva lot about these guys because I have been told that these English crooks are not so hot on shootin' people owin' to an old-fashioned habit that they have got in this man's country of hangin' killers pronto, which is one of the reasons that an English copper can get about his business without bristlin' with cannons all the time.

By this time the lorry is justa few yards from me an' I hear the driver change gear. I yank out the Luger an' I put a coupla shots through the near-side drivin' lamp which apparently causes the guy drivin' the truck to be surprised because he slows down an' I then step out into the road an' do a big stick-up act.

I walk up to the lorry an' I tell the two guys to get down into the road. I also tell 'em that if there is anybody in the back who wants to start somethin' they had better get busy because I am goin' to blow the pants off anybody as soon as look at 'em. They have a look at me an' evidently believe that I mean it because they come down an' in a minute some other guy comes around from the back.

Right now I hear a car comin' an' before anything can happen a squad car shoots round from the main road an' eases up, which shows me that Hampshire Constabulary has done his stuff an' that Herrick is on to my scheme.

I line these three guys up beside the truck.

"Bozos," I tell 'em, "the game is bust wide open, an' I got an idea that some of you palookas is goin' to have a rest cure. So just take it nice an' easy an' don't do anything we wouldn't like."

The squad car now unloads three coppers who tell me that Herrick has told 'em to hang around an' I hand these three guys over to them an' tell 'em to take 'em back an' hand 'em over to Herrick. I also ask 'em to apologise to Herrick for the way I am runnin' this business, but that I reckon that it is handled best this way, because it is goin' to save a lotta trouble to all concerned.

They say that is O.K. by them, an' I ask 'em if they will get Herrick to hang around somewhere near the dump where Carlotta ran in with her gray Cadillac, an' that I have got an idea I will be along to see him pretty soon, an' that he an' me can then go places together an' get some real work done.

One of these coppers says what am I goin' to do about the truck, an' I tell him that I am lookin' after that bit of business myself an' that they can leave it to me, an' that if all goes well an' somebody don't take my measure for a casket then I will be seein' 'em. I then find out from the driver who is lookin' like a sick hyena where this Playne Place is an' he wises me up. After which the cops pack these guys aboard an' scram with 'em.

I get up into the drivin' seat of the truck an' I start her up an' I drive down the road. When I get on to the main road I can see this Playne Place, standin' back in some grounds with a carriage drive.

The gates are open an' I drive in an' stop the truck in front of the door.

Some guy comes outa the darkness by the doorway an' calls me up.

He asks me what the so-an'-so I think I am doin' an' why do I not drive the truck around to the back of the house. I tell him that I will show him why, an' he waits while I get down from the drivin' seat. I have got the Luger in my hand which he cannot see an' I make out that I am goin' to tell him something an' as he looks at me I smack him down with the Luger. He flops an' I then drag him to the side of the porch an' leave him there because I reckon that he won't trouble me for a bit an' that if he ain't got concussion he oughta have.

I then stick the Luger in my hip pocket an' I take out the Spanish automatic I took off the guy way back at the farmhouse an' I work it up my right sleeve so that if anybody wants to start something quick I can pull a fast one myself, an' I then walk around the front door an' ring the bell.

I wait there for two three minutes an' then a big guy dressed up like a butler comes to the door an' says what do I want an' I tell him that I want to see this Mr. Melford an' I want to see him pronto because the matter is a very pressin' one.

This palooka stalls around for a bit an' says that Mr. Melford is a very busy man, an' that right now it is very improbable that he can see anybody, an' I say that is a very tough thing because if he don't produce this Mr. Melford good an' quick I am goin' to take a sock at him so that he will wonder where the thunder-bolts are comin' from. I also tell him that the matter I wanta see Mr. Meford about concerns a missing bullion shipment from the

U.S. Treasury, some of which I have just drove down here an' left outside an' what does he know about that?

He looks like he is goin' to have a fit at any moment, but he says he will go an' see if Mr. Melford can see me an' he goes off an' comes back again in a minute an' asks me if I will go along with him.

I go after this guy down a passage that is covered with a swell pile carpet an' I see that this Playne Place is one helluva place.

Then this butler guy opens a door an' holds it for me an' I go into the room.

It is a big room, furnished in red with big arm chairs an' lounges in leather. There is a lotta books around the walls an' standin' in front of the fireplace which is on the right of the room is an old guy.

He is about sixty years old, an' he has got white hair an' eyes like gimlets. He is a thin-faced feller an' looks as if he knew his stuff. He has gotta slim sorta young appearance like a lot of old guys have when they are able to take plenty care of themselves.

He smiles at me. An' he has gotta nice near-English accent.

"What can I do for you," he says, "an' to whom have I the honour of speakin'?"

I sit down in one of the big chairs an' I look at him an' grin.

"Cut out the neat stuff, Mr. Melford," I tell him, "an' let you an' me get down to brass tacks. I just told your butler—the guy who is probably listenin' on the other side of the door right now with a gun in his mitt—that I drove some of the U.S. Treasury ship-ment along here in a truck an' it's outside now. That's how it is an' I thought that I'd like to have a little talk with you justa show you that you ain't got all the brains in the world, an' that even if some of the guys like me that Uncle Sam picks to take a look after things cannot speak very pretty English, an' even if we are a bit tough sometimes, well, we can still do a little bit of fast thinkin'."

He smiles at me. He looks like some schoolmarm reprovin' a little boy who's been playin' hookey.

"All this is very interestin'," he says, "but I'm afraid I don't quite understand, an' I still don't know to whom I'm talkin'."

I get up.

I walk over to the door an' I lock it. Then I put the key in my pocket an' go back. He is still smilin'.

"O.K.," I say. "If that's the way we're breakin' around here I'll tell you. Just you sit down in that chair over there an' listen, an' if I was you I'd make the most of that chair because you ain't goin' to sit in big leather chairs for long.

"My name's Lemmy Caution. I'm a 'G' man. I reckon you know all about me. If your name's Melford then I'm the King of Siam. Your name's Harberry Chayse an' you're the lousiest son of a dog that ever put people up to do the work that he hadn't got the guts to do himself."

He goes as livid as hell, an' I see his fingers tighten on the arms of the chair.

"Look, Brilliance," I tell him. "I'm goin' to tell you a little story an' when I've told it to you you'll know why I've come along here. Here's the way it goes:

"There was once a guy who thought he was durn smart. He was a big Wall Street guy an' he knew all the right people. He'd got an adopted son who was a bit of a mug an' who used to hang around with night club dames—they used to call him Willie the Goop.

"O.K. Well this Wall Street guy found that he wasn't doin' so well. In fact he was in a bad jam an' he'd gotta get his hooks on plenty dough pronto. He used to get around with all sorts of official guys an' he meets up with a guy in the U.S. Treasury, because this guy's cousin, whose name is Mirabelle Gayford, is engaged to this Willie the Goop, an' the Wall Street palooka thinks that through this engagement he can pump the Treasury guy an' find out when the next shipment is goin'.

"Well he finds out. An' when he's found out what he wants to know he fixes that the engagement between this Mirabelle an' his adopted son is bust. He does this because this Mirabelle is gettin' burned up because Willie is still hangin' around night clubs an' she don't like it. But the Wall Street guy, whose name is Harberry Chayse, wants Willie to hang around night clubs so that Harberry can pick up the thugs he wants to do a job for him.

"Well, Willie does this, an' Harberry meets up with a first-class mobster, name of Saltierra. Harberry an' Saltierra get down together an' they fix a nice little scheme to knock off the bullion, but they are goin' to do it in such a way that nobody is goin' to suspect Harberry.

"But in between whiles some guy who is a mobster of Saltierra's, has shot off his mouth in hospital before he dies an' the Feds get busy. Also Willie the Goop wants money an' Harberry won't give him any because he ain't got any—well, not so you'd notice it; an' also because this Willie has realised by now that there is something screwy goin' on an' he has put two an' two together an' thinks that he will make plenty trouble.

"Well, Saltierra an' Hangover—a crime reporter pal of his—smell out that Willie is goin' to meet up with a 'G' man called Myras Duncan at Joe Madrigaul's club, so they fix to bump both Myras Duncan an' Willie an' they do it very nicely. The only thing that is worryin' 'em is that another 'G' man called Caution has blown into town.

"This guy Caution begins to muscle around an' the bunch realise that they gotta make it snappy, an' so after Saltierra has had one go to bump this Caution they think that the best thing they can do is to make a clean-up an' get Caution down on this Harberry's boat—which is a fast one—an' give him the works too.

"This is a good scheme because it still keeps Harberry in the background. Harberry has got some tame clairvoyant called San Reima, an' this guy starts seein' visions an' warns Harberry that the guy who killed his adopted son Willie was Saltierra. Harberry knows this durn well, but he tells this San Reima that they will have a seance down on the boat an' get everybody down there.

"This is a swell idea because it gets San Reima an' Caution on the boat where they can be bumped off, an' the boat can be used to chase over the Atlantic so's to be off Southampton in time to pick up the bullion after their English pals have got it.

"But the thing is put up to look like the yacht was snatched, because this still keeps Harberry nice an' respectable, an' outa the job so that he can still go on workin' his end.

"This Mirabelle Gayford who is a swell dame hears about this seance business, an' because Willie has told her one or two things she begins to think that there's something screwy goin' on.

She tries to stop Caution goin' on the boat because she's gettin' ideas in her head about this Harberry, but Caution gets aboard an' that's that.

"The yacht goes off an' next day Harberry says that his boat's been pinched. He makes out that he is a very indignant an' he comes over on the next boat to England, where, some three four months before, he has taken a house—this house—an' fixed up with a bunch of thugs over here who he gets to know through Saltierra, to do the stick-up of the gold train an' rush the stuff to the *Atlantic Witch*.

"But Saltierra has been a mug. He has not bumped this Caution while he had the chance, an' when Caution gets ashore Rudy has the wind up because he don't know what to do or where to go with the gold when he's got it aboard. His orders was to stick around until Hangover gave him his instructions.

"Next thing Harberry sees a piece in the paper where it says that this Caution guy is stayin' at some hotel in Southampton. He falls for this because this guy Caution is a dangerous guy an' has got to be rubbed out. So Hangover turns up—still doin' the little crime reportin' act an' tells Caution a lousy spiel about Harberry havin' found some address in England of his adopted son's murderer, an' that he will try to get this address an' tell Caution.

"Caution makes out he is fallin' for this stuff an' goes an' meets Hangover at some dump where that guy aims he is goin' to bump Caution. But he don't, he gets bumped himself. I'll find out why pretty soon.

"But the mug has bought himself a pair of new gloves in Romsey, an' the name of the shop is stamped inside an' Caution checks on this, an' so, Harberry, what with this an' that, it looks as if the game is just about sewn right up in the bag an' you can cash in your checks because it looks as if the pay off is here. An' how'dya like that?"

He just sits there smilin'. Then he takes a cigar outa his vest pocket an' bites the end off an' puts it in his mouth.

"Very interesting, Mr. Caution," he says. "An' may I trespass on your good nature to ask you just how you managed to connect my poor self with this business?"

"You slipped up three times, Harberry," I tell him, "but I ain't got the time to start arguin' points with you right now, so you'd better ring for your hat an' take a walk with me. I'm goin' to cash you in, sweetheart, an' you can work out your next crossword in the jail. This'll get you in trainin' for the twenty to fifty years that's comin' your way when we get back to the States."

He sighs. Then he gets up an' goes to the matchbox on the table, an' takes a match out to light his cigar. It don't light very well so he puts it down an' opens up a big cigar box to get another. I have been waitin' for something like this an' so when he spins around with the gun that he has got outa the box in his hand I have already slipped the automatic down my sleeve an' I do a little sharp-shootin' first that busts his hand up considerable. He drops the gun with a yelp.

"Listen, Harberry," I tell him, "I don't mind you smokin', but don't try any funny business."

He wraps a handkerchief round his hand, an' grins at me. He looks like the devil in a bad temper.

"I'm afraid you're too good for me, Mr. Caution," he says. "May I ask where we go from here?"

"Stick around," I tell him. "I'll arrange to have you collected. There ain't anywhere you can run to anyway."

He nods his head.

"I would like a little time to myself," he says. "If you would be good enough to leave me this"—he points his foot at the gun on the floor—"maybe that would be the easiest way out for everybody."

"I wouldn't know about that," I tell him, "but if you do decide to bump yourself off, do it nice an' quick, an' don't make any mistake about it. Saltierra never made any mistake about Willie, an' Hangover gave Myras Duncan two or three, an' San Reima got about five bullets before Rudy was done with him. So, Harberry," I go on, "you can't expect me to be burned up over your handin' in your dinner pail. Well, so long, maybe I'll be seein' you."

I walk across the room an' I open some french windows an' I go out, because I am not so keen on goin' through the hallway, because I reckon that the guys outside thought that the shot they heard was Harberry givin' it to me.

I find that I am at the back of the house an' I walk around until I am on the road again. I look back an' I see that the truck is still standin' outside the front of the house.

I ease round through the iron gates an' start workin' towards the truck. Right then I hear a shot from somewhere around the back an' I reckon that Harberry has kept his word an' bumped himself off, which, if you ask me, is a clever thing for him to do. When I get around to the porch there ain't anybody there except the guy I hit with the gun who is still lyin' there dreamin' sweetly, an' the engine of the truck is still runnin'.

I jump up into the cab an' I start off an' I scram along the carriage drive an' out the other gate. I keep goin' until I come to the place where I turn off for the Botley Road, because the time has now come when I reckon I would like to have a little talk with Rudy and Carlotta, who, I reckon, are waitin' for me very patiently.

Because they have gotta stick around there. I reckon that after the bullion was moved along to Playne Place that Harberry was goin' over to see Rudy an' fix what was goin' to be done next, which it looks to me would be something like this: Harberry would wait around for a bit until this gold snatch was blowin' over an' then he would fix himself with some boat that he would charter over here an' get the stuff moved to wherever he had planned to send it in the first place.

Maybe he would use Saltierra for this, or else he would have to fix some sort of pay off for that mob an' arrange to get 'em outa the country, although it looks to me when I remember what Salt-ierra said about settlin' down with Carlotta in some place, that the *Atlantic Witch* was supposed to stick around the coast here for a few hours after she had got the gold aboard so that Harberry could let Saltierra have instructions as to where he was to take the stuff.

An' the reason why Rudy, Carlotta an' the rest of that bunch will stick around where they are is because, if I know anything about Harberry, then he has not let these guys know where the gold is, just in case Rudy tries some sort of a double-cross, by which you will see that Chayse has gotta whole lot of brains.

Maybe Harberry was so burned up at Rudy lettin' me get away off the *Atlantic Witch* that he was goin' to scram off without even contactin' Rudy—because, if he did this, what could Rudy do about it? He couldn't do a thing.

I drive along slowly down the road, an' presently a car runs up alongside an' I look around the side of the truck cab an' I see that it is a squad car. I pull in on the left an' stop.

It is a sergeant guy an' I show him my pass an' tell him that the truck is loaded up with bullion an' not to let anybody else try an' pinch it. I also ask him where Herrick is an' he tells me he will drive me along.

A coupla miles down the road we turn in to a little road an' along a path, an' there, amongst the trees, is another squad car with Herrick standin' by the bonnet. Away through the trees I can see the back of the dump where Rudy, Carlotta an' the little bright boys are waitin' for me to call in.

Herrick grins. "You're havin' a good time tonight, aren't you, Lemmy?" he says. "An' it looks to me that you're usin' me just like a sorta district messengers' office. Supposin' you let me know what is goin' on."

I tell him just a little bit about what has been breakin' an' I also tell him that if he will just let me play along in my own way for another half an hour or so we will have all this business cleaned up.

He sees what I am gettin' at. He knows durn well that if he had dealt with this business in an official sorta way we shoulda got nowhere at all.

But I have a lotta trouble persuadin' him to let me go along an' tackle the Rudy Saltierra proposition on my own, but after I tell him why he says O.K.

We arrange that the three cars that are in this neighbourhood should now concentrate around the house, two on the road about a quarter of a mile away, an' the third—Herrick's car—just where it is way out at the back of the house among the trees.

He gives me a police whistle an' we fix that when I start playin' tunes on this the cops are goin' to close in an' fix these guys.

He walks a little way with me through the trees.

"I ought not to let you try this out, Lemmy," he says, "but you're an obstinate cuss an' maybe you know what you're doin', but I am not goin' to feel so good if this Saltierra tries any shootin' business with you."

I tell him to be his age, because I reckon that if I can get a little talk with Rudy before he starts any ironin' out acts then maybe he will look at things my way.

I tell him that Rudy don't know that there are any coppers hangin' around here; that he don't know about Harberry, an' that if I turn up he will think that I have done a big gumshoein' act after Carlotta's car, an' then, if I have any luck, I can do what I wanta do.

Maybe I am not feelin' so good about it myself, because Rudy is a tough guy an' he is burned up about me, an' is likely, if he feels that way, to bump me first an' talk afterwards.

But I have always found that you gotta take a chance.

CHAPTER FIFTEEN
LATE NIGHT FINAL

I KEEP goin' stickin' in the shadow of the trees around the house, an' I get around it an' start workin' towards the back where there is usually a servants' door or a sun window that I can get through.

I can't see a light any place, an' if I didn't know better I would think that the place is empty.

After a bit I find a coupla french windows lookin' out on to a little lawn around on the other side of the house. I take out my pen knife an' I start work on the catch an' in about three minutes I have got these windows open. I slip through.

I have to feel my way about because I am not takin' any chances about using a match to see where I am goin', an' this place is as dark as a black coat down a coalmine. Anyhow, after a bit I get sorta used to it an' get across the room an' find a door.

By the side of this door is a sideboard with some bottles on it, an' I pick up one of the bottles an' throw it down like I have knocked it over. I then pull the Luger outa my pocket an' start slowly turnin' the handle of the door. I take plenty of time over this so as to allow the guys to get around an' wait for me.

Then I step out into the passage on the other side of the door. I start easin' along when some guy sticks a gun barrel into my back an' tells me nice an' quiet to put my hands up an' keep 'em up.

I sorta know that voice. It is Saltierra!

I turn around.

"Well, if it ain't the punk copper," he says. "Say what is the matter with you, sap? I'm tired of seein' you around. Still it's nice of you to come on in like this. We been tryin' to make an appointment to meet up with you for some time. We got some business to talk with you."

He frisks me an' takes the Luger.

"Take care of that, Rudy," I tell him. "It ain't mine, an' I want it back again."

He grins.

"You got your nerve," he says. "You ain't ever goin' to use a gun again in your lousy life. Walk straight ahead an' look snappy."

I walk straight ahead down some passage. When I get to the end the door opens an' I go into a big room.

It is a swell room, with good furniture an' in the middle is a big table. All the curtains are drawn close, an' there is a nice fire. There are plenty bottles on the table. They have been doin' themselves O.K.

Sittin' around are a lotta the guys I saw aboard the *Atlantic Witch*. Some of 'em are boozed an' some ain't. They are a lousy lookin' lot anyhow—but tough. I reckon most of 'em was wanted for something some place.

Right at the top of the table, lookin' like the Queen of Sheba with bells on, is Carlotta. She is flushed an' she looks at me like I was a cheap rattlesnake.

Rudy makes a motion that I should sit down in a chair, an' I do. He pours me out a good shot of whisky an' hands it to me.

"Drink that, copper," he says. "It's a sorta farewell drink, because we ain't goin' to make any more mistakes about you. We're goin' to give it to you here an' now."

"That's swell, Rudy," I say, "but just tell me one thing before I start thinkin' about handin' in my dinner pail. How did you pull this off? It sorta interests me. I reckon it was clever."

"You bet it was clever," he says. "You didn't know that Hangover was playin' in with us, did you, you sap? Well, we fixed it. Directly we saw that stuff in the paper we knew that when he got here he would contact us an' get holda you, an' get you some place where we could get at you. Carlotta here reckoned that if she showed up an' let you see it was her, you would follow along like the big punk you are just because you got some silly idea about always followin' your nose. Well, you fell for it. You thought you made things pretty tough for us, didn't you, doin' that high divin' act off the *Atlantic Witch*?"

I grin.

"Well, it mixed you up a bit, didn't it, Rudy?" I tell him. "It made you cancel everything an' scram off. I suppose you set fire to the yacht an' come ashore in the motor boats.

"By the way, big feller," I go on, "I suppose you know where that gold is, don't you? I suppose that the English crowd ain't likely to double-cross you outa anything?"

I grin an' sorta look around at them nice an' pleasant. I can see by the looks on these guys' faces that I have touched a spot that is reactin' plenty.

Rudy gives a horse laugh.

"Don't take any notice of this punk, fellers," he says. "He's tryin' to pull a big scare on us just so's he can make time to think up something to get outa here. We know all about it. Carlotta here told us how Hangover wasn't quick enough for you, how he missed with the first shot an' you was quick on the draw an' got him. I gotta admit you're a good shot, Lemmy, but still the little girl was clever enough to lead you along here."

I grin some more.

"Listen, Rudy," I tell him. "Why don't you be your age. Ain't you ever goin' to learn any sense? What do you think you guys are goin' to do now?"

"I'll tell you," he says. "First of all we're goin' to iron you out because we reckon we don't like your face one little bit. You caused us plenty trouble as it is. An' after that, baby, we're just stickin' around. Didn't I tell you we was international? Well, we got organisation, an' we're still goin' to have that gold even if you did do your high-divin' act an' stall us for a bit. The coppers here ain't ever goin' to find them gold bars, an' when they're tired lookin' for 'em, well I reckon there'll be another boat for us to get 'em away on."

"That means you got some pals over here lookin' after you," I say. "But listen, Rudy, supposin' they ratted on you. If they hold the gold why should they worry about you. It's their country, ain't it, an' they're better off here than you. Maybe they'll rat on you. Alright, supposin' they do, what is goin' to happen to you guys.

"Another thing: you're wanted for murder in the States. These English coppers will get you sooner or later, an' then what? You'll go back an' you'll be fried, an' you know it."

"Yeah," he says, "that's what you think. You know all the answers—ain't you the clever 'G' man? Whadya want to know before we bump you?"

"You know what I wanta know, Rudy," I say. "Why don't you be your age an' get it over with."

He swallows some of the whisky an' he laughs again.

"Alright, punk," he says. "Well let me tell you somethin'. I ain't talkin' now, an' I ain't going to talk; an' I'll tell you somethin' else. Nobody in this country ain't got anything on me, wise guy. Not one little thing. I ain't done a thing over here. Anything I done was in the States, an' if these cops did get me, I gotta go back there to be tried an' maybe when I get back there is some friends of mine who can do a little fixin', see?"

"It don't make no difference, Rudy," I tell him. "When you go back to the States they're goin' to have you fried for ironin' out Willie the Goop."

"Howdya think they're goin' to prove that?" he says. I tell him how I went back to Joe Madrigaul's an' found his jacket with the bullet hole in it an' the letter to Carlotta from Willie.

"I gotta admit I was a sap about that letter," I tell him. "I thought Carlotta gave it to you an' wised you up to the fact that Willie was goin' to spill somethin'. But when we was on the *Atlantic*

Witch you gave that bit of business away. You told me you made up your mind to bump Willie about seven o'clock that evenin'. That was just when the post arrived at Joe Madrigaul's, an' that letter was addressed to her there. I reckon she never saw that letter—you pinched it an' opened it. You done this because you was jealous of Willie an' you wanted to see what he was writin' to her.

"I go it all weighed up an' measured," I go on. "An' I reckon that I can make a good guess at what happened from the start. Here's how I figure it.

"You find that Willie is hangin' around this dame Carlotta at some club dump, an' you fall for her yourself, an' get her that job at Joe Madrigaul's place.

"Then Hangover sees Myras Duncan hangin' around. He knows that Duncan is a 'G' man, an' that he will probably be operatin' on this proposed gold snatch business, an' after you pinched that letter from Willie the Goop to Carlotta I reckon you two got together an' decided that it was time that Myras Duncan an' Willie got theirs. So you fix it like this:

"Hangover is to take Duncan an' you're goin' to bump Willie. Hangover gets to the Club just before he reckons Myras is goin' to show up, an' you or one of your mob ring through on the telephone to the booth at the end of the passage an' ask for Duncan. While Duncan is in the booth Hangover gives it to him with your gun that has got a silencer on it, but he never had no chance to fix anything to either move the body or close up the booth because just when he is walkin' away from the telephone passage he sees me come in.

"Right then he knows that I will be workin' in on this job with Duncan, because he knows who I am, an' when I tell him that I am Perry Rice he is durn sure of it. So he has to leave Duncan in the box an' come over an' talk to me. He has gotta wait for a chance for fixin' this stiff.

"But I find Duncan there, an' I stick an 'Out of Order' notice on the booth, an' then I ask Hangover to do a phone call for me, an' like a silly punk he has to pass the other two empty booths an' look see why somebody has stuck this notice up an' if the body is still there. Maybe he thought you'd fixed to get it moved. From that time I was on to Hangover, an' I played him along, because I had to find out what was happenin'.

"Anyhow I reckon that he thought that you'd had that notice stuck on the call booth an' that this would keep anybody else outa the booth, so he comes over an' he does a bit more stuff with me, an' then just before Carlotta starts her number he eases out of the Club an' he goes round to the back door, an' he meets you there an' hands you the gun he shot Duncan with. He sticks around there until you come back with the gun an' you hand it over to him an' he scrams. Then you go to Carlotta's room an' you're there when I blow in, an' that's why you don't have any gun.

"He knows durn well that you will be taken down to head-quarters, an' I bet he has a laugh when they take me along too. So he blows along an' gets us both out of that jam.

"Next day I tell him the truth about everything, because I have always found that if you wanta mix a bad guy up the best thing to do is to tell him the truth. I also ask him to tell me where this guy Skendall lives. He tells me an' he reckons that I will go down an' grill Skendall an' he tips you the wink that this is the time to bump me.

"So you fix it, but I knew you couldn't know I was goin' after Skendall unless Hangover told you, because after I saw you had some mug watchin' the Hotel Court I scrammed around to another hotel, an' so you couldn't have followed me down because you didn't know where I was.

"I was waitin' for you to try that bump-off, an' when you tried it I knew I was dead right, an' that I was on to the real guys."

I take a drink of whisky an' I look at him an' grin.

"It looks like I know something, don't it?" I say.

He grins back.

"You make me laugh, copper," he says. "Maybe you know somethin' an' maybe you don't, but if what you told me is all you know you can go fry an egg. I'm goin' to be as dumb as a clam. If the English cops ever do get me they can apply for extradition an' send me back to the States. I reckon I can stand trial O.K."

"Don't make me laugh," I tell him. "You reckon you can stand trial. Why, you big mug, even if you stand a chance of gettin' away with the Willie the Goop bump-off what about this guy San Reima? You shot this guy on the *Atlantic Witch*. Howdya think you're goin' to get away with that? You'll have to be pretty good, Rudy."

"Maybe I am good," he grins. "But when the time for the trial comes you won't be there to give evidence."

"So what?" I tell him. "Supposin' I am bumped. Howdya think you're goin' then?"

He grins like a hyena.

"Maybe I won't do so bad, copper," he cracks.

"You mean you reckon you got somebody who can frame you outa this?" I say. "Well, they'll have to be durn good, Rudy, an' that's a fact."

He don't say a word, he just sits there lookin' in the fire an' drinkin' the whisky an' grinnin'.

Round on the other side of the table is the guy Kertz. He speaks up.

"Listen, Rudy," he says. "What is all this palaver about? Bump this guy an' have done with him. He knows plenty."

"Swell, Rudy," I say, "an' then there'll be another rap to beat. An' I suppose the big guy behind all this, the guy who is goin' to get you outa all this if the English cops did get you an' send you back, is your old pal Harberry Chayse?

"Well, let me tell you something an' I hope it'll make your ears burn, Harberry Chayse is as dead as mutton. He bumped himself off about half an hour ago after I had a little talk with him an' told him that the works was bust wide open.

"An' here's something else. We got that gold. We got it in a house not far from here where the old guy was storin' it. Now laugh that off!

"The other thing is that I'm takin' you back to the States an' you're goin' to the chair, an' these palookas are goin' to do some sweet stretches—about twenty to fifty years I should imagine— an' how do ya like that?"

There is a silence. Sorta ominous.

"You make me laugh," I tell 'em. "You think you're crooks. Why, you're so dumb you ain't got enough sense to know when it's rainin', an' as for your lady friend Carlotta she gives me a pain in the ear. Even if she looked good I wouldn't like her. You can think about her, Rudy, an' about that little *hacienda* you was goin' to have, while you're waitin' on Death Row for the chair. I reckon she'll just be sour milk to you then."

Rudy looks grim. He raises the gun, an' I don't feel so good.

Then she breaks in:

"Just a minute, Rudy," she says. "I reckon this guy thinks he's smart. Well maybe he's pulled a coupla fast ones an' maybe we're in bad, but there's just one little thing that I'm goin' to do. I'm goin' to give it to him myself. I'm goin' to kill that lousy copper if it's the last thing I ever do."

She is lookin' at me with them green snakes' eyes of hers, an' she starts walkin' round the table until she gets to Saltierra.

"Give me the gun, Rudy," she says. "I'm goin' to show you just what I'm goin' to do to this lousy Federal dick with his little tin badge an' his hot-pertater wisecracks."

Rudy grins. He is lookin' like a burned-up toad. He hands her his gun. All around the table these rats are sittin' grinnin'.

"Give it to him in the guts, sweetheart," he says. "It hurts more."

I get up.

She moves over to me, an' as she is comin' towards me, I think that I have never seen a dame move like this one does. She is like a graceful tiger.

She stops opposite me an' she raises the gun.

I look into her eyes. Just for one minute I see 'em sorta change. Then as she spins around an' turns her back on me, I start laughin'.

"Stick 'em up, Saltierra," she says in a voice that is like a piece of cold steel, "an' all the rest of you put your hands on the table. The first person to move gets it!"

Do they have strokes? I tell you the petrified forest ain't in it! Rudy's jaw is saggin' open. He looks like he is goin' nuts at any moment.

I stand there laughin' like I am goin' to die. Then I start in.

"Don't take it too bad, boys," I say. "I was as big a mug as you. All the time this dame has been tryin' to get next to me; all the time she has been tryin' to tell me that she is the dame that Myras Duncan wanted to contact me up with at Joe Madrigaul's place.

"And was I dumb? She tried to get me along to her apartment to tell me an' I wouldn't go. I thought it was a frame-up of Salt-ierra's. She was the dame who let me get outa those handcuffs on the *Atlantic Witch*, an' I thought I'd been the clever guy an' done it myself.

"But tonight I got it. When I went around to that garage to keep that date with Hangover he was waitin' upstairs on the top floor for me. He was waitin' to bump me like he bumped Myras Duncan. An' this little girl four-flushed you that she was goin' down there to lead me along here. You big saps, she went there to pull a fast one for me, an' it wasn't until she shot Hangover just when he was drawin' a bead on me that I got wise to it.

"You big punks," I tell 'em. "Do you think I was sap enough to come back here on my own if I hadn't known that if I'd had coppers bustin' around this place tonight some of you guys might have got wise to what she'd done an' put a coupla slugs into her?"

I look at Rudy. He looks like he is goin' nuts.

"She shot Hangover," I tell him. "She knew Hangover was goin' to wait in that garage for me, an' so she pulls one on you that she should go down there an' lead me along here so that you guys can fix me. She comes back an' tells you that Hangover had a shot an' missed an' that I did some quick shootin' an' got him, an' that I will follow her along.

"You're a mug, Rudy. That paper you showed me on the *Atlantic Witch* about the gold movement was typed on a follow-on sheet with the same watermark as the note I got from Harberry Chayse. That told me all I wanted to know about him, that, an' the fact that your pal Hangover was the guy who fixed up the arrangements for the seance, so's you could get the boat, bump that guy San Reima an' get me, an' all the time you could keep your big boss Harberry outa the job, so that if anything went wrong he could still look after you mugs.

"As for you, Carlotta," I say. "Well, if you ain't the original little sweetheart, then I am the President of Cuba, an' I'll think up some more compliments for you later. In the meantime we gotta get busy."

I give her the police whistle I have got from Herrick an' she gives me the gun.

"I'll look after this circus," I tell her. "Just run outside an' stand on the doorstep an' blow that whistle, an' when Herrick comes along an' you feel you wants faint just come back here quick so's I can catch you, because even when I hated you like hell I wanted to squeeze you, an' if anybody's catching you when you do a faintin' act it's goin' to be me."

She gives me a little smile that makes me feel like I am the King of China on celebration day, an' she scrams. In a minute I hear the whistle an' in five more I hear Herrick an' the English cops bustin' around.

The mob are still sittin' around. Are they burned up or are they?

While they are handcuffin' this bunch, she comes over to me.

"What's all this about this faintin' business, Mr. Caution?" she says. "I don't faint. . . . I'm not that sorta girl."

An' while she is sayin' it she sorta gives a little gasp an' faints.

I catch her as she flops, an' while she is lyin' in my arms an' I am doin' a first-aid act—an' likin' it—I get around to thinking' that when I have got this besuzuz cleaned up, then maybe I will go for this dame Carlotta in a big way, because my old mother always told me that a guy needs three things—nourishin' food, lots of sound sleep an' a swell dame.

An' did Ma Caution know her stuff or did she?

THE END